What the critics are saying

Discover for yourself why readers can't get enough of the multiple award-winning publisher Ellora's Cave. Whether you prefer e-books or paperbacks, be sure to visit EC on the web at www.ellorascave.com for an erotic reading experience that will leave you breathless.

www.ellorascave.com

Secret Submission
An Ellora's Cave publication

Ellora's Cave Publishing, Inc US
Ellora's Cave Publishing, Ltd UK
1337 Commerce Drive #13
Stow OH 44221

ISBN: 1-84360-811-1
ISBN: MS Reader (LIT) 1-84360-754-9
Other available formats (no ISBNs are assigned):
Adobe (PDF), Rocketbook (RB), Mobipocket (PRC) & HTML

Edited by *Pamela Campbell*
Cover Art by *Scott Carpenter*

SECRET SUBMISSION

Diana Hunter

Chapter One
A new idea

A widow by the age of 30, Sarah Simpson-Parker spent the obligatory one year in mourning and then moved on with her life. Her husband, a soldier for his country and a munitions expert to boot, had died two years ago in an ironic off-base traffic accident. It had taken her a year to start thinking again; in her opinion, the Victorians probably had it right when their social customs dictated a year-long mourning period.

She felt much freer this time around on the dating circuit. Both she and her husband had been throwbacks to an earlier time, adhering to an increasingly outdated morality; when they'd married, they both were virgins. After five years together, they realized a little more experience would have gone a long way towards making sex satisfying. As it was, their sex life was adequate, but nothing more.

At least then she'd had a sex life. In the two years since her husband's death, Sarah had remained chaste, and she was getting darn tired of it. Age was beginning its slow slink into her limbs; recently she'd found a white hair mixed in with her long, shoulder-length brown waves. A critical look into the mirror showed her a reality she had to face: her still-fit body and long, carefully brushed hair were ever-so-surely creeping into middle age. She wasn't even sure why she was still on the pill anymore, it had been so long since sex had been a part of her life.

She'd had a few kisses from the men she'd dated, but most of the men she'd gone out with just didn't do anything for her – until she met Phillip.

The first few dates with Phillip Townsend had gone so well, Sarah had agreed to more. Tall, dark, handsome, rugged; she almost had said "no" the first time he'd asked her out. She guessed he was slightly older than she—at least he'd looked it in the grocery store where they'd met when each of them chose the same orange at the exact same moment. Older, perhaps, and a bit rugged; clean shaven, but no gray yet in his hair. She liked the way his dark hair curled and was glad he'd left it just a little on the long side. In fact, had his hair been buzz-cut short, she probably wouldn't have given him a second glance – she liked to run her fingers through a man's hair, and Phillip had just enough to play with. On their dates, she'd noticed women notice him—and throw glances full of venom in her direction. He was Hollywood handsome and she'd been worried the beauty had only gone skin deep. But it hadn't and he'd caught her interest. Tonight they'd done the dinner and a movie thing and then gone for ice cream and a walk along the beach. It was late, or rather early now—and Sarah was glad tomorrow was Saturday and she didn't have to work. No cares, no commitments, just a day to relax.

The moon was full and the soft white light bathed the empty beach. Phillip pulled her close and kissed her once, twice. Sarah returned his kiss, liking his smell, his touch. His hands began to wander and she let them, liking how they made her feel.

"I like my women compliant," he whispered in her ear.

And compliant she was feeling. The moonlight, the anticipated day off, his touch; they all combined to put her in a tremendously relaxed mood.

"Would you do what I asked you to?" he asked her, nuzzling her ear. Phillip Townsend knew what he liked in women. Never married, he had been through several long-term relationships; each one had run its course and the break-ups had been mutual. He dated more selectively now that he had grown older, and theoretically wiser. Sarah's blush when their fingers met on the orange had prompted the first date—her intelligence had dictated several more since then. Tonight he would find out if she was worth any more of his time. He sincerely hoped she was.

Of course, it wasn't only her brain that intrigued him. While not drop-dead gorgeous, she was still a beautiful woman. That set of freckles scattered over the bridge of her nose gave her a pixie-like quality that belied the severe cut of her shoulders. Obviously that was where she carried all her tension. He saw those shoulders as a bit of a challenge — would she be compliant enough to relax with him?

"Yes," she murmured her answer, his touch arousing her.

"Would you come back to my place and do what I asked you to?"

This was exactly what she'd hoped for. She'd been a virgin until marriage, then monogamous throughout it and chaste afterward. It was high time she was naughty. "Yes," she murmured again, an impish smile dancing in her eyes.

He took her hand and they worked their way back to his black Corvette, the sand of the beach squishing through their toes. He did not kiss her again, nor touch her except for holding her hand. Pausing at the car only long enough to brush the sand off their feet, Phillip held the door for her as she sat and refastened her sandals while he slid on his docksiders. A moment more and they were on the road.

* * * * *

The ride to Phillip's cottage wasn't long – he lived out of town in a cottage separated from his neighbors by several acres of woods. They talked of small things along the way, getting to know more of each other's opinions; he liked brussel sprouts and she didn't; he hated washing dishes and she found it relaxing. As he pulled into the long drive and parked the car up near the house, the two of them fell silent. The Corvette was his one extravagance; certainly it seemed out of place beside the simple cottage. Putting the stick in neutral, he let the engine idle for a moment as he turned to the beautiful woman beside him.

"Now, Sarah, I need to ask you again. Once you step out of this car, I want total control over you. Are you willing to give that to me? I promise, I will not hurt you."

She hesitated, suddenly realizing the position she was in and what she'd agreed to. Her physical desires warred with her practical nature; did she really want to give this guy *total* control?

Seeing her hesitate, he leaned over and kissed her gently. From the few statements she'd made about her dead husband, he knew she was really not prepared for what he was asking. "I will give you a word—a safe-word—and if you say that word at any time, I will stop what we are doing and we will talk. Will that make you feel better?"

Swallowing hard, Sarah nodded.

"Then the word I will give you will be 'orange'. How's that? Just think of the day we met and you'll remember it."

She nodded again in response. Part of her couldn't believe she was actually doing this, the other part of her was so excited, she didn't trust her voice.

"Remember, once you leave the car, you will do as I say."

The warning tone was implicit, yet Sarah knew he meant it. She nodded again and took a deep breath at the sudden arousal his words caused inside her. She was voluntarily giving up all control—letting someone else take the lead. She, who prided herself on her ability to think through every problem she'd been given; she who led an entire set of teams at work. What would her friends and co-workers say of her now, agreeing to give up control to a man she'd met only a few times? She didn't care. It had been far too long since she'd had sexual relations of any sort. Putting thoughts of everyone and everything else aside, she opened the door and stepped out.

Shutting the door, she stood next to the car, suddenly uncertain as to what to do now. Just how far did this control thing go? Could she walk to the door without being told to do so? On unfamiliar territory, she felt the world wrench sideways a bit.

He smiled at her nervousness and came around the car, taking her hand. "Come with me, for you are now mine."

Frowning, she searched his face for signs of a power hungry fanatic and found none. He was still the same; smiling the way she'd enjoyed earlier. Stepping carefully in the dark, she followed him to the door of the cottage.

"Stay here and let me get the light." He unlocked the door and went in, closing the door behind him. Inside she saw a light come on as she waited. An owl hooted somewhere and she jumped. But then he was back, opening the door for her to enter. She sensed she still had the right to back out; but once over the door, she was committed.

She stepped over the threshold.

Only one small lamp was lit near the door; the rest of the place was in shadow. Phillip stepped behind her and kissed her neck. Her eyes closed as his hands moved down her body, exploring her. She swayed as he moved his kisses along her neck to her cheek, her ear. He pulled her hands behind her and she did not resist. There was a coldness around her wrist, a small click, and she was caught.

"You are mine," he whispered in her ear. The thought caused her knees to go weak, although she remained standing. She hadn't expected bondage to be part of the evening, but the thought of it gave her a small thrill. His voice was quiet in her ear: "You cannot prevent me from doing to you all that I want to do."

His hands now slid to her breasts, still covered by her blouse, still confined in her bra. So far, so good. She wasn't yelling or screaming at him to let her go. In fact, she seemed to be enjoying herself. How far could he push her tonight? What would her limit be? Was she the one he'd been looking for? Phillip pushed the last thought down. Too many times in the past he'd gotten his hopes up only to find his partner throwing walls up when he least expected it. Better to just enjoy the evening and leave the future where it was. He rubbed her breasts with his open palm, and her nipples stood up under all their layers. "Yes, you do find this exciting, don't you?"

For answer Sarah moaned and sagged against him, her mind reeling with pleasure. She hadn't known how wonderful the lack of movement could be. His words echoed in her mind and she whispered, "Yes."

"Yes, what, my dear? Do you have something more to say to me?" His fingers pinched her nipples gently through the layers of clothing and she moaned again, wanting him to undress her, wanting him to take her.

"Yes, Sir." The word came easily and a corner of her mind wondered just what had prompted her to give him that title. Was it because her need was growing and if he wanted the words, she would give them to him? Did he want that designation? It didn't really matter. If it would lead to a real orgasm, she'd call him anything he asked her to.

Phillip steadied her, then stepped around to read her face. "Look at me," he commanded and she couldn't resist. Her eyes met his and she saw now the latent power in his being. Not power-hungry, but raw power, natural. She gasped as she saw him unveiled and her arousal grew.

"Follow me." He turned and did not look back to see if she obeyed him or not. He knew she would—and she did. The darkness gave way to a short corridor; she followed and turned when she saw him disappear into the blackness to her left. There she hesitated. It was too dark to see and she couldn't tell where he'd gone.

A match flared as he lit a candle. In the small light, she could discern little, but it was enough to give her guidance. She stepped into the room and faced him.

"Good." That one word, spoken fairly flatly, gave her a bit of satisfaction. She didn't entirely understand this game, but she was apparently learning quickly. And there was no denying how aroused this game made her.

Phillip knew the candle didn't light much of the room — that was his intention. No use scaring her away. Better to ease her into the ideas he intended to introduce her to. He was glad she'd followed him without question, but it was obvious she was nervous. Stepping toward her, he slowly unbuttoned her blouse.

Sarah's body ached for his touch, but he was too careful: his fingers touched only the buttons, nothing else. She squirmed a bit and pushed out her breasts, hoping he might touch them again, but he seemed not to notice.

Deliberately, slowly, he pulled her blouse out of the confines of her pants, letting it fall to her sides, opening her bosom to his inspection. Then, using the front closure on her bra, he opened it, letting her breasts hang down. She blushed, knowing she was being examined. No man other than her husband and her doctor had ever seen her breasts.

Stepping forward, he cupped a breast in one of his hands, sliding the other around her waist. She leaned toward him, giving him better access to her body. It had been too long — and her husband had never excited her like this. "Anxious, are we?" he laughed.

For answer, she grinned at him.

He turned her and led her to the wall. In the dim light, she couldn't make anything out, but there did seem to be something glimmering above her head in the candlelight.

Phillip turned her to face into the room again and stepped behind her. Now came the first real test. He had told her he liked his women compliant. The truth was far more complicated. What he liked were women that would willingly hand over their bodies for him to play with. Not only did he enjoy the exchange of power, but he liked to think he made the time worthwhile for the woman as well.

Sarah felt the handcuffs release. Quickly now, he pushed the blouse and the bra off her and let them drop to the floor. Then, raising first one of her hands and then the other, he fastened them above her head, elbows bent. She felt the leather cuffs wrapped neatly around her wrists and tried to pull her hands through, but she was most definitely caught. The thought caused a whole new set of feelings to flood her—arousal, panic, arousal. She groaned a little and stretched, experimenting with her restrictions.

For his part, he simply stood and watched as she tested her bonds and discovered her vulnerability. He didn't want her to get frustrated, however, not yet. He wanted her aroused. Picking up something from a table nearby, he stepped forward again, leaning in to whisper in her ear, "You cannot escape. You are mine. And you like feeling helpless, don't you?"

"Yes," she murmured.

"Yes…what?"

"Yes, Sir," she amended, the title still sounding odd to her. But she liked this new experience too much to let a little word stand in her way.

With his foot, Phillip pushed against her feet and Sarah backed up against the wall. But doing so put her a bit off-balance and she leaned forward ever so slightly.

"Just right." Sarah hadn't minded the cuffs, could she take a more personal binding? With a quick movement, Phillip lassoed one of her breasts in a loop of soft clothesline, pulling it tight before she realized it was there. She gasped, feeling the pain, the sudden influx of pleasure.

"You have never had your breasts bound before, have you?" he asked. She shook her head no in response. "Would you like me to stop?" Again she shook her head no. "Remember, you have a word you can use if you want me to stop at any point."

Only briefly did she consider using the safe word. But the pain in her breast was swelling to full arousal and she had only one thought on her mind now: reaching a climax. She shook her head again. She would not use the safe word.

Smiling at her willingness, Phillip wrapped the cord around her breast several times, giving it a collar of rope. Then he turned to its mate, giving it similar treatment. Finished, he stepped back to survey his handiwork.

Now she blushed in earnest. There was no way she could or would stop him. His fingers brushed her swollen nipples and she gasped in shock. A thrill ran through her, right to her toes. With her breasts bound as they were and her hands hung high, her sex was awakening. Oh, she definitely liked this game.

He stepped forward again, circling her with his arms, his hands on her back pulling her into his embrace. Her tied breasts crushed against his shirt as he kissed her, his tongue probing, forcing her mouth open as he took possession of it. She yielded gladly, feeling her stomach give a small, pleasant flip as she did so.

Releasing her, Phillip bent down, taking one of her nipples in his mouth, kissing it, licking it. He enjoyed her taste. Sweet and yet slightly musky. She moaned in response, feeling her knees go weak and he smiled — she made wonderful noises. Yes, he could have quite a bit of fun with this woman, if she let him. For a few seconds, she hung by her wrists as he gave his full attention to her sensitive nipple. She got her feet under her again just as he took the other nipple in his mouth, lightly tugging on it with his lips making it warm and firm; her knees threatened to buckle again. The first nipple he'd kissed, still wet from his tongue, stood straight in the air, cold and hard.

His hands moved to her waist, touching the zipper of her twill pants. She flinched so Phillip possessed her mouth again, and as their tongues entwined, he unzipped her pants, sliding his hands in and around her hips, squeezing her rear. "No panties?" he whispered into her mouth.

"No," she whispered back, suddenly realizing what that made her look like.

Without another word, he stepped away from her and pulled down her slacks. He put aside her clothes, then, again without speaking, he reached over and took an ankle in his hand. Pulling her leg to the side, he fastened a cuff around it. What was it his grandfather used to say? 'In for a penny, in for a pound.' Well, she hadn't stopped him yet and he definitely enjoyed pushing her limits.

Sarah watched him. The cuff Phillip now locked around her ankle was attached to a bar about two feet in length. He did the same with the other ankle. Acutely aware that she stood before him wearing nothing but ankle and wrist cuffs, her breasts bound by his hand, her own hands secured to the wall above her head and her legs spread wide, for the briefest of moments, she quailed. What was she doing? Letting a man chain her to a wall to ravish her? What was she thinking? Her breasts bound and her legs spread like...like...like a woman who needed sex—who wanted it so desperately she would play such games to get it. Feelings of desire coursed through her.

Quietly he lit two more candles in the room, but her eyes did not stray from him. For now he stripped off his shirt and she saw the tremendous muscles in his chest. He moved with the grace of a cat, no, a lion, as he picked something up from a table in the dark. Coming to her, he brushed his hand again over her nipples, causing her breasts to ache for more of his touch. Another possessive kiss, and he stepped back. So intent was she on his eyes, that she saw only a flick of his wrist and a quick blur before she felt the soft flogger between her legs.

She cried out before she could stop herself.

"Would you like me to stop?" he asked, standing casually in front of her, running the soft leather of the flogger through his hand.

"I'm sorry, I didn't mean...it didn't hurt. You took me by surprise, that's all."

He still stood, not making any move other than to watch her, still running the flogger through his hand. She wondered if she'd said something wrong, then realized what it was. "Sir. You simply took me by surprise, Sir."

He nodded his approval and a small thrill of satisfaction ran through her. She was learning how to play this game. The thought of being whipped into submission brought images to her head from the occasional romance novel she read. Those images never failed to excite her. The reality of actually being flogged, however, was much more arousing than she ever expected.

He swatted her gently several times; sometimes on the stomach, sometimes on the arms, sometimes the legs. But then one landed on her bound breasts and she gasped. "Do you like that?" He let it land there again and the urge to come was strong.

"Oh, yes, I like that very much, Sir." The title came easily in her need and surprise. She *did* like this. Why? What was this saying about herself?

He flicked it over her pussy and her moan was vocal. "Like that?"

"Oh, yes, Sir!" The psychology of why she was responding to this faded into the background of her mind, replaced by desire and need. She writhed in her bonds, wanting desperately to come now.

He flicked it again. "What do you want? Tell me."

"I want to come…oh, let me come!" She felt like such a slut asking a man if she could come; in the past, she controlled her own orgasms. But the bondage and her lack of power and the flogger had done their work. She wanted to come and was willing to beg for it.

"No."

The word was flat, final. He turned, putting the flogger on the table behind him.

She cried out in frustration. This wasn't fair! She wanted to come, but because of her bonds, could not. How dare he get her all worked up and then leave her? Before she got enough breath to speak her mind, however, he was back, facing her.

"You are mine, tonight. I command you. You may only do what I say." He brushed a hair out of her face. "Do you accept this?"

She just stared at him. Then, slowly, she repeated, "I am yours, you command me, I may only do what you say." Fine. She'd play his game, come, and go home.

"What?" His voice was soft, his lips so near her ear she could feel his breath. She squirmed in her bonds. "You need to learn to say it. To accept it."

Her breath was ragged, her need intense. "I am yours, Sir. You command me, Sir and I may do only what you say." She paused before adding, pleading, "Sir."

For answer, his lips pulled on her earlobe, one hand playing with her nipple, the other reaching down and brushing the hair on her mound. She moaned and pushed against his hand as he held her, slipping one finger down to touch her clit. Her body moved towards a climax and she pushed against him, once, twice, three times.

And he stepped back. The sudden removal of his hand left her unable to come—again—and she whimpered in frustration. He took her chin in his hand and turned her face up toward his. "Open your eyes," he commanded. She did so, unable to refuse. "You will come when I tell you to. You will come when I want you to. And you will keep coming until I tell you to stop. Do you understand?"

She had no words. The constant arousal and the bondage were beginning to tire her. She hung from her wrists and nodded her consent.

He could see she was almost ready. But it was time to give her a rest before continuing his training. For training her he was. Breaking her, slowly, without her knowledge. Each time he pushed her a little further and she did not resist, his hopes went a little higher. Sarah just might be the submissive he hoped she was. Gently, he removed the ropes from her breasts, letting the blood flow to them once again. As it did so, she breathed deeply, her breasts rising and falling, tingling.

He caressed each one, softly planting kisses on the base of her breast where the ropes had left their marks. Massaging them, he waited until he heard her whimper again, knowing her desire was still strong. Leaving the cuffs on her wrists, he detached them from the wall, letting her hands fall to her sides.

She sagged against him as blood flowed to her arms. Her legs, still spread about two feet apart, kept her off balance. He held her, then scooped her up, spreader bar and all, and carried her over to a still-dark corner of the room.

She was aware that the surface under her was soft and warm as he laid her face up. Once again he took her wrists and raised them over her head, stretching her arms to fasten them; this time she could not bend them at all. Nor did she have the strength to.

He lit a few more candles now and in the increased light, she realized she was not on a bed, as she had surmised, but on a high table covered with a thin mattress. He secured the spreader bar to the table, then moved out of her sight for a moment. When he returned, he again carried something in his hand.

"You need to learn obedience to my commands. You need to learn who is in control tonight." He held up a small, butterfly-shaped object. "Do you know what this is?"

She shook her head no, and he bent down closer. "What was that?"

"No, Sir, I do not know what that is," she murmured, nervousness making her voice tight.

"It is a clitoral stimulator. Let me show you." He reached between her legs and her back arched in response. "Yes, I know you are eager. But not yet." He placed the butterfly in its position against her sex then turned it on to its lowest setting.

She gasped as the vibration sent its waves through her entire being. Her arousal began to grow again. She writhed on the table, trying to get the pressure she needed in order to come.

"Do you wish to use your safeword? Know that if you do, I will let you come now. Say the word and you can come and then I will take you home."

She looked at him, long and hard. Wasn't that what she'd wanted earlier? He stood there, not gloating over her, but genuinely concerned for her. He brushed a hair from her face and the tenderness in his touch moved her. "I don't want to say my safeword, Sir." She was surprised at how easily the title came.

"Do you like being in my control?" He smiled kindly at her and she smiled back, surprised at her own answer. "Yes, Sir."

"Very good. But I am afraid you still will not come. Not until I say so." Using the straps attached to the small machine, Phillip fastened the stimulator against her body. He turned a knob and the vibrations grew slightly more intense. Sarah had not only withstood, but seemed to enjoy the light breast bondage and the light flogging—but could she handle his demand for total control of her body as to command her orgasm? Deciding to push this limit as far as he could, he turned and blew out all but one candle. "And now I must leave you for a bit, my dear. Enjoy."

What? He was leaving her like this? Her body stretched on a table and unable to come? She had played his game, where was he going? The vibrations coming from her clit made her breathless and her cry was strangled with despair and arousal. Sarah watched as Phillip sauntered to the door with the one remaining candle, blowing it out as he reached it. In the sudden darkness, she heard the door shut.

It is said that the mind is the body's most sexual organ and Sarah's was working overtime. What if he never came back? What if something happened to him out there and he needed help? Each fear only added to her feeling of helplessness, which fueled her need, which heightened her desire. She lost track of time—alone in the dark, she squirmed on the table, trying to find relief. Her breath came in short gasps and tears fell from the sides of her eyes. The moans of before were now whimpers.

Listening to her in the darkness of the room quickened the blood in his veins. His stomach tightened as he realized how much she was enjoying this. Never before had he had a partner who so quickly gave her trust the way Sarah had tonight. Granted, it had been a while since she'd been with her husband—and Phillip knew she'd been with no man since. But still, she responded to his commands as if being dominated was a deeply-held secret she now let her body reveal.

Beside her ear he whispered in the dark, "You will only come on my command. I control your body, I control your mind."

"Yes, Master," she whispered, not even realizing she'd changed his title.

Inside his heart, he smiled. "You may come now." With his hand, he pressed the butterfly up against her body. Her reaction was immediate and violent. Wave after wave crashed over her, through her. Conscious thought fled and she knew only the pleasure of the waves that carried her as her body convulsed time and time again.

How long her climax lasted, she had no way of knowing. Exhausted at last, she lay limp on the table, unable to move. Dimly she realized he had brought her hands to her sides, and taken away the bar between her ankles.

"Here, my slave, drink this." She felt his arm under her head and shoulders, lifting her. A cup was in his hand but she could not take it from him; she had no strength left at all. He held it to her lips so she could drink. "Water. Just clear, cool water."

Phillip laid her back on the table so he could remove the butterfly. Once done, he scooped her up as if she weighed nothing and carried her out of the room; he would not be taking her home just yet. The poor woman was exhausted. Instead, he carried her to his bedroom, her arms wrapping themselves around his neck. Crawling into bed beside her and pulling the covers over them, he felt protective of her as her body folded itself against his own, snuggling her body to his warmth.

She lay contented. Never before had she had such an intense orgasm. Still basking in the wonder of it, she drifted off to sleep.

* * * * *

The sound of a bird's call outside the window woke Sarah in the morning. Sunlight streamed through the window and she stretched, forgetting for a moment where she was. But the feel of cuffs around her wrists made her stiffen as she remembered. The entire night came back to her in a flash: the bondage, his dominance and control over her; her begging for release, the incredible climax. All Sarah had wanted was a romp in the bedroom; she certainly had not intended to stay the night. However, after last night's activities, it was probably best that Phillip had not taken her directly home.

Throwing the covers back, she checked her ankles. Same as her wrists; cuffed, but not fettered.

"How are you this morning?"

Sarah looked up to see him leaning against the doorway, already showered and fully dressed. She had been too far into her own need to come last night to fully appreciate the physique of the man who controlled her. His frame filled the doorway with his wide shoulders and imposing height. A shirt now covered his strong chest muscles, the sight of which had actually registered in one part of her brain while the rest of her was busy. She appreciated anew the straight line of his clean-shaven jaw and the aquiline profile of his nose. Was it possible such a handsome man was really interested in her? Or was he only after one thing? Naked before him, she resisted the urge to pull the covers over her again. Smiling to cover her sudden nervousness, she answered his question, "I'm fine. Thank you." Was she still supposed to say 'Sir?'

"Not sore?" Phillip came in to sit beside her on the bed.

Surprisingly, she wasn't. She shook her head and made room for him to sit. His nearness caused her breath to quicken; to her knowledge, he had not come the night before. Well, she was ready to do her part. He'd been incredible and had showed her parts of herself she'd never even known existed. How she felt about that, she would think about later.

He reached out and caressed her breast with the back of his finger. The nipples already stood out straight from the sudden chill when she had thrown off the covers, but now they hardened at his touch. Sarah remembered the game they'd been playing the night before; the cuffs were testament to that. Time to find out how far this game went. Putting on a demure demeanor, she knelt on the bed and affected a meek tone. "What would Master like this morning?"

He laughed at her playacting. "You would make a fine slave, my dear." He leaned in to pull her earlobe with his lips and whispered, "You do know that, don't you?"

She bent her head towards him, feeling the desire brewing inside her. His touch turned her to jelly all over.

But then he pulled back, and she realized he held a key in his other hand. Deliberately, he took first one wrist and then the other, unlocking the cuffs, removing them and Sarah looked at him in confusion. When all four cuffs lay beside them on the bed, he took her hands in his and addressed her directly. It was time to lay it on the line to her.

"I would like very much for you to be my slave. But you need to realize I am not asking you to play a game, and there would be no playacting. If you agree, I will be your Master—in every sense of the word."

Sarah looked deeply into his eyes for signs that this was a joke. But all she saw was an open honesty, and that raw power she had glimpsed the night before. Her brow furrowed with yet-unasked questions. He held a finger to her lips, silencing her.

"If you accept, it will not affect your outward life. Your co-workers need never know. In fact, you do not even need to give up your apartment; you'll continue to live there during the week. But on Friday nights, you would come here, and leave from here on Monday mornings. During that time, you would be mine and would follow my commands."

Phillip understood the risk he was taking. It was quite possible the woman would bolt at his proposal. But after her responses last night, he was in danger of becoming emotionally involved, and his heart was too much to risk in another fruitless relationship.

He stood and pulled her to her feet. "Take your shower now, and think about it. The offer will be open for a while." He walked to the door, then turned and smiled, his manner not betraying his inner turmoil. "I release you from your promise of last night. I will not command you in this. It is a decision you must weigh carefully. But know that I will take care of you—my slave."

His words rang in her ears. "My slave." She considered his proposal as she readied for her shower. The bathroom was just off the bedroom and she ran the water hot as she thought. "My slave."

Stepping into the shower, she threw her head back, letting the water cascade over her body. Now she examined her breasts for marks made by the ropes last night. There were none. Her ankles had a thin, red line where the cuff had pressed her during the night. The same on her wrists. And she could not deny the fact that she had enjoyed herself.

But what did that say about her? She, who had so prided herself on her independence, on her ability to lead, was actually considering being a slave? Voluntarily? She must be nuts!

Finishing her shower, she turned off the water and toweled dry. She wrapped her hair in one towel, and took another one to wrap around her. No, she could not agree to this. The only reason she'd even come home with him last night was because she'd been feeling so naughty. And surprisingly, she had no regrets. It had been a wonderful night and she had to admit, she loved the bondage. But to actually be a slave? No. She finished her toilette and walked back into the bedroom.

The bed had been made while she was showering. Neatly placed on the coverlet were the cuffs she'd worn before, their open locks dangling from the closure. Sitting on the bed, she picked one up, turning it over in her hands. There was no denying the desire they provoked. To be cuffed, to be owned by one man—a Master. She sighed. There was something wonderful in that thought. No worries, no decisions. Only pleasing him.

She saw her clothes neatly folded on a chair in the corner. She ignored them for the moment and firmly tucked the bath towel around her. Picking up the two wrist cuffs, locks and all, she went to find him.

Finding the kitchen was easy enough. She walked over to where he sat at the small table. "I can't believe it, but I am actually considering your proposal."

He leaned back in his chair, looking her over. She was chewing her bottom lip, holding the two cuffs as if she were weighing them against her own independence. He would not rush her. After the very first date, he had known this woman had possibilities, and after last night, he was sure. Yes, he wanted her. He wanted her to be completely his to subjugate and control. But he only wanted her if she were willing.

"Give me the cuffs." He was pleased when she handed them to him without hesitation. Now he weighed them before her as she stood. "Give me today. Be my slave without question for the next twenty-four hours. Audition me, if you like. If tomorrow morning you wish to leave, then we will part as friends." He looked deeply into her eyes.

"I will even ask you to keep your safe word for this time. But know, if you agree to be my slave after tomorrow morning, you must trust me completely."

It was a fair offer. She had no plans for the day—and no date for the night. Instead of a quiet, relaxing weekend, she was getting something far more intriguing. Could she do it? Could she be a slave for a whole day? This arrangement would give her a better glimpse into what she might expect from him. She smiled, "I accept." She held out her wrists to him. "For the next twenty-four hours."

Chapter Two
Audition

Gravely, Phillip took her wrist, fastening a cuff to it, smiling gently at her as the locked clicked into place. Taking her other wrist, he did the same. "Then you are mine, slave."

She felt a shiver at his use of the word. It was what she volunteered for, but hearing him call her that still surprised her.

"Go and comb out your hair; return to me wearing nothing but your cuffs."

She smiled and sketched a small bow before leaving him. It didn't take long to fulfill such an easy command, although once the towel around her body was gone, she did feel naked in more than just a physical sense. Completely nude but for the cuffs, she stood in the bedroom doorway for several moments before she had the courage to walk the short distance to the kitchen. Swallowing hard, she forced herself to take the first step, then the second. A few more steps and she was back at the kitchen where she paused, feeling a little timid and more than a little nervous.

For her obedience, she was rewarded with a smile. Boy, she liked those smiles more and more. His right cheek dimpled so nicely and there was a twinkle in his eye.

Phillip couldn't stop smiling. Sarah was wonderful! He'd given her back her freedom, half expecting her to leave. Until she walked back into the kitchen, he didn't really know for sure if she truly enjoyed the bondage or not. The thrill of dominating someone who voluntarily gave her trust coursed through him and made him hard. Last night was for her; this morning would be for him.

"Kneel before me, my slave." Again the word sent shivers through her and she did so.

He undid his pants and lowered them. It was the first time she had seen his cock and her eyes grew wide with pleasure. Not huge, but well formed, long and slender. And hard.

"Keep your hands at your sides, slave, and make me come, using only your mouth. Be sure to accept all my come; I do not want to have to change my pants."

His orders excited her and she knew she was growing wet. His command was no more than she expected. It pleased her to know he also had desires and needs. Her only worry was that she wasn't experienced in this matter. Only a few times had she ever taken her husband in her mouth, and the experiences had been far from pleasant. But that was another place, another time.

Hesitatingly at first, then with more assurance, she put her lips around the tip of his cock, feeling him, tasting him. To her surprise, she liked his taste, liked his smell. She took in more of him now, feeling along the head of his cock with her tongue, exploring him.

Tempted as he was, Phillip held back. He would not lose control as he reveled in the feel of her warm tongue as it circled and dipped. She obviously didn't have much in the way of experience, but he could teach her that later. For now, he simply stood and enjoyed himself.

"Good, slave. Now go deeper." His voice from above her gave her courage and she opened her mouth wide, taking in a much of him as she could. On instinct her hands moved upwards, but then she remembered his command and slowly she lowered them again, moving in and out on his cock as she did so.

The harder Sarah sucked on his cock, the wetter she became. Kneeling before a man at his command...In and out; flicking her tongue all along his shaft, she felt him and tasted every inch she could reach.

"Get ready to accept my come," he growled from above her and she sucked harder, hoping to be able to take it all. She was rewarded with a salty taste in her mouth as the white liquid pumped into her mouth. She wanted to please him, to show her willingness to follow his orders, but swallowing all he gave her was too much. His come dripped out of the sides of her mouth, falling to land on her breasts.

Phillip's rocking slowed, then stopped. Only when she was sure he was done, did she let go and sit back on her heels.

Sarah's desire to please him and give back to him a little of the same pleasure he'd given her the night before endeared her to him. "Very good, slave. You have done well. Do you want a reward?"

She smiled at his words of praise, glad she'd done her first real slave command correctly. Did she want a reward? Yes. Did she expect one? That was harder to answer and she wasn't sure where the boundaries were.

"No, Sir. I do not want a reward. I only wish to serve my Master."

Phillip knew it was still a game to her; he could tell by the tone of her voice. That was all right; she'd come to truly serve him in time. He smiled at the sight of her, kneeling before him, her chin and breasts covered with his mark. "You have not yet eaten, slave. Come on," he held out a hand to help her up. "I ate earlier, but I'll prepare your breakfast, too." The smile turned to a grin. "Go ahead and wash up, then come on back and sit here." He indicated the chair he himself had recently vacated. Near a window, her nudity would be exposed for any passerby.

Sarah hesitated only a moment. The area of woods that surrounded the house would protect her from peepers, she decided. Washing quickly, she slid into the chair as he prepared and served her an omelet.

"I thought I was to serve you, Master," she teased.

With a twinkle in his eye, he set the plate before her. "You did, my dear—and you will again, in many, many ways, my slave."

There was a faint, ominous sound to his voice and she studied him in alarm. But there was only mischief in his eyes and she relaxed again. The omelet was delicious, as was the orange juice. She ate her fill as he watched. Their conversation was again of small things; anyone listening would have thought them simply a newly married couple. Only her nudity and the cuffs around her wrists pointed to another story.

She helped him wash the few dishes there were; feeling her nudity each time she did a "normal" activity. How strange it felt to dry a dish, the towel occasionally brushing against her bare skin, reminding her of her promise and her compliance. Each time it did so, she grew wet again.

There was a purpose to having her do such mundane tasks in the nude, of course. Phillip knew the simple, everyday activities would take on a sexual atmosphere and would serve, not only to remind her of her position, but to keep her in a perpetual state of arousal. That was exactly where he wanted her.

The morning chores done, he took her by the hand and led her into the same room where he'd tied her the night before. Sunlight now streamed through a window she'd not noticed in the darkness, giving her a first clear look at the furnishings. He stepped to the side and let her take her time taking it all in.

On the wall to the left, on the same side that had the window, she saw a board nailed to the wall with two rings hanging from it like small doorknockers. Chains hung down from the rings and she realized this was what she'd been attached to the night before. Her cheeks burned at the memory of her wanton behavior and how she'd begged him for release.

The table was also there, covered in its thin leather mattress. Another table stood against the wall, but it was covered with a dark blue cloth. She was pretty sure she could see the outline of the flogger he'd used on her last night among the several bumps under the cloth. Several other larger shapes in the room were similarly covered with the same cloth. Phillip now uncovered a low, rectangular shape.

It was a small cage, not even as high as her waist. Long and narrow, she thought it large enough for a very large dog.

"I'm afraid you need some punishment, slave." Time to find out just how compliant she could be. Although he was concerned about pushing her too far, he needed to determine whether she could handle being punished for infractions. This was an audition and he wanted her to be fully informed of what would happen to her. But there was no reason the audition couldn't also be a time of training, whether she recognized it or not. He gestured into the cage.

She looked at him as if he were crazy. "What? What do you mean?" The game was no longer fun if he thought she was going inside that thing.

"You swore to do as I asked for twenty-four hours, and you have already broken that twice."

"How?" She was indignant. She'd done exactly everything he'd asked her to. But a seed of doubt was planted. Had she done something wrong?

"I told you to keep your hands at your sides and take me only with your mouth. You moved your hands." His manner was quiet and calm.

"But I didn't use them!" She took a step back toward the door.

"And you didn't keep them at your sides." He stepped closer and she could see he meant every word he said. The raw power in him was strongly evident—only now she was slightly afraid of it. He advanced on her, pushing her emotions.

"That alone would have been a small punishment, however." Sarah's back braced against the door as he towered before her.

"Do you know what else you did that does not please me?"

She racked her brain, but could not think of a thing. They'd done the dishes and had a pleasant conversation. She shook her head.

"You did not tell me the truth, slave. And that is something you must always do. Do you remember when I asked if you wanted a reward?" She nodded, her eyes wide and heart pounding. "You told me you didn't want one. But you did, didn't you? You wanted me to take you again, to let you come again."

She could not lie to him. Trembling, she nodded. She hadn't told the truth.

The scared look on her face almost caused him to back down, but he held his ground. He didn't like having to be so forceful, and yet, he knew it had to be done. While Sarah was far from her physical childhood, in the world of submission she was but a newborn and had much to learn. He would very much enjoy teaching her, if only she would now do what he commanded. With a gesture that bordered on impatient, he pointed again to the cage. "And now, my slave needs to learn that she will be punished if she does not tell me the truth the first time I ask her. Crawl into the cage, slave."

Fear in her eyes, she did as she was told. This wasn't fun anymore, but she was afraid to challenge him. He instructed her to turn so she was facing the narrow part of the cage, her back against the bars and her legs spread wide. He locked her cuffed wrists to the far opposite ends of the box, then reached in for her ankles, spreading her legs and locking them wide apart with the cuffs he'd apparently gotten from the bedroom at some point. There wasn't room to sit up straight; with her arms and legs spread wide, she couldn't have anyway.

"I have some chores to do. You will stay there until I decide I would like to let you out." With that, he turned on his heel and walked out of the room. The door was still open and she could see him put on his jacket. When she heard the front door open and close behind him, her fear got the best of her.

"You can't do this to me! Let me out!!! Let me out!" she screamed, hoping he would return, knowing he would not. She was locked in a cage like an animal. She pulled on her bonds, trying to get her hands through the cuffs, but they were too tight. Helpless, naked, alone, she took a deep breath and calmed herself.

"Now think, girl. There has to be a way out of this." She tested her bonds again, but they remained as restrictive as ever. Tugging on them caused her juices to flow as the feeling of total helplessness overwhelmed her again. She was at his mercy. Completely and fully his to do with as he wanted.

And wasn't that what she'd agreed to? The thought brought a flush to her cheek as she felt a thrill through her entire being. Completely at his mercy. That was what being a slave meant. He was not fooling around; this was not a game. If she agreed to be his slave, it meant uncompromising obedience on her part. But what did it mean on his?

The time went by and she had no idea of its passing. Had she been here an hour yet? Less? More? There was no clock in the room and the sun had gone behind a cloud. She bit her lip, thinking about what it was he wanted from her. The question was, did she want to give it to him? Especially if she were going to be punished for what she considered a relatively minor infraction.

Well, okay, she should've been upfront with him on the reward thing. She liked to come and she liked the way he motivated her. She'd played the game, and lost. Or had she? No, perhaps not. She didn't like being in the cage, but it wasn't painful. The bars weren't the most comfortable seat she'd had in years, but there was no permanent damage being done. And if he was the Master, didn't he have the right to discipline her?

Suddenly she realized where her thoughts were taking her and stopped them. No, this was a game to her; she'd signed on for twenty-four hours and that was it. She wasn't a quitter; she'd do her time. Tugging her arms and legs in their bindings again only aggravated her helpless feeling and caused those juices to flow. But there was nothing she could do about it—no way to get relief. Instead, she sighed and waited, getting hornier and more frustrated by the moment.

She heard his step in the hall and tried to sit up straight, forgetting her bonds would not let her. It was hard to turn her head very far, but she could see most of the doorway. He stepped into it and she caught her breath. Why did he have to be so gorgeous?

Phillip hadn't gone further than the front porch. From the window there, he could peek into the room and keep an eye on her without her seeing him. He'd seen the struggles and heard her early yelling. But she'd quieted fairly quickly—more quickly than he anticipated. He deemed a half an hour to be long enough punishment—he doubted *he* could take much more. She looked so deliciously sensuous in that cage. Putting on his 'stern face,' he reentered. "How are you doing, my slave?"

She almost answered with an automatic "fine" but thought again. She was not fine. Her legs and arms ached from the position she was in, she was getting horny and not liking it at all. Her body betrayed her; in her mind she knew she didn't like this discipline thing at all, but the wetness of her sex said otherwise. Tears formed in her eyes as she struggled with the question.

Phillip waited patiently, seeing the war going on inside. Good. The slow training was working. She was now considering what yesterday she would have dismissed out of hand. He knelt and opened the cage, unlocking her ankles first and then her wrists. Sarah rubbed her arms; they tingled as feeling came back to them.

"Crawl out of there now and kneel before me."

Slowly, she did so. Once she cleared the cage, she stopped, kneeling on her heels.

"No, slave," he said kindly. "That is not how one kneels to one's Master. Spread your knees a bit and sit up." She did so without question, the tears falling quietly down her cheeks.

"Now put your hands behind your back and clasp them." His tone was that of a quiet teacher and she responded to his commands, not fighting him. "Push your shoulders back and gaze straight ahead." Her breasts stuck out when she did so making her feel vulnerable and weak. With an effort, she brought her chin up and gazed straight ahead, her vision clouded with still more tears.

"That is the position you will take when I tell you to kneel. Do you understand, my slave?" She glanced up at him and saw only kindness in his gaze on her. She nodded, trying not to sob outright.

"Stand now, my slave." Phillip reached down to help her to rise, then put his arms around her. "Come with me." He led her into the living room and set her on the couch, leaning against him. Pulling down a blanket from the back of the couch, he covered her, holding her as the sobs came in earnest now.

He kissed the top of her head and held her close, letting her tears fall. Perhaps he had been too hard on her. At least now she knew what he wanted. Did she see that she wanted it as well? The woman responded to being tied up, and that disturbed her. His hand brushed along her cheek as pity moved his heart. There was so much she did not comprehend about her own sexuality. As her sobs subsided into the occasional hiccup, he kissed her forehead. She looked up at him, her face stained and red from her cry. "I'm so sorry, Sir. I don't know why I'm crying."

"Don't you?" He kissed her temple. "I do." He smoothed the hair from her face. "For years you have trained your mind to think in one, specific way."

He kissed her face again. "But your body always knew something was missing. You just didn't know what it was." He kissed the bridge of her nose. "I am training your body." Kiss. "And your body likes what it is discovering." Kiss. "But your mind doesn't accept this new training." Kiss. "And so it has gone to war with your body." Kiss. "Unfortunately, your heart is stuck in the middle."

He kissed her lips then and she answered with hunger. He was right on every count. Something had been missing from her life. Was this it? In many ways, she liked his domination over her. Unwittingly, her heart moved a step toward him and in her answering kiss, she took the first step to submission.

He accepted her small step without words, encouraging her to lean on his shoulder, feeling the warmth, the security, the safeness of his presence. Relaxing, she drifted off to sleep.

* * * * *

When she awoke she could hear him rustling about in the kitchen. With a start she looked at the clock on the mantelpiece. Almost noon! She threw the lap blanket back and stood, her glance falling on her naked body and the ever-present cuffs. They were symbols of her slavery, she knew that now. Nodding, she went to the kitchen to find him.

"Have a nice nap?" He grinned at her, still mixing something in a small bowl.

"Yes, Sir." Her brow furrowed and she sniffed. "What is that, tuna fish?"

He laughed. "I need to get some groceries. All we have for lunch today is tuna fish sandwiches or peanut butter and jelly."

"Tuna fish sounds good to me!" Her stomach growled and they both laughed.

They sat together at the table, eating their lunch and enjoying each other's company. It was a measure of how far she'd come in that she only gave her nudity a passing thought.

Again she helped him with the dishes, folding the towel and hanging it when they were done. "Come with me," he instructed and she followed him almost eagerly. She still hadn't come yet today and very much wanted to.

They went back into the bedroom again and he pulled the covers down almost off the bed. With a gesture of his head, she knew he wanted her to lie down and she did so, leaving plenty of room for him to join her. He smiled, "Move into the center, my sweet, and put your hands above your head."

She grinned as she realized he was going to tie her down. Last night had been the first time she'd ever been immobile and she had liked it very much – her climax had never been so intense. Eagerly, she raised her arms, resting them on the pillows as he fastened her cuffs to the headboard. She pulled a few time, experimenting, even though she knew she was caught fast.

"Spread your legs." For a moment, the command warred inside her. In one way it seemed such a demeaning thing to say, even if she wanted it. But she conquered her mind and opened her legs to him.

But he did not fasten them to the bedposts as she expected him to. Instead he held up a small, pink butterfly. "Look familiar?" He grinned, knowing the stimulation it would provide would increase her desire, but not let her come. She almost groaned—not that! He fastened it to her clit then stood. "Close your legs now, slave."

Puzzled, she did so. Wasn't he going to take her? It was what she wanted last night and still wanted today. She raised her head and watched him lash her ankles together, then use a large, thick belt to wrap around her legs just above the knees. Another rope to secure her feet to the footboard and she was stuck. She squirmed, feeling the butterfly between her legs, but she could not get loose.

"I need to go get groceries. This will keep you entertained while I am gone." He reached over and turned on the control to the butterfly. A low vibration moved against her clit and she moaned as her muscles relaxed and responded to the stimulation. He chuckled and left the room. "I'll just go get my jacket and be back to check on you."

When he'd picked Sarah up for their date the night before, he hadn't really thought to turn their evening into an all-weekend tryst. But the timing had been right and he knew how to improvise. Problem was, he hadn't done the shopping; he hadn't lied to her at lunch time – there was little food on hand. He had tied her safely and knew she'd be very tormented in the short time he'd be gone. Thank goodness there was a small store only two miles down the road. Grabbing his jacket, he slid his arms into the sleeves as he poked his head in the bedroom door.

Seeing him in the jacket, Sarah realized he really did intend to leave. "Sir…" she started.

"Do you have something you wish to ask me? Something to say to me, slave?" His voice was kind and he stepped into the room to examine her bindings. They would hold—and not hurt her, despite the fear in her eyes. He offered her a way out if she wanted it. "A safe word to use perhaps?"

She shook her head no. "No, Sir, I will be fine." He nodded and moved the dial on the control. The intense vibration shot through her and she tried to arch her back, but could get little purchase with her legs bound together.

"Good. I will return shortly." With that, he gave her a kiss, long and deep. Standing, he strode out of the room without another word.

* * * * *

Sarah could see the clock from her position on the bed. After checking it fifteen times in fifteen minutes, she decided she preferred the morning alone time spent in the cage, when she didn't have any frame of reference for the passing of time. The little butterfly vibrator hummed along between her legs and she could get no relief from it. She squirmed a bit early on, but it was hopeless. Of course, that realization only made her need greater.

It was actually almost soothing once her body got used to it. She took deep breaths, feeling the vibrations all the way through her, relaxing every muscle but the ones by her pussy. She could almost go to sleep.

She twitched and realized she had in fact drifted off. A quick look at the clock showed her not much time had passed by – only five minutes from the last time she'd looked. So far he'd been gone only twenty minutes.

"Wonder where the store is?" she thought to herself. "Never thought of asking, did you? No, you were too into this slave thing to ask a simple question. And he probably would've answered you, too!" She sighed another big breath and wriggled some more.

"Mmm, I can't wait till he makes me come," her thoughts continued. "Last night was the single most incredible orgasm I have ever had." But thinking about it reminded her of her need and the vibrations added to it. The desire was stronger, but she knew there would be no relief until he returned.

But what if he didn't return? A sudden, awful, horrendous thought hit her right in the bottom of her stomach. She'd seen an old movie once, called <u>The Pit and the Pendulum</u>. She remembered very little other than it starred Vincent Price. But there was a part where, for whatever reason, he and a young lady had descended to the dungeon of this old castle where this ingénue of the movie had been intrigued by an iron maiden. The Vincent Price character had locked her inside, gagging her even, so she could get the full effect. But then the climax of the movie had occurred and he'd been taken out in chains or killed or something. Anyway, the movie ended with a shot of the girl, still locked and gagged in the iron maiden, her eyes wide, no one knowing she was there. And the whole audience knew she was doomed to a slow, painful death.

She had never forgotten the look of fear in that actress' eyes. The similarity between that character's fate and her own suddenly came home to her. What if her date were hurt? Or worse, killed in a car accident? Scenarios of doom began flooding her brain as she thought of more and more possibilities. And no one knew she was here! Her own family lived far away, and, while some of her co-workers knew she had a date Friday night, none of them knew with whom. She might be reported as missing, but she'd be dead before anyone found her.

Her fear rose. "Panic. We mustn't panic," she thought. "Get your mind under control." The possibility of any of her horrible scenes really happening was remote, she realized. He'd return – and soon – she was sure of it.

But the adrenaline rush caused by her fear attack had to go somewhere; her arousal deepened. "I need to come," she cried out, starting to move in earnest on the bed. Trying to find a way to bend her legs or get a hand loose.

And that was how he found her: writhing on the bed, tears flowing freely from her need. He reached out and took off the belt around her legs and she opened her eyes, realizing he was back. "Oh, thank God. Please, Master, please let me come!"

He shook his head and sat next to her on the bed, suppressing a laugh. Hearing her moans, he'd rushed right into the bedroom, fearing the worst. But the vibrator and her own thoughts had been far more active than he anticipated and his little slave had simply gotten herself horny. Reaching over, he pinched a nipple fondly as he brushed the hair out of her face with the other. "No, my slave. Not yet." He turned down the intensity on the vibrator's control and she cried out in anguish. He waited till she calmed and then leaned in to whisper in her ear. "I have possessed your mouth with my tongue and my cock. It is mine and I own it." He took her mouth again, his tongue sliding in and over hers. She moaned, the pleasure of it coursing though her.

He pulled back when he was done and looked at her sternly. "I am going to release your bonds, but you are not to touch yourself, or in any way try to please yourself. Am I understood?"

She nodded and he untied her feet from the bottom bedrail. She desperately wanted to cross her legs to get the friction she needed, but with an effort of will, she lay still. He undid her arms and helped her to her feet, noting her obedience.

Again he led her to the room she was beginning to think of as his dungeon. It didn't matter that this wasn't an old English castle; it didn't matter that it wasn't in the basement and sunlight streamed through the window. It had all the right equipment. She just hoped there was no iron maiden.

"Put your hands behind your back." She did so and heard the by-now familiar click of the cuffs being joined. She was not facing the table that held his toys, nor did she turn to look when he went to it. He came back with a different rope than the one he'd used last night and tied her breasts differently this time. He liked using different tie-ups—each one had a specific purpose. Today he wanted her breasts to feel confined, yet he still wanted access to them. Passing the rope around her body and under her arms four times, he had most of her fairly ample breasts confined. Not in big circles, but squeezed flat. The ends of the rope ended up in the back and he brought them around her upper arms. Gently, he pulled on them and she felt her arms being pulled together behind her. Her breasts now pushed against the bindings and Sarah knew her pussy was so wet it was dripping. She gasped as he knotted off the ropes.

Coming around the front, he surveyed his work and smiled at her mild discomfort. "Oh, yes, slave. I like this look for you very much." He reached out and fondled her breasts in their ropes. Rolling a nipple in one hand, he kissed her again, possessing her mouth. For a moment she struggled, wanting to put her arms around him. But that movement was denied her and instead she leaned against him, her knees getting weak.

"Come here, my slave. You need something to lean against." He led her over to one end of the mattress-covered table and let her lean her hips against it. Then he bent down and fastened one of her ankle cuffs to the bottom of the table legs. He did the same with the other and she was effectively immobile once more. With her arms pinioned behind her, her breasts jutting into the ropes and her legs spread wide, she had again become his toy.

He paused to admire her body — bound to the table, unable to move away. She was at his mercy and the thought aroused him. At every step, he half-expected her to use her safe word, but she remained silent, wanting to explore this world as much as he wanted to show it to her.

He stripped off his shirt and stepped close to her; she could feel his bare chest against her arms. Reaching his arm around her, he held her about the waist with one hand while the other pinched and rubbed her nipple. Moaning again, she leaned back into him, her eyes closed, enjoying the sensations. He nibbled on her ear then held something before her eyes. "Look at this," he commanded.

It was a long, black, rubber tube with small rings attached to either end. "Do you know what this is?" She shook her head no and he continued. "It's a bit. I want to put it in your mouth now. But I have no fasteners on it, do you see?" She nodded. "I can put it in, but you can spit it out and use your safe word any time you want. Do you understand?"

She nodded again and he fit the bit to her mouth. Her tongue was under it and she could taste the rubber. It added a thrill to her situation while still giving her a measure of control. But then he added, "You'll want it to bite into."

Before she could figure out what he meant by that, he was behind her again, holding her in place with his arm around her waist. Once more he pinched her nipple and she closed her eyes, letting her head fall back, and so she did not see the nipple clamp he held in his hand. Not until she felt its bite did she realize his intention.

She squealed and looked down at her breast. A small, silver clamp gripped her nipple, a light chain hanging from it. As she watched, he scooped up the other end of the chain and she realized the clamps were a set. He fastened the second one and stepped back.

For a moment she thought about spitting out the bit and begging for their removal. She had never known such an intense pain. Small fires burned at the tips of her breasts and she shook them from side to side, trying to cool the heat. Very quickly, however, the pain turned to a surprising pleasure and she calmed, wanting him to continue without her interruption.

When the bit did not go flying, he smiled. He thought she'd like this. Pain could be very seductive, very alluring, and *very* arousing. Not that she needed the latter. He finished stripping and stepped behind her again, now as naked as she.

"I have possessed your mouth. It is mine and now you wear the gag that I have given you. This afternoon, I will take possession of your ass."

Sarah gasped as she realized what he intended to do. For a moment she struggled in her bindings, but the bit stayed in place. With a sudden shame, she realized she wanted him to be the first to enter her virgin ass.

Gently he pushed her forward until she was leaning over the table, the nipple chain just brushing the mattress top. Even that little movement of the chain sent new waves of pleasure/pain through her entire being. She heard him kneel behind her and felt his hands on her, separating her cheeks. Something warm and wet trailed down along the crack to her hole and she realized his tongue was doing exactly what he said he would do — taking possession of her ass.

He circled her hole several times with his tongue, slowly, languorously; his hands never leaving her cheeks as he squeezed and fondled them. She longed to feel his touch on her clit, knowing her orgasm would come immediately. But he was deliberately avoiding it and the anticipation was almost painful.

The circles around the hole got smaller, and then she felt him push against her with his tongue. Moaning into the bit, she leaned forward to give him better access as his tongue penetrated her ass.

He leaned back on his heels and she felt something liquid dribble down between her cheeks; she sighed in relief when he set a bottle of baby oil on the mattress in front of her so she could see what he was using. With his fingers, he spread it around her hole, pushing on her anus and letting her feel the wondrous sensations that emanated from her rear.

Now he began working her hole in earnest, sliding just the tip of a finger inside. Her moans were louder now as he began to finger-fuck her ass. Gently he slid a finger in and then pulled — first to the front, then out; then sliding in again and pulling to the side. Bit by bit, he stretched her.

Her need was almost unbearable now. She wanted his cock inside her — she wanted him to possess her. Again she leaned forward, the clamps themselves just a hairsbreadth from the mattress. He was being so careful with her, so gentle so he would not rip her. Knowing this did not make it any easier for her to bear.

At last she felt something larger against her now-stretched hole. "Ready?" he asked her; she nodded "Yes." His hands were on her hips and with one motion, he entered and took ownership of her ass.

She bit into the gag as she screamed. For several heartbeats, her ass burned as her interior muscles protested the intrusion. But then she relaxed and Phillip pulled out, pushing in again with slow deliberation. Each time he withdrew, her muscles relaxed more and Sarah gave herself up to the helplessness of her situation.

Phillip thrust in again and she realized he was moving deeper inside her each time. One more thrust and she felt his balls brush the lips of her pussy. It was too much. As he moved in and out, she could no longer control her body and she convulsed with the first surge of her orgasm.

Sarah's muscles contracted around Phillip's cock as he held it inside her, nestled in her tight little hole. As she moaned into her bit and came, he relinquished the control he had held for so long. With a groan of his own, he came inside her and together they rocked against the table as wave after wave took them both.

How long it lasted, she had no idea. All thought fled, leaving only sensation. She continued to moan as the orgasm lessened, then stopped. Once again, Phillip had given her one heck of a climax. He wrapped his arms around her as he went soft inside her, then backed away and cleaned himself. His juices flowed from her ass and trickled down her leg to mingle with her own. He grinned — he was not done with her yet — not this time.

Coming to her from behind again, Phillip held her with his arm around her waist as he had earlier — with one small difference. The vibrator still hummed along and with all the other sensations, she'd almost forgotten it. Now he turned the button and raised the vibrations; she gasped — she was going to come again.

"Keep the bit in place — you will want it," he instructed. Her eyes were beginning to glaze but he could tell she understood. With one hand he reached down to push on the vibrator, the other brushed her now very sore nipples. She came. Loudly. Her body thrashed against him as the more intense climax took her.

Just as it started to lessen, he removed a clamp and her body thrashed again — the pain giving her another climax. Tears streamed down her face and her teeth left marks in the bit. Now she knew what was in store for her when he removed the other one. Her climax lessened and he gave her a moment's respite. Her breathing slowed and he deemed her ready — he removed the second clamp. Again a climax wracked her body.

But she had no strength left for this one. If he had not held her upright, she would have collapsed along the table. The last climax faded and she was limp in his arms, exhausted.

Gently he lay her down, knowing the pressure of the mattress against her bound breasts and sore nipples might cause her body to climax a fifth time. He was not disappointed. Small twitches wracked her body as she came again, the waves this time leaving her barely conscious.

Gently he removed the bit; she didn't even open her eyes. Kneeling, he undid her legs, then the knots on the ropes binding her arms. Once her bindings were removed, he picked her up and carried her into the bedroom, settling her exhausted body gently onto the bed. Quietly he tiptoed into the bathroom to get a warm cloth to bathe her, but she was already asleep when he returned. He bathed her anyway, letting the soothing warmth add to her comfort.

His hands lingered over the task. The soft, round curves of Sarah's sleeping form invited his caress. Bathing her skin kindled a warmth inside him that he had not felt for a very long time. This time he did not push the thoughts away. He had violated her ass and she had enjoyed it. He dared to hope.

Phillip draped the wet cloth over the small wastepaper basket that stood beside the bed and looked his fill. He was to blame for her exhaustion and the thought amused him. This afternoon, Sarah had reached heights she'd only glimpsed through the clouds of her morality before and it was his doing. If he was right about her—they were heights she'd want to scale again.

The afternoon's activities had tired him as well. Pulling the covers up over them, and snuggling into the bed, he spooned his body against hers and together, they slept away the rest of the afternoon.

* * * * *

The room had gone dark by the time Sarah awoke. She felt his arm over her and lay there, feeling his protection. What a glorious afternoon it had been. She had never known pain could bring such pleasure. Carefully, so as not to disturb him, she reached up and squeezed her breasts gently, feeling around the nipple. There was only the mildest memory in them of the pain they had earlier felt. Moving slowly, she rose from the bed, not disturbing his slumber.

She went to wash up, only to discover she'd already been washed; his thoughtfulness touched her. Her husband certainly wouldn't have done such a thing. Not because he was a bad person, but because it just never would have occurred to him to do such a small service for her. In the kitchen, she turned on a small light and looked at the time. Almost 7:00. No wonder her stomach was growling! Peeking into the fridge, she saw a bowl of beef, already marinating. Upon further investigation, she found other indications of what he'd intended for dinner.

Donning an apron, she decided to let him sleep and surprise him with dinner. Was it a slave-type thing to do? She shrugged. Maybe, maybe not. No way to learn but to do it and see. She crossed the kitchen clad in her cuffs and apron, stopping about halfway across at the feel of the cloth against her skin. This was the most amount of clothing she'd had on since she'd arrived almost twenty-four hours earlier. The thought made her smile – and horny again.

But the full apron, slipped over her neck and tied around her waist, was a necessary item when working with the stovetop. She didn't want to splatter and burn her stomach—or anywhere else for that matter. Puttering around the kitchen, she started the dinner then set the table for two. On a sideboard, she found a set of candlesticks, the candles in them already burned about a third of the way down. She set them on the table—a romantic dinner by candlelight. Just what she would've ordered, had she been the Mistress.

Quietly she went to the bedroom door and checked on him – he still slept soundly. Dinner was still a half an hour away; she'd let him sleep. Back in the kitchen, she pulled a stool up to the counter to wait.

She was still very puzzled by this slave thing. He said earlier that her body had always known something was missing. How had he known that? She examined the leather cuffs. There wasn't much special about them that she could tell: just a wide belt but made for a wrist. A lock held it in place, making it difficult for her to remove. It was a small lock and she probably could pick it or just break it open by slamming it with something, but there was more to it than that. It was a symbol of her slavery.

How often in her daydreams had she imagined cuffs or ropes binding her wrists? How they felt so real sometimes that she'd look for the rope burns. She'd always laugh it off, saying to herself that perhaps she'd been chained in a former lifetime. But now she wondered, what if it wasn't a former lifetime? What if it was a desire for something in *this* life? She shook her wrist, hearing the little tinkle of the lock against the clasp of the cuff – it just sounded *right* in her ear.

The potatoes boiled over and she jumped from her reverie. Turning them down, she stuck a fork in them – done. Time for Master to get up.

But he beat her to it. She turned from the stove and he was standing in the doorway. Only the stove light was on and his face was in shadow. He was naked, but was he angry that she'd cooked for him?

Phillip had awakened to the smell of dinner cooking and had lain there for several minutes, just enjoying the fact that she'd taken the initiative to go ahead and get it started. Listening to her bustle around the kitchen, humming a snatch of a tune caused that warm feeling to grow again in the pit of his stomach. What was this woman doing to him? Did he really dare to dream?

And when the tension in his belly got too strong, he had gone out to the kitchen. Only one small light burned over the stove—and fluorescent wasn't flattering for any face. Except hers. There was no mistaking it. Sarah Simpson-Parker was a beautiful woman.

"I see my slave has been busy while I slept." She still could not tell his mood from his voice. "Y...yes, Sir," she stammered. "I thought to surprise you—and serve you for a change."

He stepped into the light and with relief she saw his smile. "I like that my slave wants to serve me." He pulled lightly on the apron. "I also like that my slave has enough common sense to protect herself in the kitchen." He leaned forward and kissed her lightly on the mouth. "I'll go shower; will it be ready soon?"

"Yes, Master. By the time you return."

He left and she almost danced across the kitchen. He liked her surprise! Quickly now she finished the dinner, mashing the potatoes and setting the meat and vegetables out on a platter and bowl respectively. The water stopped in the shower and she lit the candles.

When he returned, he had dressed in a dark pair of slacks and a crisp white shirt, open at the collar. Sockless, he looked very handsome, and very sexy. Her breath caught in her throat as he seated himself while she placed the food on the table. Taking off her apron, she sat next to him, her nudity now more comfortable than the apron.

To her surprise, he said grace. She served him first, making sure he had plenty of everything before filling her own plate. Waiting for him to take the first bite, she tried to do what she thought a servant would do.

They talked all through dinner and into the night. Where they'd grown up, about their families, what life had given them and what they'd made of it. One of the candles guttered and went out before they realized it was almost midnight and the table was still littered with the dinner's remains.

Laughing, they cleaned up the mess, and did the dishes. The simplicity of the act aroused him as he watched her padding barefoot and naked around the kitchen, tidying up. Phillip caught her in his arms and covered her mouth with his kiss. After their nap, neither was tired; Sarah could see the desire in his eyes and knew it matched the desire in her own.

"Come, my slave. I want to play with you one more time before I sleep."

Thrilled, she followed him to the bedroom. With a sweep of his arm, he cleared the bed of sheets and blankets and gestured to her to once more stretch herself out along the bed. When she made a move to put her hands over her head, he stopped her. "No. Tonight you will lie with your arms at your sides. They will not be bound – but you will not move. This is my command."

She realized he was testing her resolve. Smiling, she lay in the center of the bed, her arms at her sides, her legs together. He smiled at her determination, and set to work weakening that resolve of hers. Moonlight streamed in through the window and backlit him as he undressed for her.

Slowly and with a cat-like grace, Phillip unbuttoned his shirt. Button-by-button his chest was revealed until his smooth skin was bared to her sight. Strong muscles gleamed in the moonlight as he tossed his shirt to the side and stepped toward her naked body; he was the predator and Sarah trembled to realize she was the prey.

His eyes never left hers, holding her in his gaze. She tried to look away, but the slow removal of his clothes mesmerized her. His gracefully long fingers now bent to unzip his pants. As they fell, Sarah saw he wore nothing underneath—only the thin fabric of his shirt and his pants had been between them all evening long. Naked in the moonlight, his eyes locked on hers as his cock grew to its wonderful length.

Sarah's breasts rose and fell as her breath quickened. Using all her willpower, she kept her hands at her sides, even though her fingers cried out to caress that magnificent shaft of his. She wanted to feel the velvety softness with her hands—a softness she had already experienced with her lips. Opening her mouth now in remembered service, her tongue crept out to lick along the side as desire coursed through her.

With the graceful stride of a lion, Phillip moved out of the light to stretch beside her on the bed. He brushed her nipples with the palm of his hand and leaned into her ear, licking along the edge. She moaned at the pleasure and squirmed.

"Do not move, my slave." She stuck her tongue out at him and lay still. He laughed. "I think I can find a better use for that tongue." He kissed her then, reminding her that he'd already claimed possession of her mouth. Their tongues entwined and again she needed every ounce of her willpower to keep her hands to her sides.

Phillip's kisses moved away from her mouth and down her neck, traveling to her soft, ample breasts. His lips sucked each nipple in turn and Sarah gasped as his tongue circled and sucked, fondling her breasts as he parted her legs with his knee. Obediently and eagerly, she spread wide for him. He grinned as he moved in between them. "My, my, slave. Do you want something?" He tugged on her nipple and she moaned in remembered pain and pleasure. "Answer me, slave. Is there something you want?"

"Oh, yes, Master," she breathed.

"What is it? What is it you want, slave?" He rolled the nipple hard between his fingers, causing her to cry out in desire.

"You, Master! I want you. Inside me."

"I have possessed your mouth and your ass, slave. Do you wish me now to possess your pussy?"

She arched her back as his fingers now trailed along her stomach and stopped, petting the hair covering her mound. "Yes, Master. I want you to take possession of me—all of me."

He smiled and let his fingers continue downward, caressing the wet lips of her pussy. She wriggled under his touch and he needed to remind her again. "You may not move, slave. I have commanded it."

For answer she moaned in frustration, but lay still. His finger slid along her clit and she cried out again, but did not move. Ever so slowly, his slid his finger inside her, feeling her warmth and willingness to have him. Sliding his body down the bed, he dragged a pillow along with him. "Lift your hips," he commanded. When she quickly complied, he pushed it under her bottom, raising her to a more convenient level.

Now he leaned down and she could feel his breath on her pussy lips. No one had ever eaten her before—ever. She felt his tongue slide over and between her lips and gasped as it found her clit.

"Oh, Master! I'm going to come!"

"No, you aren't. Not yet. You will hold it until I say so. Understood?" His voice was muffled by her legs. She didn't know if he saw her nod, but she didn't trust her voice. Instead she grabbed the sheet under her hands, holding on as if for dear life.

Phillip's tongue licked along her pussy, over her clit, then down again, parting the lips as they went. He had tasted several women in his life and each one had their own distinctive scent and taste. Sarah was slightly salty, her musky scent filling his nose as he flicked his tongue out to lap up a generous portion of her juices. There was no doubt the woman liked his handling of her. Again that full feeling of satisfaction settled in his belly as he pushed deeper with his tongue.

Sarah felt his tongue enter her, possessing her the way he'd possessed every other part of her. Her breasts heaving, she held back tears as she tried desperately not to come.

And then he was leaning over her. "Are you ready for me, slave?"

"Yes, Master. Please!" She ended on a scream as he thrust into her, possessing her body with his cock. He pulled out his entire length and pushed into her again. She moaned, her body writhing, her control in tatters.

"Now, slave. Put your arms around me now and come with me."

Yes! She wrapped her arms around his shoulders and her legs around his waist, opening up for him, letting him in, riding him as he rode her. His mouth covered hers and his tongue entered her as she responded with passion. Sarah tasted herself on his tongue—a taste she'd never known before. Abandoning reason and thought, she opened herself to him and gave him her entire being. Eagerly her tongue sought his, wanting to lick her own juices from his mouth. He slammed into her body, forgetting to be gentle as the lion inside of him responded to the submissiveness that now awakened in her. Together they reached their climax and Sarah felt Phillip's cock pulse as he emptied his seed inside her—marking her—making her his own.

The realization made her climax again — he had claimed her; she was his. Over and over they rocked together, their voices groaning as one as their orgasms ran their course.

Afterward, they lay entwined for an eternity — for time had ceased to have meaning. How long they made love, she did not know — did not care to know. He explored her with his mouth and she did the same to him — wanting to know every inch of him. Phillip's fingers gentled, letting his tongue bathe her skin; making her shiver in the waning moonlight. Sarah too, joined in the bath — sucking his nipples and tasting the hollow that ran from his neck to his stomach. But as the fire of their passion lit anew, his fingers grew more insistent and her mouth more eager. When he grew hard once more, he took her, at her fervent invitation.

Their bodies almost spent, this time they rode the gentle waves of an orgasm together, softly rocking in each other's arms. He came inside her again, and Sarah felt the sticky wetness add to the ample amount of come already between her legs. Too tired to move, the two fell asleep, her head on his chest, his arm around her waist.

* * * * *

She woke up in the morning uncuffed. Surprised, she sat up, examining her empty wrists. How odd they felt. The water shut off in the shower and she waited for him, expectantly.

The door opened and he came into the bedroom, toweling his hair dry and completely naked. Her breath caught in her throat at the sight of his muscular body. With a sudden lurch, she realized this was the first opportunity she had been given to see him totally nude. Yesterday morning he was already dressed by the time she awoke. And during their lovemaking in the afternoon, she had felt his naked skin next to hers, but he had been behind her the entire time. Last night she glimpsed him in the moonlight. This morning, he stood there in all his glory.

And glorious he was. Those broad shoulders, now shirtless, lived up to the potential discovered by the exploration of her fingers the night before. She knew those shoulders to be hard-packed and tight with power. His wet hair dripped onto his skin and droplets rolled down along his chest; her eyes followed the little trail of water as it coursed along his smooth, well-muscled chest to gather in the little hollow in the center of his flat stomach.

He was not erect this morning, yet even in a dormant state, his cock impressed her—had she really taken that entire length into her ass? She squirmed and shifted as she continued to watch him. He had a runner's thighs and she watched his muscles ripple and stretch as he moved across the room.

Phillip took his time in the doorway. He was vain enough to realize her gaze was an appreciative one and he let her look her fill before crossing to the bed.

"Morning!" He smiled at her and she rose for a kiss. He gave her a light one, and a tap on the bottom. "Take your shower, my dear. I'll be in the kitchen."

She hurried through her morning ritual. Every moment away from him was a moment of the day lost. Still, washing the remnants of last night's lovemaking from her pussy, Sarah smiled, feeling very contented with her weekend. Phillip filled her mind and she wanted to be with him.

Coming back into the bedroom, her hair still wrapped in its towel, she saw her clothes had been moved from the chair to the bed. The meaning was clear: she was to dress. With some trepidation, she did so. Did this mean he was done with her? What if she wasn't done with him yet? Putting aside her sudden doubts, she picked up her panties and slipped them on.

The clothes felt awkward on her—she'd been naked all weekend and had just gotten used to the feeling of freedom. Now her clothes confined her in a way she'd never realized before and made her self-conscious. Dressed, she made her way to the kitchen, where he sat just as she'd found him the morning before. But where yesterday, her nudity made her uncomfortable, today her clothes did. For a completely different reason, she found the ground this morning just as shaky as she had before.

"Please sit down, Sarah." It was the first time since Friday that he'd used her name. It sounded odd, but she did as she was told.

He took her hand and looked at her gently. After their coupling of the night before, he knew setting her free would be difficult on the both of them. And yet, it had to be done. He wanted her as his slave—but she needed the freedom to come to him on her own. Only that way would he truly own her—only that way would she truly be owned.

"I have to release you now, Sarah—our twenty-four hour trial is over. Besides, you have other things to attend to this weekend and so do I. I will take you home soon and you will resume your life just where you left it on Friday." He paused, searching for the right words. "It is my hope that you will come here at the end of the week."

She caught his meaning. He was releasing her—during the week she would live as she always had—on the weekend, she would become his slave, if she wanted to.

"I will not ask you to make a decision today—in fact, I don't want you to. You need to take the week. Put some distance between your experiences here and get back to your life before. Only then can you decide."

She knew what he was saying was wise. Right now, her decision would be based on emotion alone. The weekend had been filled with glorious sex, but little else. And she wanted more. It was comforting to discover he did too.

She nodded her understanding. "Yes, Phillip, I understand. When I make my decision, how can I let you know?"

"I will be here on Friday. Once work has finished for you, drive here instead of going to your apartment. Pack a change of clothes, because, if you do come, you will not leave until Monday morning when you leave for a regular week of work."

There was no mistaking the authority in his voice. The latent power stirred her and she knew if she showed up at his door on Friday, he would make good on his statement. The thought thrilled her.

"But now it's time for me to take you home, Sarah." He stood and she followed suit, her stomach growling. They both laughed. "What say we go have breakfast before I take you home?"

"Definitely!" She grinned and they headed out the door. She had a decision to make this week, although she already had an inkling what it was going to be…

Chapter Three
A second try

All week Sarah thought about Friday night. She'd gone to work Monday morning, just as usual. She had gone about her normal, everyday tasks, same as she always did.

But she wasn't the same. And she was surprised that no one noticed. Everything was tinted differently and Phillip's presence was with her every moment. Even doing innocuous activities such as bending down to pick up a fallen document, or reaching up high to get something off the upper shelf; she'd remember being in similar positions with him. Tied. Unable to move. Controlled. His toy. She blushed with remembrance. His slave.

Every little moment like that made her wet. She had taken to bringing an extra pair of panties with her to work and changing at midday. A constant state of arousal had been her manner all week.

Her "normal" week.

And now it was drawing to a close. Finally! She'd put together a small suitcase of clothes for Monday and put it in the trunk of her car that morning. How she'd made it through the day, she had no idea, but at last she was out of the building and driving down the highway.

It was almost 6:30 before she pulled into his drive. His car was already there and she remembered he said he'd be waiting. Desperately hoping she hadn't made him wait long, she practically flew out of the car and up the path to his door. But once on the porch, she paused to collect herself. She was making a fool of herself, running this way. She was behaving like a slut that needed to rut. She made a wry face. Which wasn't so far from the truth.

There was no bell, so she knocked. Softly at first, then with more courage. Would he be mad at her for the traffic's delay? Would he even still want her? "What ifs" ran through her head as she waited, trying not to bounce in impatience.

The setting sun lit his powerfully built frame as he opened the door and stood smiling at her. Again dressed in a crisp white shirt and dark slacks, his appearance took her breath away. Tall and rugged, the sun made shadows in the deep dimples of his cheeks. His shirtfront half open, the soft evening light caressed the smooth skin of his muscled chest and Sarah's heart beat a bit faster. How could she have forgotten how his hair curled over his ear like that? She stood grinning and speechless.

He stood in the doorway, blocking it with his incredibly handsome body. "Good evening, Sarah. Have you come to spend the weekend with me?"

She blushed and lowered her eyes. "Yes, Sir, I have."

He nodded. "I'm glad you came. You know the rules now. Are you ready to enter my house?"

She raised her head and looked at him, her voice and manner steady. This was what she'd waited for all week. "Yes, Sir. I am ready to enter and become your slave."

He stepped aside and she crossed the threshold.

* * * * *

The corridor was at once familiar and strange. Everything was exactly where she remembered it being, but she was a different person entering now. She'd seen the house in different lights throughout the previous weekend, but this time she was here, knowing what she was in for.

Phillip walked straight into the living room, certain she would follow without being told and was pleased when she did so. Certain now that she was here. His week had been spent getting ready for the moment she returned. If she returned. Hearing her car in the drive had been the sweetest sound on earth. Now he would test the strength of her resolve. He sat comfortably in one of the large easy chairs while she stood, chewing on her lip in uncertainty.

"Undress for me, slave." His voice was quiet, commanding.

Her fingers trembling with nervousness, she unbuttoned her white silk blouse, pulling it out of her skirt. She let it slide off her shoulders and fall gracefully to the floor. She had to hide her grin as the blouse landed exactly as she'd practiced all week long. Reaching behind her to find the zipper to her skirt, she pushed out her breasts to give him a bit of a show.

A smile twitched at his lips. The little minx wanted to play! Delighted, he sat back to enjoy her performance.

She slid the knee-length skirt down her legs and stepped out of it, looking for a place to set it down. Spotting an empty side chair, she stooped to pick up her blouse and took the two pieces of her outfit to the chair, clad only in her bra, panties, stockings and heels.

Returning to her position, she reached behind her again to undo the clasp of her lacy white bra. For a moment, her breasts pushed against the cups and then fell as they were released from their confinement. With a deft toss, the bra landed neatly on top of her folded clothes.

Now she pulled down her panties and stockings together, her breasts hanging forward as she did so. She kicked off her heels, and took the entire pile to the chair, then came back to stand before him, clad only in her earrings and a gold chain necklace she'd forgotten she was wearing.

With an appraising eye, he enjoyed her performance. She was very sexy—and she knew it. He would have fun with her body and her mind this weekend.

Without moving from his chair, he commanded her again. "Kneel."

This, too, she'd been practicing all week. She knelt without hesitation, her hands clasped behind her back and her elbows slightly together so that her breasts pointed out in front of her.

Already she could see the nipples sticking out. Keeping her chin parallel to the floor, she gazed straight ahead, waiting for his next command.

She felt rewarded when he told her, "Good, slave. You remembered." A thrill went through her and she could not contain her smile. But she dared not move her eyes to look at him. She remained still.

He now uncoiled from the chair and again she was reminded of the slow grace of a wildcat, moving out on the hunt. She watched him from the corner of her eye as he moved around her, examining her from every angle as she knelt before him.

Her cheeks reddened, aware of his scrutiny. All week, she'd practiced this position, the only one he'd taught her. She was up to almost 10 minutes before her muscles would cramp and she'd have to move. Only the grin on her face gave away her own pleasure—knowing he was surprised at her endurance—and pleased.

"Stand."

Gracefully, for she had practiced this as well, she stood, only wobbling a little as she rose. She still kept her eyes front, but brought her legs together, leaving her hands behind her.

He nodded his pleasure, smiling. "You are ready for another position, my slave. Put your feet about a foot apart."

She looked down to check how far a foot apart was. Her pussy was more available now, but still comfortably covered. Returning her gaze forward, she gripped her hands tighter, the muscles in her arms beginning to twitch.

"Now move your feet out another foot."

Without looking she did so, her inhale sharp as the cooler air of the room hit her now spread pussy lips. With her feet so far apart, she was open, vulnerable. Her eyelids fluttered a little as elation thrilled through her.

Walking behind her, he saw her arms trembling. "Let me help you here," he whispered into her ear. His breath so close increased her desire. She felt the familiar leather around her wrists and heard the familiar "click" as he locked the cuffs in place. Now she could relax her arms a bit, letting the cuffs take some of the pressure of keeping her arms pinioned behind her.

He rubbed her arms for a moment, feeling her relax under his hands. Moving up to her soft, round shoulders, he massaged them, helping her release some of the tension of a work week made longer with anticipation.

But he did not want her too relaxed. Not yet. He let his hand slide down over her breast and smiled at her gasp as he passed lightly over her nipple. Letting his hand continue downward, he felt the small roundness of her belly, and lower, the downy hair that covered her mound. She leaned against him and a moan escaped. There was no doubt about her need. Or his.

And then her stomach growled. Her eyes flew open in embarrassment and he laughed out loud. "Hungry, my slave?"

"I was too excited to eat lunch, Sir. I haven't eaten since breakfast," she admitted.

He tilted his head sideways as he considered. "Good." He stepped in front of her, standing close. His scent intoxicated her and her head swam a little. "Then let's make sure you have an excellent appetite, shall we?" Lightly his hands traced over her shoulders and down her arms, one hand settling on her derrière, the other scooping around to steady her back. His kiss was not gentle.

The ferocity of his unleashed passion took her by surprise and she recoiled. But he held her tightly and crushed her to him. Her own body now responded and she opened her mouth, letting their tongues entwine, her own ardor matching his. A need echoed in her belly, but it was not food she now was hungry for. His hand squeezed her ass and she leaned into him, wanting him, wanting him to feed her pussy with his sex. Having her arms locked behind her frustrated her, increasing her need.

Roughly he broke from their kiss and with a small growl he picked her up and tossed her over his shoulder as if she were no more than a sack of potatoes. She squealed, and tried not to wiggle lest he drop her. In the bedroom, he threw her on the bed, rolling her over and unlocking her cuffs. Rolling her again onto her back, he grabbed her hands and dragged her up the bed, locking her wrists to the headboard.

Never had she been treated so forcefully. But she wanted him — needed him. All week Sarah had thought of nothing but his command of her. Her body ached for his touch as he practically ripped the clothes from his own body, then pulled her legs apart, locking them into place. Only once she was bound and helpless to stop him did he pause to survey her — spread and ready for his pleasure.

"I am going to take you like the slave you are. Your body is mine to use — and I intend to use it hard." His voice was rough and gravelly from his desire and the sound of it thrilled her.

"This pussy," he paused to grab her, sinking his fingers inside her and rubbing her juices with his hand, "this pussy is mine, isn't it, slave?"

She writhed with the need to come building inside her. When she didn't answer, he pulled her, several fingers still buried deep inside, his thumb on her mound. "Answer me, slave. Who owns this pussy?"

"You do," she gasped. "You do, Sir." Above her head, her hands clenched as she arched her back, giving herself to him.

"And what are you?" He pulled on her again and she cried out.

"I am your slave, Master. My body is yours. I am your Slave!" Her voice cracked on the last word, her breath gone, her mind wanting only to feel him inside her — to have him take her and take her hard.

Phillip pulled his hand away and knelt between her legs, reaching under to grab her ass, pulling her onto his knees. Positioning his cock, swollen with the desire he had denied himself all week, he saw with satisfaction the gleam of the juices that pooled in her pussy. With a single thrust, he entered her, slamming her body back onto the bed.

Riding her hard, he thrust in and out, long thrusts, as she rose to meet each one. But he could not hold out for long. As the muscles in her pussy contracted with the first wave of her orgasm, he came and the world ceased turning for them both.

Wave after wave of powerful contractions shook them, their animal passion spending itself after a week of denial. Feeling him slam into her as if she were nothing but a whore for his use, she came again and again, all thought gone. His cock battered her pussy, his repeated thrusts bruising her tender flesh as she came again, her wordless cries filling the room.

Her sounds drove him wilder as the animal inside rutted against his slave. All week he had thought about her, wondered if she would return. His heart was lightened when he heard her car in the drive and he used all the control he had watching her taunt him with her striptease. Now that control was gone and as she screamed again and he felt her pussy muscles contract around his cock once again, his own climax came, forceful and violent.

A small, still-sane part of him knew he was hurting her, but he could not stop. His seed spit forth and filled her as his own groans echoed in his ears. Only when his cock was completely empty did he stop, his momentarily exhausted body collapsing on top of hers.

As his motions slowed Sarah's body relaxed and the orgasms lessened, then stopped. Panting, they lay entwined as the intensity of their passion passed.

Slowly awareness came back to her. His full weight was upon her, and far from feeling suffocated, she relished his warmth. Never had she been so forcefully handled, so forcefully taken. Knowing that his need had been as great as hers made her feel as warm inside as his body made her feel outside. There was comfort and satisfaction in the realization that she could make him lose control.

He stirred, raising his head to look at her. "Are you all right? Did I hurt you?" His concern was obvious.

"Mmmm, you just gave me a most wonderful gift—besides the several orgasms, you showed me a side of you I didn't know existed. And I'm fine," she added as the concern in his eyes did not ease.

With her reassurance, he slid off her and pulled a blanket from the bottom of the bed over the two of them. Raising himself on one elbow, he caressed her face, still nestled between her bound arms. "I have thought of very little this week but you. Last week you showed such a willingness to learn, to please, that I'm afraid I got my hopes up quite a bit for this weekend." He grinned and she saw a bit of shyness there she'd not expected. "I was afraid you would change your mind and not show up. And then when you were late..." his voice drifted off.

"I am very sorry about that, Master. I left work on time, but the traffic was particularly bad. I can try a different route next time."

He smiled and kissed her forehead. "That's all right—you take the safest route. I can put up with a little delay, knowing you are on your way." His hand stroked her breast now, circling the nipple. "Seeing you kneeling so obediently before me, ready to serve me, pushed my control over the edge and I wanted you more than I have ever wanted anything before. Mostly I keep the animal in me caged, to let it out is dangerous. But be assured, I will never hurt you."

Sarah suspected he had bruised her, but that had only led to stronger climaxes. By morning, she would be fine and so she said nothing. For the first time she found she wished her wrists were not bound. More than ever, she wanted to put her arms around him and hold him—he looked vulnerable for just the briefest of moments and she knew she'd glimpsed a part of him he showed to no one. A stirring in her heart warned her he was fast becoming more than a mere dalliance—she was falling in love.

"I know you will not hurt me," she whispered. Then she grinned with a naughty smile on her face. "Well, at least not hurt me more than I can take!"

He laughed outright at that and the moment passed. Her stomach growled again, this time answered by his. Laughing, he released her from her bonds and helped her off the bed. Phillip dressed, and Sarah, wearing nothing but her customary ankle and wrist cuffs, accompanied him to the kitchen, from which were coming the most delicious smells.

She set the table, noticing he'd placed two new candles in the holders. They ate by their light and caught up on the week's events. It seemed perfectly natural now for her to be sitting in the nude at the table, her cuffs jingling as she ate, while he wore his customary white shirt and dark pants.

Dinner and dishes done, he led her to the couch, where they snuggled in front of the fireplace, talking through the rest of the evening. By ten o'clock they were both yawning, tired from the day of work, a good meal, and their earlier passion. He took her by the hand, led her to bed, and they fell asleep in each other's arms.

* * * * *

A deep sleeper by nature, Sarah woke to find the sun up long before she was. Apparently Phillip had been up and busy as well. She tried to roll off her stomach, only to find her hands tied to the opposite sides of the bed. Her ankles as well were tied, and she could not move.

"Good morning, slave. You seem to be stuck."

She could not see him—he must be somewhere at the foot of the bed. "Yes, Sir," she answered, sleep leaving in a hurry, replaced by a feeling of vulnerability. She shivered as he sat next to her and ran his hand over her ass. Lulled by his caress, the slap made her gasp.

"I had a very nice time talking with you last night, slave." He slapped her ass again. She couldn't remember the last time she'd been spanked—her parents hadn't used that form of discipline very often.

"It was a wonderful evening, Master."

Slap! "Yes, slave. I know you enjoyed it. But mostly it was a conversation between equals and today you must learn your place." Slap!

Her cheek was burning where he'd hit it and she knew it must be turning red under his hand. After each spank, his hand rubbed the spot and she was intensely aware of her arousal.

"What is your place, slave?" Slap! He moved his hand to the other cheek and she was totally unprepared for it.

"My place?" Her brain thought furiously. "My place is…"

Slap! "You're thinking too much, slave. Answer me, where is your place?"

He spanked her again and her voice tight, she blurted out, "My place is at your side, Master!"

"Close, slave. Try again."

But he hadn't spanked her. His hand still rubbing her ass, she thought and then answered, "My place is at your feet, Master."

"Very good, slave." She felt him get off the bed. There was the familiar snick as he unlocked her ankles and then she saw him move to her hands, releasing her wrists.

"Go use the bathroom and do not dawdle."

She scampered into the bathroom, her rear end still stinging from his blows. There had been a certain playfulness about them, yet she sensed a deeper seriousness. She could not deny that his use of her this morning aroused her on a very deep level. There was no doubt in her mind that she was the slave and he the master. Quickly she finished and returned to the bedroom, where he sat on the edge of the bed.

"Kneel."

She did so, taking again the position he had taught her. Spreading her knees and clasping her hands behind her back, she knelt with a straight back, looking forward. He leaned down and took her chin in his hands, angling her head up so that their eyes met.

"I am going to push your limits today, Sarah. Know that I will not harm you and remember you can use your safeword if you need it. But today I intend to teach you the meaning of the words 'obedience' and 'discipline.' Do you understand?"

She wasn't sure she did. She knew what the words meant—but obviously his definitions must be a little different than hers. And he'd used her name—that meant he was extremely serious. Well, she was here to be his slave—and exploring this part of her personality was certainly exciting. She nodded, accepting his words.

"Stand."

Rising gracefully, not teetering this time, she stood before him. She was surprised when he bent down and removed her ankle cuffs, then took her arms and removed those cuffs as well.

"Then, slave, listen carefully to my instructions. You are to take your shower, then replace your cuffs. In the kitchen you will find a note listing what you are to prepare for breakfast. I will be leaving for a while—breakfast should be on the table when I return. You are not to touch yourself in any sexual way. Do you understand, slave?"

She nodded. The instructions weren't difficult—well, except for the last one. He kissed her lightly and left. A moment later she heard the front door close and a moment after that, the car started and pulled out.

Feeling a little strange, she took her shower, cleaning herself, but not even tempted to awaken her sex. She was distracted and couldn't figure out how she felt about his commands.

Returning to the bedroom, the cuffs lay on the bed where he'd placed them. Thoroughly dry, she picked up one for her wrist and fit it, snapping the lock shut. While such an act certainly aroused her, it was much more satisfying when he put them on her.

Jingling her cuffs, Sarah made her way to the kitchen. The note he'd spoken of was easy to find on the otherwise empty counter.

> "*Slave,*
>
> *Cook my breakfast and have it ready on the table — hot — when I return. Cook my eggs sunny side up; the two strips of bacon should be crisp and the toast light. Use the potatoes in the refrigerator for hash browns. Set the table for one.*
>
> *Master*"

As she set about finding the pots and pans she'd need, something inside rankled her, but she couldn't put a finger on it. Slicing the potatoes, she stopped and picked up the note and re-read it.

There it was. "Set the table for one." That was the phrase that bothered her. She was cooking his breakfast, but was not going to be allowed to eat with him? He was treating her as someone to be ordered about — a servant! Or a slave. Her cheeks burned as the realization hit home.

Tears stung her eyes as she donned the apron and turned on the heat under the potatoes. A frown furrowed her face as she pulled one plate out of the cupboard and set it on the counter. With a lump in her throat, she set his spot at the table, and looked wistfully at the chair she usually occupied.

This was a side of slavery she'd never even considered. Submitting to him when they had sex was easy — this was not. And it was not fun. If this was what he'd had in mind, she wasn't sure she wanted to be a part of it.

But she'd committed to the weekend, and if the man wanted a maid/cook/cleaning lady/slut for the weekend, well, she'd do it. But she wouldn't be back.

Pushing the browning potatoes to the side of the pan, she laid the strips of bacon beside them, stepping back as they splattered a bit. The bread she set in the toaster, ready to be pushed down the moment she heard his car.

He pulled in just as she had everything ready. Pushing the lever of the toaster down, she broke the eggs into a second pan to fry up quickly. He entered and she heard him in the corridor. Should she greet him? If she left the stove, the eggs might burn. She was saved from her indecision.

"Smells good, slave. I will be served now." He sat in his favorite spot at the table. Phillip knew he was pushing her—he could tell that anger simmered just under the surface. Appearing nonchalant, he watched her fulfill his orders, his gut wrenching as he wondered if he had pressed her too far.

Sliding the eggs onto his plate, Sarah scooped out the hash browns and laid the bacon over the top. The toast popped and with a quick swipe of the knife, she buttered the two slices and set them on the side. Carefully carrying the plate, she brought it to the table, remembering at the last minute the old rule: serve from the right; take away from the left.

"Kneel by my side, slave." Yes, there was anger in her silence, but something else warred in her eyes. Turning so that she would remain in his field of vision, he casually watched to see if she would follow his command.

Surprised and uncertain as to why he wanted her to kneel beside him, she did so, her chest out proudly and her eyes looking along the length of the table. She might not like being treated like this, but darn it, she'd take what ever he dished out. He'd see the iron side of her yet.

"Take off the apron." With a pull on the strings, the apron came loose and Sarah folded it neatly, setting it on the chair she normally sat in.

"You may kneel at rest, slave."

She wasn't sure what this command meant, but she leaned back onto her heels and let her hands rest on her thighs. When he didn't offer any further instructions, she relaxed a little. He had opened a paper he'd brought in with him and was engrossed in reading and in eating the food she'd prepared for him.

Phillip's eyes roamed the page, but his attention was completely on the woman kneeling at his side. He had meant what he said about the obedience this morning. Modern women were not used to being treated as servants and he suspected Sarah was no different. If things worked out between them, they each would find their spaces in the Dominant and submissive roles, but for now, he intended to push her limits and find out just what she would—and would not—take. He turned the page, eating his breakfast and pretending to read as his slave knelt silently at his side.

After a bit, Sarah's legs started to ache from kneeling for so long. She glanced up at him without moving her head, but he was still involved in the paper and seemed to have forgotten her. Briefly she thought about saying something; this wasn't fun and she certainly wasn't getting aroused. Before she could, her stomach rumbled—loudly.

If he heard it, he gave no sign. But after a few moments more, Phillip set his paper down and pushed his chair back. Looking down, he complimented her. "You have been very good, slave. For that, since you are hungry, you may finish what I did not eat. Clean up and do the dishes and then come to the playroom." He rose and left the kitchen.

She stared at his retreating back. *I may eat his leftovers? Did he really say that?* Standing, she took his plate. He'd only eaten one egg and one slice of bacon. Both pieces of toast were gone and about half the hash browns. Obviously he'd not intended to eat it all and had her prepare enough for the both of them.

But the thought of eating leftovers from his plate was abhorrent to her. What was that he'd said earlier about testing her limits? Well, here was one. She'd go hungry rather than eat someone else's leavings. She scraped the plate into the garbage. There weren't many dishes and she did them quickly.

Remembering the apron, she returned it to its hook before going down the corridor to what he called the 'playroom,' but she still thought of as the dungeon. Standing in the door, trying not to glower, Sarah waited for his next instruction.

His back was to her, yet he'd heard her enter. Without turning around, he gestured to the wall where the rings hung down. It was where she'd been fastened their very first night together.

Since he didn't speak, she decided she wouldn't either. Almost defiantly, she walked over to the wall, turned and faced him, absently noting that there were actually three rings evenly spaced on the board fastened to the wall above her.

He was pushing her—wanting to see how far he could push before she'd rebel. His face stern, the power in him evident, he stood before her. "Raise your arms."

A part of her ice melted at the kind look in his eyes and she did as she was told. How could he do that do her? What was there about him that made her want to submit? He took her left hand in his, stepping closer to fasten her wrist cuff to the outside ring and she inhaled the scent of his cologne. Her eyes drooped a moment as she fought becoming aroused.

Shifting his weight, he picked up her other hand, pausing to place a kiss on her palm before raising it to fasten to the opposite outside ring. The light pressure of his soft kiss sent another gentle wave toward the center of her sex and again she fought the arousal, the feeling of vulnerability it always provoked.

His hand brushed a stray hair from her face; in spite of her anger, the ice melted a little more. "Did my slave enjoy her breakfast?" he asked quietly.

"No, Sir, I did not." Her cheeks turned red, knowing she did not do as she was commanded. It didn't help that her stomach rumbled at that point, giving her away.

He noted the sounds of hunger coming from her belly. His fingers played over her breasts, lightly touching them, a feather-caress only. "Why did you not?"

Her head dropped — his hand was there on her chin, pulling it back up. "Tell me why you did not enjoy your breakfast, slave."

Sarah raised her head and lifted her chin from his fingers as her independent streak broke free. "I didn't like the idea of eating your leftovers. I'm better than that."

She discovered he could raise a single eyebrow. "You are my slave. You are to do as you are commanded." His voice was stern, but he did not raise it. Phillip was actually glad to see her independence come forward. A slave who willingly gave that independence to him was much more of a whole woman than a slave who came with a trainload of baggage and dependencies. Still, he was not about to back down — he needed to know if this was a hard limit for Sarah or a negotiable one.

Tears formed in her eyes. Was it such a big thing he was asking? After all, he'd been careful not to eat that egg — and the hash browns had been separated from the others. Why was she making this an issue? "I'm sorry, Sir. I just couldn't do it," she whispered.

He nodded and took a step back. "Understood, slave. But you must understand I will test that limitation — and together we will find what you are too 'good' for." He picked up the flogger. Lightly, he dragged it over her breasts, her stomach, her mound. Her anger dissipated in his manipulation of her body and a moan escaped her lips.

"At the moment, I will neither discipline nor reward my slave for her actions this morning." He reversed the flogger and put the handle between her unbound legs, rubbing the end in the white cream that he knew would already be there. He almost smiled when she opened herself a little wider to allow him access. "But know we are not finished with the matter." He would take his time in breaking down her walls of propriety. In time, she would submit to him on every level, but not yet. He wanted her walls broken, not her spirit.

The handle of the flogger pushed upwards against her clit and Sarah's eyes drooped to half-mast, longing to come at his hand. But even as she acknowledged the desire building in her, she recognized its selfishness. If she was his slave, and submitting to him, then shouldn't she be more concerned with his welfare than her own?

Phillip leaned in, his tall frame towering over her, his lips at her ear, kissing the edge and whispering to her. "Tell me, slave. What do you desire?"

He pulled up more on the handle of the flogger, causing her to gasp and raise herself on tiptoe. Her anger departed as a misty haze on a hot summer day, replaced by an ache only he could fill. Sarah knew her answer and spoke it from her heart. "I desire to please you, Sir."

Phillip pulled up again, forcing her onto the very tips of her toes. She moaned and his tongue flicked out to taste along the inside of her ear. "Yes, slave," he whispered. "You desire to please me with your sex — your wantonness and lust." He moved the handle back and forth, soaking it in her juices that flowed freely now. "But I want your desire to please to extend beyond sex — beyond the lust of your body. It is *my* desire for you to want to please me in *everything* you do."

The handle of the flogger was driving her mad — she would have spread her legs further, but she was so far up on her toes it was impossible. He expected an answer and there was only one she could give him. "Yes, Master. I will try to do better next time."

"Try?" He pushed the flogger upward once more so that one foot was now off the ground.

A wordless cry came from her throat. "I will do better next time, Master. I will." Her head leaned back against the wall and he could see her discomfort reflected in her eyes. With a deft movement, he withdrew the handle, flipped the flogger over in his hand and struck her with it across the breasts.

The shock of it made her cry aloud. Again the flogger fell, making red marks that quickly faded. The blows stung, and she put her breasts out for more. She would show him that she would take whatever he gave her. She suddenly wanted to do anything he asked of her.

Phillip recognized her move into that un-thinking mode — the mode where all one wanted was release from the tension building inside. She would promise him anything now — do anything. But he also knew she would resent any promises made while she was in this state. She was at her most vulnerable when her passion overtook her mind — and he knew some masters took advantage of their slaves at this moment.

He landed a few more strokes on her unprotected breasts, careful not to overdo it. She couldn't say no to him now, so he'd have to say it for her. Setting down the flogger, he came over to rub her red breasts.

His touch was soothing to her — the skin on her breasts was just beginning to burn when he stopped the blows. He massaged them, kissing them, licking them of their light wounding. Her nipples were hard little nubs and as his tongue caressed them, Sarah moaned. "Spread your legs," he commanded.

She did so with no thought to how demeaning the command had sounded to her the first time she'd heard it. She enjoyed it now — and the slutty way it made her feel. He knelt down and fastened her ankles to the wall, her legs stretched as far as they could be. She hung from her wrists now, her legs spread too wide to support her. Not even realizing she did so, her hands grasped the rings above her.

His intent was to take her deep into that subspace mode. Picking up a coil of rope from the table, he came back to her, passing a length of it around her waist, pulling it tight. She gasped and drew in her breath and he pulled it a bit tighter. "Hold your breath," he told her and then knotted the rope to make a tight circle around her waist. "You may breathe again."

Her breath came out all at once, but she found with the rope tied so tightly, she couldn't take such a deep breath in again. Once more her head rested against the wall behind her as her eyes closed, savoring the sensation, aware that her juices gushed again by the way the air moved over her spread crotch.

Phillip stepped back to watch her enjoying the tight bondage of a simple rope. Waiting until she grew used to it, he tugged on the rope a few times, pulling her waist out toward him. Secured to the wall as she was, she could not fight him, nor did she try. But the creamy white liquid from her pussy glistened below.

Stepping toward her again, he passed the rope around her back, tying it securely and then bringing it down through her deliciously sweet crack, passing by her tiny asshole, and up through her soaked pussy lips. He made sure it was snug against her clit then tied it securely to her waist rope, pulling it tight as he did so.

Her moaning grew louder, to be invaded by such a simple thing! Desperately she tried to rub her clit onto the rope, but it didn't move—and neither did she. The most she could do was squirm in her bindings, the rope digging into her need and driving all thought but one from her mind.

He leaned in again to whisper in her ear, one hand on the wall beside her head, the other fondling her slick pussy lips. "Perhaps my slave will consider shaving her pussy for me by next weekend." It was only a suggestion, and this would be the only time he would make it. But it was a way to test her resolve—her desire to truly please him.

Sarah heard his words echoing in her head without meaning. "Shaving...pussy...slave." Over and over the words ran through her head. Yes, she would shave for him—it was not something she'd ever considered, but if he'd hand her a razor, she'd do it now. She'd do anything for him.

He pulled on the crotch rope and she moaned again — yes, this was what she wanted — to be his slave. Her eyes were closed and her spirit open. Let him do with her what he wanted.

She felt him undo her ankles, letting her feet touch the floor again and more out of instinct than thought, she let her legs take her weight. He undid her right wrist, guiding her arm down or it would've fallen. Then her left as she leaned against the wall.

"Open your eyes, slave. Obey me!" He had to order her twice before she recovered and looked at him. "Stand up on your own two feet." He needed to see how far she had descended into that subspace mode. When she stood and her eyes cleared and focused on him, he knew he could proceed. If she could come back to him only on a voice command, she wasn't ready to come yet, no matter what she might beg for.

Desire ruled her body and mind. Desire to please him. She longed to do what he wanted. The crotch rope still held her sex prisoner and she had to will her hands not to touch herself now that they were free.

He pointed to a spot near the wall. "Kneel there, slave, facing me." She did so, the rope rubbing against her, increasing her craving. Dutifully, she placed her hands behind her back, grasping them and pushing out her breasts, no longer red now, but still sensitive. Her knees were apart, giving him access if he wanted it.

But he ignored her sex and the rope for the moment, instead kneeling beside her and pulling her hands back to her ankles. "Grab your ankles," he instructed and she did so. The familiar snick of the lock informed her she was stuck in a kneeling hogtie. A modicum of awareness had returned and she tested her bindings wanting to be sure she could not move. A few tugs convinced her that her wrists were firmly attached to her own ankles.

Phillip stood before her, again examining his willing captive, her pussy lips swollen with desire at the point where the rope disappeared between them. Did she understand how great an aphrodisiac her blind obedience was to him? How his body thrilled to see her tied and helpless, completely dependent on him for release? No. Not yet. She was a submissive and might never understand the other side. Bending once more to check the rope and reposition it right over her clit, he indulged himself for a moment, slicking his fingers with her wetness.

"Open your eyes, slave."

Sarah saw him, down on one knee before her, his fingers held before her face, dripping with the cream he had scooped from her. She watched as he slowly licked his fingers clean, obviously enjoying her own salty taste. Her lips parted as she bit her lower lip, wanting to suck those fingers of his—anything to show him her servitude.

With a satisfied smile, Phillip saw that look of longing and knew she was almost ready. Reaching up, he pulled down a rope that ran through a pulley in the ceiling, and fastened it to the rope around her waist. It was the work of a few moments to attach the other end of the rope to a small cinch attached to the table. A manual affair; as he turned the handle, the rope wound up on the cinch and pulled at her waist rope which in turn tightened in her pussy and on her clit.

Bit by bit she felt herself pulled up, helpless to stop the rope now biting into her ass and pussy. The tension on her clit was almost unbearable. Almost. He seemed to know when to stop— the right moment just before she screamed. He let her hang there a moment, feeling the pressure from without build the pressure within.

Again he knelt beside her. "Look at me," he commanded. Her look was colored with pain and desire, but otherwise clear. "I am going to give you the bit again. You will again be able to spit it out if you want. Or do you want to use your safe-word now?"

For a moment she thought. How much more could she take? Her desire to serve warred with her desire to be freed. She shook her head. "No," she said, the word strangled with her passion. "No safe-word. I want to please you. I'll take the bit."

Now he was on dangerous ground and knew it. She couldn't use the safe-word, even if her body cried out to her that she should. But she also had a need to please and wouldn't be happy if he now pulled back from what he'd promised her. He placed the bit in her mouth and without another word, fastened a clamp on first one, and then the other nipple.

Tears now fell unbidden. Her head fell back and she pushed her breasts out further then tried to wiggle the clamps off. But the wiggling caused the rope to burn in her pussy and after a moment, she was still.

"Open your eyes," he commanded gently. He wanted her to see what he was going to do to her next—if she weren't prepared for it, the sensation could take her too much by surprise.

She opened her eyes and saw he held a glass of ice. Reaching in, he took out one ice cube and ran it around her sore nipple. She gasped at the relief it gave her, knowing the rope between her legs was thoroughly soaked with her juices now. He set the glass down when it was obvious this was pleasurable to her and took a second cube, running it around her other nipple as well.

After a moment, he slid the melting ice cube down along her belly, running it around her navel. The cool water dripped down along her stomach, reaching her thighs and her crotch cried out for the same relief.

And he gave it to her. Taking a fresh cube, he traced around her mound, soaking the hair there. He ran it along the rope, stopping where it disappeared into her flesh, coming back up to her mound. She moaned into the bit and tried to push her hips up to him—she wanted that coolness on her pussy.

The ice cube was smaller now and he ran it along the rope from her navel straight down, this time gently pushing through her pussy lips and running it all the way around to her ass. The cold water gave relief to her hot skin while heightening her desire. Her chest heaved as her breathing grew more and more heavy and the nipple clamps made her aware of every breath.

He saw the change in her breathing and that her head had fallen back once again. She was ready. Taking a fresh cube, he ran it along the rope and stopped for a moment at her asshole, listening to her muffled whimpers. The cube melted quickly and he brought it back up to her pussy. Separating the lips of her sex with one hand, he pulled the rope aside just enough to slip the small piece of ice inside her vagina, to melt there. Keeping her lips spread, he bent down and gently blew on her clit.

And she exploded. Her body jerked to a rhythm of its own making—and each movement sent new signals to her brain. The clamps pulled at her nipples, the rope burned her clit and her ass and the ice melting in her pussy, the awareness that she was totally his and that he could do anything to her that he wanted, all combined in her mindless pleasure.

Sarah couldn't think. Her mind drifted among the clouds, reaching ever higher as each wave pushed her along. Blue and lavender and rose-colored clouds sailed beneath her as the waves of her orgasm deepened to royal blues and dark purples. She knew she screamed into the bit, but she could not hear her own voice as her climax crested, then ebbed, the colors returning slowly to pale pastels.

Phillip watched as she came, his own sex hardening at the sight. He had driven her to this—he controlled her body—and increasingly, her spirit. The power he held concentrated itself, coiled and tense and immensely satisfying.

After several moments, her body slowed, then stopped and hung loosely. But for the crotch rope pulled up tight by the pulley and winch, she would've collapsed onto the floor. He undid her arms from her ankles first, then lowered her body to the floor, one hand on the winch, the other arm guiding her down.

Perception of the world outside her own being gradually came back to her and she followed his movements absently—as if he were dealing with someone else or she were far away. Lying on the floor while he untied the long rope from her own simple rope harness, she brought one hand up and removed the bit. Licking her lips, she swallowed hard a few times, but said nothing.

He stowed the longer rope and came back to her with a bottle of water and a straw. "Here, drink some." Lifting her head, he guided the straw to her lips and saw her take a long swallow.

"Ready to sit up?" She nodded and he helped her to a sitting position. The rope still bit into her, she was wet from the ice and the clamps still bit into her nipples, but her head was clearer now.

"You are doing well, my slave." His words of encouragement made her smile. He smiled in return and the world lit up for her. "Stand now." The command was gentle, and she obeyed simply because he'd asked.

He led her to the table and helped her onto it so she could lie down. He spread her legs a bit, but did not fasten her down in any way. Instead, he untied the rope that encircled her waist and her sex, gently removing it so it would not burn. Quickly he inspected to be sure there had been no damage — there was none. Her pussy lips, clit and ass were irritated and red, but would recover quickly. The sensitivity there would fade as well, and he wanted her to come when he did.

His voice gruff again, he commanded, "Stand now, slave, and face the table." Trembling a bit, she did so. She wasn't sure how much more she could take and the clamps were really starting to hurt. "Lean over." She leaned over the table, her elbows bent and taking most of her weight. "Spread for me." Her face burning at his tone, she did so.

She didn't need anything more to get her ready to take him, he could see that right away. Stripping himself of his garments, he stood behind her and entered her pussy with one thrust. She cried out and almost immediately started pushing back against him.

This was what she wanted! The feel of his cock inside her made her tremble all over. She hungered for it and pushed her pussy back on him, wanting to take all of him—eat all of him with her pussy. Her movements guided by nothing but pure animal lust, she rutted with him until they both exploded in a geyser of passion. Tremors shook their bodies, shuddering through them as they rode each wave; the two moving in unison for one long, eternal moment.

And then it passed. Slowly it faded until time and memory returned. Together they lay, spent, on the tabletop, until Phillip gathered the strength to reach around and take off her clamps; she groaned with their removal. Massaging her breasts to lessen the pain, he felt himself soften inside her and stepped back, slipped out. His juices, mingled with hers, dripped down along her leg.

Scooping her up, he took her to the bedroom. Drowsy with sex, she clung to him, caring about nothing in the world. He put her down and crawled in next to her, covering them both with the blankets. Nestled together, they slept until early afternoon.

Chapter Four
Punishment

Phillip awoke with Sarah's body still spooned into his—his arms wrapped around her, holding her. For a moment, he buried his face in her hair, inhaling deeply the scent of her. She slept on, exhausted from their morning activities. Gently, he unwrapped himself and stood, gazing upon her sleeping form.

She had been so compliant in everything so far—except for the food that morning. He would try that again later. He wanted her for his sub, his slave. Her enthusiasm to serve him with her body gave him hope she would be willing to serve in other ways as well. But he wanted that servitude *only* if she were willing and *only* with her spirit unbroken.

He went to the dresser and quietly pulled out a drawer, taking out a present he had bought for her. Laying it beside her on the bed, he tiptoed out, letting her rest. He'd try her enough in the hours to come.

Upon awakening an hour or so later, Sarah discovered she was alone in the bed. Rising, she made her toilette and cleaned up from their earlier lovemaking—although a week ago she never would have coupled anything so violent with the act of making love. And yet, they were compatible.

Since her cuffs were still in place, she did not shower, but simply used a washcloth to clean and make herself presentable. Her stomach growled loudly and she remembered she hadn't eaten breakfast. The clock on the dresser read 2:15—so she'd missed lunch as well!

It wasn't until Sarah went to straighten the covers on the bed that she found the lingerie he'd laid out for her. Holding up the bra, she saw that, although the material was black, it was sheer and hid nothing. There were sheer black stockings as well, and a garter belt to hold them up. She'd never worn real stockings before, only pantyhose. A little experimentation with the clips on the garter belt, however, and she figured out how they worked.

There was a small scrap of cloth left on the bed and she picked it up as well, turning it about to figure out its purpose. "Oh!" She covered her mouth and checked the door to see if he'd heard her surprise as she realized what it was. In her fingers she held the smallest pair of panties she'd ever seen — and realized it was a G-string.

But she couldn't wear these! She'd feel like…well, she'd feel very naughty in them, that was certain. She put on the bra to see what it looked like. It was the right size — a fact which was not lost on her. How had he known? She colored as she realized her clothes had sat on the chair all last weekend and he must've looked. The fact that he'd gone shopping for her this week, and lingerie shopping at that, made her smile with delight.

Eagerly, she pulled on the G-string, stockings and belt, fastening the front clasps easily enough. The back ones were a little harder to reach and she twisted around several times trying to catch one. She giggled as she realized she must look like a dog making his bed turning around and around like that. Finally catching it, she fastened the back of her stockings and stood to look at herself in the mirror.

And the word popped into her mind again. Slut. Standing there in such sexy garments — garments she never would've had the courage to purchase for herself, her pert nipples made the sheer fabric stick out. Her pubic hair showed around the tiny scrap of the G-string and she remembered his request when she was tied. He wanted her to shave. Could she? Her hand ran through her soft hair and toyed with it a moment. Could she actually do that? Swallowing hard, she knew she would. Briefly she remembered the incident about breakfast and how she'd determined she wouldn't be back next weekend. And here she was actually contemplating fulfilling an action he wanted her to do outside of their time together.

She turned to look at herself from another angle and knew, dressed like this, she looked the part. She was a slut—a slave for his use. She needed to look those words up in the dictionary when she got home. Was there a difference between slave and slut—or whore? There was suddenly so much she didn't know.

Her cheeks flushed a deep crimson as she realized he wanted her dressed this way. It was how he expected to see her when she went to him. It was her master's will that she look this way. Sarah had to sit down on the bed as the thought took hold.

Phillip wanted her to look like a slut. What must he think of her to want her to dress like this? By buying her these clothes and putting them out for her to wear...were they like a costume? Was this a part she was to play? Or did they represent something more—something he wanted from her. Yes. Her heart beat hard. That was it right there. The relationship they were developing was not a game to him—he wanted a slave—a real slave who would do what he wanted when he wanted without question and without hesitation. If he needed a cleaning lady or a cook, he could command her to be that. If he wanted a slut, then he expected her to dress like one, to act like one, to become one.

Her head reeled with the implications. Images of the morning flashed before her inner eye—his mastery of her, and her need to be mastered. There was no doubt her body responded to his manipulations. In fact, that was why she'd come back this weekend. She liked the way Phillip controlled her. And she liked pleasing him. His cheeks would get this cute little dimple in them each time he smiled and she liked getting him to smile.

Standing again, she took another look in the mirror. Was he right? Was there a slut hiding inside her? Throwing her hands up in frustration, she slapped them on her thighs and sighed. Well, she wasn't going to find out here. Only time with Phillip would give her that answer. Taking a deep breath, she turned from the mirror and went out.

He was spread out on the couch, his face buried in the newspaper he had bought that morning. For a moment, she hesitated. He hadn't called her; how should she approach him? Finally she walked around to the front of the couch and simply knelt in her customary position, waiting for him to notice her in her new finery. Putting her hands behind her and spreading her knees put stress on the fabric and she closed her eyes briefly against the sudden thrill.

Hearing the rustle of the newspaper, her eyes flew open and she looked straight ahead as she'd been taught. He set the paper on the low table before him and commanded her, "Stand, slave."

She rose, keeping her hands behind her. "Put your hands at your sides and turn for me — show me your new clothes."

She relaxed her arms and began a slow turn for him, a smile playing about her lips. Tossing her head, Sarah shook her shoulder-length hair at him, hiding her self-consciousness at being dressed in this manner. Glancing back at him as she turned, she saw that dimpled smile and giggled. She was actually enjoying showing off for him! The G-string up the crack in her rear only accentuated the fact that her cheeks were bare. Continuing her turn so that her back was to him, she did not realize he had risen until he put his hands on her shoulders, stopping her.

"Very nice, slave. I like seeing you in the clothes I have purchased for you. Do you like them?"

Her voice was unsteady with the desire to please him and to find out about herself. "Yes, Sir — I like them very much."

His hands slid down off her shoulders, along her arms, coming to rest on her butt cheeks below. His mouth nuzzled her ear. "Do you like them well enough to wear them this week for me?"

Her head spun for a moment—wear underwear like this to work? A flush started at her neck and colored her whole face as she whispered, "Yes, Master. I would wear these to work for you." And she would—she could hardly believe it of herself, but she would. Her stomach fluttered in nervousness at the thought. She would shave herself and she would wear sexy underwear, simply because he'd commanded it and she wanted to please him.

Phillip smiled behind her. He had no intention of letting her wear them to work; she needed to be able to concentrate on her job. All he'd wanted to know was how willing she was to please him outside of their weekend agreement. Her answer pleased him a great deal. She was starting to discover the hidden side of herself.

Moving around in front of her, Phillip simply commanded, "Follow me," and she went along behind as he led her to the room they both were starting to call the dungeon.

The furniture in the room had been shifted. The large, covered object from the corner was now pulled out to the center, still hidden behind its blue cloth. With a deft tug, Phillip revealed the cage beneath. It stood almost to the ceiling—a good two and a half meters tall at least. But it wasn't very wide or very deep. He opened a door on its front and gestured to her.

Images of The Pit and the Pendulum crept into her mind and she almost balked. But she glanced down at the cage he had put her in last week, now covered and in the corner. That hadn't been too bad, not after she'd gotten used to it. Biting her lip, she stepped inside.

The door slammed behind her and she flinched. The lock went home and she knew she was trapped. In the tiny space she had, she turned around quickly to look at him, fear in her eyes. She swallowed hard and calmed, seeing him still there, smiling gently at her.

"Yes, slave, this is a cage for you. Feel how it has you locked in—a place for me to keep you." He pulled up a wing-backed chair he'd gotten earlier from the other room and sat comfortably, leaning back with his legs outstretched. "Perform for me, slave. Let me watch you in your cage."

"Perform? I do not understand." She looked at him, confused.

For answer, he just cocked an eyebrow at her.

"I do not understand, Master." How could she forget his title? He sat there, obviously her master, since she was caged and he was not.

"I want to see you perform, slave. You are here to entertain me. Make me want you."

Slut. He didn't say the word, but it hung heavy in the air. He had dressed her like one, now she was to perform as one. Swallowing hard, Sarah tested the limits of the bars, finding out just how much — or how little — room she had to maneuver. She didn't know how to perform the way he wanted, but she'd seen a few movies in her time. Trying to copy the moves of the girls on the poles, she arched her back for him, pushing out her breasts against the sheer fabric that barely confined them. Grabbing the top of the cage to steady herself, she twisted and turned, letting him see her from every angle.

The confinement of the cage was turning her on. She couldn't move much, but there was something about being locked inside the bars, performing for him, that started to arouse her. It made her feel naughty and sexy. Perhaps Phillip was right and there was a sexy siren buried deep inside her. She turned around, saw the bulge in his pants and turned again so he would not see her smile. She wasn't the only one enjoying this.

Phillip relaxed, watching her primitive attempts at being sexy. The fact that Sarah was enjoying herself, however hesitantly, proved his instincts about her had been correct. It was equally obvious, however, that she needed direction. Direction he would be happy to provide. "Play with yourself, slave — make yourself ready."

Play with herself? She barely did that alone in the privacy of her own bedroom and he wanted her to do it while he watched? Trembling a little, she put her hands to her breasts, her fingers circling her nipples.

"Good, slave. Make them stand out for me—get them wet."

She put a finger into her mouth, got it wet with her spit then ran it around one of her nipples, soaking the bra. Her nipple sprang out to meet her finger and she was surprised by the sudden arousal it caused. With more assurance, she got it wet again and did the same to the other nipple, soaking a pair of small circles on her bra.

"Pinch them, slave. Make them good and hard."

She did as he instructed. Pinching her nipples hard under her thumb and forefinger, she felt a familiar wetness gathering between her legs. She pulled on the nipples, constrained from pulling too far by the sheer bra. Her fingernail, digging deep around the base of her nipple caused a soft moan to escape from the depths of her growing desire. She closed her eyes and let herself enjoy the feelings coursing through her, no longer questioning them.

Her inhibitions fading, she let a hand fall down to the G-string. She wanted to take it off, but there wasn't room to bend inside the cage. Instead, she let her fingers work their way down to her pussy. Gathering some of the wetness there, she brought up her wet fingers and rubbed the warm liquid around her nipple, soaking the dark bra further and causing the hard nipple to show even more. Going down again with her hand, she trailed her fingers over her clit this time before bringing up more of her juices to soak the other nipple.

Phillip stood and approached the cage. Smiling at him she offered him her breasts, but instead he took her wet hand and pulled it through the cage, licking her fingers clean of her juices as he watched for Sarah's reaction. His cock was so hard, it was getting painful, but he would not relinquish to it—yet.

Sarah's knees melted, feeling his mouth around her fingers. Unconsciously, her other hand slipped down into her panties again, soaking her fingers and rubbing her clit. There was something very sexy about being so close to him, yet separated by the hard, iron bars of the cage.

Phillip reached in and took her other hand, pulling it away from her sex as well. Now he held both of her hands in his. Again he licked the fingers, sucking them, cleaning them of their juices. She moaned as her arousal grew and she pushed her hips against the side of the cage, wanting him to touch her, to lick her there.

But her desire was young yet, and he was not going to let her finish her performance so soon. He let go of her hands and stepped up onto a small stool that sat to the side of the cage. "Raise your arms, slave."

She did as she was told and he fastened her cuffs to the top of the cage, preventing her from touching herself again. She moaned in frustration, tugging at her bindings, even though she knew it was futile. He stepped down and moved to the front of the cage again, reaching in and taking hold of her hips. Slowly he pulled her forward and she went eagerly, hoping to feel his touch under the G-string. The need for release was building inside her.

When he stopped her, less than an inch from the bars, she tried to move forward on her own. At least he could let her rub against her cage! He laughed at her antics and held her firmly. The sound of his laugh only increased her need. It reminded her all too well that she was his slave, his plaything to use — or not use. The animal nature in her responded and she cried out in desire.

He let her hips go and guided her gently back until she was standing. But before she could move again, he'd retrieved a short length of rope from the table and was at her side. Deftly he passed the rope through the bars, and between her legs. She spread herself for him, hoping he would touch her sex. But it was not to be. He pulled her leg out toward the bars of the cage and tied it firmly to the bar. Passing the rope around her thigh several times so it wouldn't cut into her, he at last tied it off. Coming around to the other side, he kicked away the stool and did the same thing to her other leg. Her toes just touched the floor unless she straightened her arms and hung by her hands.

He stood back to admire his handiwork—and her performance. Tied as she was, horny as she was, she could do nothing to help herself. "Yes, slave," he murmured, "you look very sexy tonight—all dressed up for me in the clothes I bought you."

She hung there, helpless, her nipples still pushing against the fabric now drying stiff from her juices. The stockings and the garter only added to her sexiness whether she knew it or not. He circled the cage, admiring her.

She knew she was blushing at his examination. Never had she felt so on display—and in such a position! Her legs spread for him, wanting to feel his touch on her sex; her desire to please warring with her desire for release.

He approached the cage and reached in, running his hand along the line of the bra. She moaned with pleasure and he smiled—he liked the noises she made when she was aroused. He pinched her nipple and was rewarded with a gasp. Letting his hand drift downward, he paused at the top of the G-string before plunging beneath it, burying a finger inside her sex.

She felt so vulnerable at that moment. Knowing she could not prevent him from doing anything he wanted; knowing that she would not prevent him. She groaned loudly and tried to move to close her legs on his hand, but, of course, could not. Her juices freshened at her helplessness. Slowly Phillip's fingers moved in and out then up over her clit, toying with her. She squirmed in her bindings, and he appreciated the dance she did for him.

She was almost ready. Phillip pulled his finger out of her panties and listened to her frustrated groan. Bringing his hand up to her face, he told her, "Open your eyes and look at me slave." She did and he could see them heavy with her lust. "Suck your juices from my fingers." Obediently, she opened her mouth and he put his fingers inside. She sucked them, wishing it was his cock she had in her mouth. And his come instead of her own salty juices.

He could feel her readiness—but now it was time for her to learn the second of the two words he had told her earlier. She learned "obedience" fairly well—with the exception of breakfast. Now was the time to learn "discipline." He pulled his fingers from her and stepped back, admiring her in those stockings and bra—caged and helpless.

"Now, my slave, I will leave you." He paused at the sound of protest that came from her, but saw her swallow hard, willing herself silent. "You did not eat this morning as you were told—that may be a limit for you or it may not, we shall see. But the fact remains that you did not do as you were told. And so this shall be your disciplining. You will stay there, caged, tied, helpless. Wanting to come, and being denied, until I feel you understand what the word 'discipline' means and why you are getting it."

With that, Sarah was forced to watch him walk to the door in the fading light of the room, turn for one, long appreciative glance at her, and then leave the room, shutting the door behind him.

This time she could not hold in her cry—"Master! NO! Please! Don't leave me like this. I'll do it—I promise, next time—oh, please, MASTER!" She pulled on her bonds, trying to get loose, trying to get relief that would not come.

Phillip stood on the other side of the door, listening intently to Sarah's yells. She was pleading, begging with him, but she was not panicking. That was his biggest concern. She'd done well when left 'alone' the week before, but the circumstances this time were much different. Today, he had deliberately tied her in such a way that she would become uncomfortable quite quickly.

But he needed her to take the time to think—and to break down the walls she had spent so many years building. Only when her shouting quieted did he leave the door, circling around to watch her from the porch once more. The sight of her framed by the double border of the window and the cage, aroused him again. Yet he denied himself, knowing he needed to be alert to any changes in her predicament. Instead, he pulled up a stool and satisfied himself with just watching.

Obedience and Discipline. The words took on importance in Sarah's thoughts when it became obvious Phillip wasn't going to return just because she yelled at him to. She could not help but think of the words as if they were written in big capital letters—he might as well have painted them on the back of the door. Obedience and Discipline. This was all about the fact that she hadn't eaten that stupid breakfast. In frustration, she pulled at her bindings again, her face twisting with the effort.

"Blast it!" she muttered, reviewing her actions that morning. Was it such a big deal that he'd asked her to take her meal from his leavings? He'd been respectful enough of her to separate what he didn't intend to eat from what he did. And really, he hadn't eaten as much as he usually did. Phillip had deliberately left her the lion's share of the food. And what had she done? Thrown it in the garbage.

She felt the tears welling inside her. She'd disappointed him. That was the problem. He'd asked her, commanded her to do something simple and she'd refused. When she'd admitted earlier that she hadn't eaten the food, she'd seen the look in his eyes - the sadness.

Her thoughts went back to their first weekend together— was it only a week ago? He had explained a bit about what he was looking for in a slave. She thought she'd understood, but realized now, that her definition of the word did not go far enough. She also thought she'd understood the word 'Obedience' and realized that definition did not go far enough either. What he wanted was total compliance on her part—a total submission of her own will to his.

And she wanted to give it to him. She stopped squirming as the realization came home. Never had he said it would be easy — he said they'd test her limits. With a start, she realized she understood what 'Discipline' was as well. This time in the cage was again a test—it gave her time to think about her 'disobedience' and put it in perspective. He was, in effect, 'disciplining' her mind to accept or reject his commands.

Sarah swallowed hard, the need to come vanishing. After years of unexciting sex with her husband, Phillip offered her a whole new lifestyle. He was prepared to give her the bondage her innermost being always wanted, but had been afraid to admit to, even to herself. What he asked in return, was her obedience when she was in his house. Could she discipline herself to accept his demands? In her heart, she already knew the answer: Yes, she wanted to be his slave—to do what she was told to do. Hanging her head, she prepared to wait out the rest of her time in the cage.

Time lost meaning for her and she didn't know if she'd been there ten minutes or twenty. Or an hour—it was irrelevant. All she wanted now was a chance to show him how sorry she was for her earlier behavior. She had disappointed him and the look in his eyes haunted her.

Tears spilled now as Sarah realized just how much she was falling in love with Phillip. He had touched a deeply hidden part of her, brought it into the light and shown her it was all right. It was okay that she wanted to have someone look after her—it was okay that she didn't want to have to be the strong one every single moment. He was willing to let her relax and just exist—and for no other purpose than to be his slave and to please him.

The room had grown dark by the time he reentered. He had spent the entire time watching her; her tears almost made him give in and come to comfort her. In the long run, however, it was right that he not interrupt her thinking. When she hung there, spent from her own emotional turmoil, he returned, knowing she had reached a decision. Without turning on a light, he untied her legs, grateful to see her put her own weight on them. He pushed the stool over and undid her arms and she let them fall to her sides. In a few moments they would start to tingle as feeling came back into them. Phillip unlocked the cage and opened the door.

Sarah stepped out on unsteady legs and knelt in front of him, her stockings and garters twisted from her gyrations in the cage, her bra with two small white spots where her juices had dried over her nipples, her face lined with the salty remains of her tears. She attempted to put her hands behind her, but the lack of feeling in them prevented her. Instead, she just let them hang at her sides.

"I'm sorry, Master. I am sorry I disappointed you. Please let me try again."

"Then come with me, slave." It took all his will to not bend down and kiss her, to pick her up in his arms and carry her to a place of honor at the table. Of her own volition, she had given him his title! But he knew he had to remain strong and let her carry out her need to prove herself. Clenching his fists so he would not caress her, he turned on his heel and walked through the door.

Unsteadily, she stood and followed him. The table was set for one as she expected it to be. "Kneel in your place, slave," he instructed as he went to get his own dinner—just a pre-made salad tonight; he had been too concerned with her welfare to take time to cook. He had thought to have her carry it to the table and serve him, but she was too spent.

Meekly and without a word, Sarah knelt beside his chair. Leaning back on her heels, her hands resting on her knees, she tried to keep herself from moving. It didn't take him long to finish his salad and when he stood, he looked at her and gave her the command she'd been expecting. "You may eat from my plate, slave, then put the dishes in the sink. Do not wash them—come to me when you are finished."

He left the dining room and she bowed her head. Was she allowed to sit while she ate? Or did he expect her to eat while she knelt on the floor? Too tired to try and figure it out, she stood then sat at her spot—or what had been her spot—at the table. She pulled his plate to her and saw that he'd set utensils for her. Touched by his thoughtfulness and picking up the fork, she hungrily ate the remains of the substantial salad and drank the fresh glass of water left at her own place.

Taking the dishes to the sink, she let them sit and went to find him. Again he was on the couch in the living room, reading by the light of a single lamp. Exhausted, she started to kneel before him, but he patted the couch next to him and she gratefully sat down and rested in his arms.

"Tell me what you have learned today, my slave." The warmth and tenderness in his touch and in his voice caused the tears to well in her eyes again.

"I have learned that I want to serve you, Master. I want to be your slave and do as you order me. I have learned what "obedience" is — true obedience, that is."

When she fell silent, he prompted her. "And what is the difference between 'obedience' and 'true obedience'?"

"Obedience is doing something because you have to do it — because someone told you to and you know it has to be done. But 'true obedience' is doing it because you want to please the other person. When it's true, your own feelings don't matter — you want to obey just to make the other person smile."

She looked at him and he couldn't resist — he smiled at her and was rewarded by a smile of her own. He kissed her on the forehead. "And what else has my slave learned today?"

"I have learned what discipline is — and that it isn't always unpleasant." He cocked an eyebrow at her and she explained. "You wanted me to think about what I had done — or hadn't done, rather. By building, then denying my need and leaving me alone like that, I had little else to do *but* think about it. You focused my mind very well." A wry grin twisted her tired face and she continued.

"I didn't like it at first, but after a while I realized it wasn't so bad — and I realized something else, too." She hesitated then plunged on. "I discovered that the orgasm was only the icing on the cake. It had always, for me, been the be-all and end-all of sex.

The only reason to have sex was to get to the release. But the buildup can be just as much fun. I never understood that before." She twisted around to look at him. "See how much I have learned...Master?"

The title came from the depths of her own heart; he knew she bestowed it willingly upon him. He had earned her trust. For answer, Phillip kissed her deeply. "Yes, slave, you have learned a great deal. But there is something to be said for that release." He guided her hand down to his cock and she felt his hardness. She giggled.

"Come with me to the bedroom, slave, and let's get both our needs taken care of, shall we?"

He took her hand and led her to the bedroom, stopping at the foot of the bed to kiss her deeply. She had pleased him with her revelations — and he knew he had made the right choice in her. Willing to explore her submissive side, willing to accept his discipline, she was exactly what he'd been looking for. In the darkness of the bedroom, lit only by a shaft of moonlight streaming through the open window, he held on to the woman of his dreams.

There were no bindings as he took her tonight — Sarah gave herself completely. Phillip accepted her gift, cherishing it, giving himself in return. They made love for hours, exploring every part of the other. And when at last he mounted her and they rode together, their mutual bliss united them once more.

* * * * *

Later, when again they lay in a jumble of legs and arms, Sarah couldn't help but remark, "I can't believe I still have another whole day before I go back to work. It seems like today lasted forever!"

He idly played with a strand of her hair. "Is that a good thing?"

She picked up her head to look at him. "Oh, yes, Sir! It is a *very* good thing." She nestled down again. "Do I dare ask what you have planned for tomorrow?"

He smoothed her hair and decided just how much he'd share ahead of time. "Well, in the morning, I usually attend church services, and I'd like you to go with me. But in this, I will not command you."

"I usually go to church on Sunday as well, Sir, but I did not go last week," she confessed.

"So you will accompany me?"

She nodded, glad to discover his spirituality was important to him.

"Then afterward, we will return here and you shall continue your training."

"Mmmm, my training." She sighed. "Why does that send a thrill through me? Don't answer, that was a rhetorical question."

Smiling in the darkness, Phillip reached down and pulled the coverlet over them and snuggled her into his arms. It may have been a long day, but it had been a very, very good one. Before long, they both slept, comfortable in each other's arms.

Chapter Five
His toy

"Come on, sleepyhead! Church!"

She rolled over and sat up, surprised. Her cuffs were already gone and the bedroom was empty. In the kitchen she heard the whistle of the teakettle abruptly stop. Gathering her wits together, she hurried into the shower and got herself ready for the day.

A long pier mirror hung on the wall at the foot of the bed and Phillip stood before it, brushing his hair when she reentered. Clad only in a towel wrapped around her head, she hesitated. What was she to wear to church? "Sir, I'll need you to get the bag from my car—I never brought it in Friday night and it has the clothes I'll need."

He smiled mischievously. "Who says you'll need your clothes for church?"

She was shocked. "SIR!" She swallowed hard. "I cannot go to church in my birthday suit!"

"No, you cannot," he agreed, laughing. "Here, while I was shopping for the lingerie, I saw something else and bought it for you to wear if you decided to go with me. You are mine in every way on the weekend," he continued when she looked confused. "When you cross that threshold, you give up your will and do what I command. That means you also wear what I instruct you to."

He went to the closet and pulled out a beautiful, conservative, navy blue suit. The top had white piping around a wide collar and buttoned in the front; the skirt was a solid navy with two white piping stripes around the hem. "And of course, you'll need stockings and shoes." Laying the dress on the bed, he pulled a small shoebox out of the closet as well and handed it to her.

Inside she found a pair of navy stockings with a garter belt to match. Also laid on top was a navy blue bra — as sheer as the black one she'd worn yesterday. This one, however, had underwires that would give more support and shape to her breasts. Carefully she set these things aside and pulled out the shoes.

The first thing she noticed were the heels — much higher than the one-inch pumps she usually wore. The tapered heel was at least three inches high, with a strap that went around her ankle. The toe section was a solid strip of navy.

"Get dressed, slave. We leave in ten minutes." He left the room.

She didn't even think about not complying. The suit was beautiful and was one she might have picked out for herself. She combed out her hair, then put on the bra and looked for the panties. There were none. Briefly she considered wearing hers from Friday, but then realized her clothes were not in their customary place on the chair. She sighed and pulled on the stockings and belt, fastening them before trying on the skirt.

There was no doubt he'd figured out her size — the skirt fit beautifully. But the hemline was above her knee — not much, but she hadn't worn a skirt that short in years. Slipping her arms into the top, she buttoned it and looked in the mirror.

The bra definitely gave her cleavage — and it was apparent in the low-cut neckline of the suit top. No matter how she pulled it, the top of her breasts still showed. She was not indecent, but showing much more skin than she was accustomed to. With another sigh, she slipped her feet into the heels.

The tightness of the skirt, combined with the heels, allowed her only to take small, ladylike steps. No tomboy could ever wear this outfit! With still a few minutes to go, she went into the living room to model her outfit for him.

He whistled when he saw her and she blushed. "Very nice, slave. You look good in the clothes your master has chosen." He held out his arm and she took it as they made their way to the car — and to church.

* * * * *

The service was more wonderful than she ever remembered church being. Maybe it was because she was on the arm of a very handsome man who had opened a whole new world to her. Many of the parishioners knew Phillip and greeted him afterward. He introduced her simply as a friend, but the possessive way his arm encircled her waist subtly let everyone know she was more than that to him.

Afterward, he took her out to a nice restaurant for brunch. Their conversation was easy and to anyone looking on, they simply saw two people who were falling in love with each other. They might have remarked on the fact that his suit was the same shade of navy as her outfit, but there was nothing in their demeanor to suggest any other relationship.

But she knew. All through the service, all through the introductions and even as they walked into the restaurant, she was conscious of the fact that she wore garters and stockings — and no panties at all. It was their secret and it made her blush at odd moments.

Back in the car, he turned toward home and she sighed with relief.

"What's that sigh for, slave?"

She grinned — he'd called her Sarah all morning in public. "I'm grateful to be going home, Master." It was the first time since they'd left the house that she used his title and he grinned back at her.

"You like being called slave?"

"Yes, Sir — as much as you like being called Master."

"Did you ever think you would like such a thing?"

"NO!" She shook her head emphatically. "Not in my wildest dreams. And if anyone else ever tried to call me that, I think I'd kick him!"

He laughed out loud, but sobered quickly. "But someone may call you that someday, slave."

"What do you mean?" She was puzzled.

"You are my property — and at some point, I would like to show off my property."

Her mouth fell open. Show her off? As a slave? Her cheeks flamed as she thought of herself on display as she had been for him last night. Surely he didn't mean that?

"Don't worry, that's a ways in your future. But know that there are other Masters and even Mistresses out there — and know that someday you will meet some of them. And you will act as a good slave ought to act."

She swallowed hard and stared out the window a moment before answering, "Yes, Master." To his credit, he was being fair and giving her fair warning. He was always up front and honest about his intentions — which was more than she could say for most of the guys she had dated.

They turned into the long driveway, parked; he came around to open her door, as he had every time. Helping her out, he took her arm to guide her, since her heels were really not made for the rough path. Once inside, he dropped his keys on the little table by the door and turned to her.

"Let's both get a little more comfortable, shall we?" He went straight to the bedroom and she followed. "Just sit there a moment while I change."

She sat on the chair in the corner, prim and proper in her suit. Her knees together, her hands resting, clasped together in her lap; sitting like the lady she was taught to be. He saw her automatic posture and smiled, then began a small performance of his own.

The suit coat he took off with little ceremony, hanging it on the hanger and putting it away. But then he caught her eye and dared her to break contact. Staring at her, the animal he held inside beginning to surface, he untied his tie, coming to stand before her. "Take off your top," he commanded.

His look of smoldering passion made her heart start to tremble. With suddenly nervous fingers, she undid the buttons of her suit top and took it off, placing it beside her over the arm of the chair. He was standing too close for her to be able to stand – he loomed over her like a villain from an old movie.

"Hold out your hands."

She did so and he looped the thin material of the tie around her wrists, securing them tightly together. The sensuous silk against her skin made her tremble as her pulse quickened.

His waist was at eye level and she watched, mesmerized as he undid the clasp of his belt and slowly slid it out of his pant loops. Once it was free, he draped it around her neck. "Hold this for me, slave." She didn't dare move.

Now he began on the shirt buttons; first the sleeves, his long fingers unbuttoning the right, then the left, flipping back the cuffs to tease her with a glimpse of the dark hair on his arms. Then from the neck downward, he unveiled his chest to her— one button at a time. Pulling his shirt aside, Sarah's heart leapt at the sight of those smooth muscles, knowing the power they wielded. Leaving his shirt on but open, Phillip unzipped his pants and let them fall. Only the briefest of briefs contained him and Sarah could see that little scrap of cloth would not hold him for long. She longed to lean forward and suckle him through the thin fabric.

"Finish undressing me, slave." With her heart now pumping wildly, she reached down with her tied hands and helped him out of his pants. Then, gently taking his cock out of his briefs, she brought the garment down and helped him remove that as well. Now only his shirt remained. He took a pace backward so she could stand and she pushed his shirt off first one shoulder, then the other until she had his arms and hands free of it.

He turned her away from him then, so that her back was to him. For a moment, he was tempted to run his fingers over her breasts; he loved feeling their soft weight in his hands. Instead, he decided to concentrate on another part of her wonderful anatomy, reaching down to slide his hand up under her skirt to touch her sex. She knew she was already damp and she moaned softly when his fingers touched her pussy lips. He probed deeper, sliding a finger inside her reveling in her tightness. She would gladly spread her legs for him, but the narrowness of the skirt prevented her.

"Bend over, slave."

The command in his voice gave her a chill and a counter-warmth spread between her legs. Leaning forward, Sarah rested her bound hands on the chair seat then bent further until her elbows rested there as well. He raised her skirt and Sarah felt another rush as she realized how open she was to him.

Slowly he pulled the belt from around her shoulders and she shuddered in spite of herself. What was he planning? She tensed the muscles in her cheeks and put her head down, preparing for what she was sure was coming next.

He smiled at her reaction. While a whipping might still be in her future, he wasn't sure she was ready for it yet—or that he wanted to give it to her. No, he had something else in mind entirely.

And so, when she felt his hands looping the belt around her waist, her brows furrowed in confusion. He tightened it around her waist and she drew in a breath.

Slap! His hand hit her bottom and she jumped, not expecting it. She gasped and he used the moment to cinch the belt even tighter. Exhaling, she found that, once again, she could not take in a deep breath. Her pussy oozed her feelings about being confined in such a way. Already her juices threatened to spill down her thighs.

He rubbed a finger over her wet clit and again she had to lock her knees to stay upright. Gently he traced a wet line from her clit through her pussy and up to her anus. She shivered as he did it again — and again. Soaking her hole and pushing his finger against it, getting her ready.

Then he slid his finger in, just the tip of it, and pulled her a little. She couldn't stop moaning. Oh, she liked it when he did this to her! Getting her juices on his finger again, he slipped his finger deeper this time, going in all the way to the knuckle. Slowly, carefully, he stretched her.

But he did not intend to take her this way — certainly not yet, anyway. Instead he held a small object down where she could peek at it between her legs. Cone-shaped and bulbous, she wasn't sure what it was. A string came from it to something she could not see in his other hand. He lubricated the object with oil then slipped it into her slightly stretched asshole.

The plug did not go in deep, but she could feel it there, pressing against her; her body wanting to expel it, but it not moving. The tightness in her belly grew stronger and she moved deeper into that wonderfully unfocused part of her mind where all awareness was of her own body.

Phillip felt her slipping into that wonderfully free state she was learning to enjoy. One hand on her waist steadied her as he played her body, helping her go deeper.

His fingers slipped along her slippery pussy lips again, separating them and teasing her clit. Hanging her head on her hands, instinct made her lean forward to give him better access. Something cold touched her there then slid with ease into her vagina. Dimly she was aware of him belting something else around her waist then a pressure on both her asshole and her pussy as the belt was tightened.

He stood her up then, helping her as the blood rushed from her face to her toes. After a moment, her head cleared. When it did, he commanded her again. "Stand as you have been taught, slave."

She put her feet apart, but with her hands bound, she could not put them behind her. Instead she let them drop in front of her, resisting the urge to touch herself. She pushed her feet a little further apart, feeling the cool air rush in against her wet pussy.

A sudden vibration from that direction caused her to inhale sharply. It was gone as quickly as it came as she looked at him, puzzled. He stood before her, nonchalantly running a brush through his hair. He turned from her and she felt the vibration again—only now it was in her ass! Then both together were turned on full and she almost fell to her knees.

But again, it stopped as quickly as it started. He laughed at the expression on her face and held up the remote he hid in his palm. "I control those vibrators, slave—you will feel them when I wish you to." Her ass started to buzz again and her eyes closed in pleasure. Her hand started to creep to her pussy with a mind of its own.

"Oh, no, you don't!" He laughed, pulling on the end of the tie and raising her hands. "I see you need some help here. Stand at the end of the bed."

She moved to the foot of the bed and turned to face him. He left the room for a moment, returning with several lengths of good, stout, cotton rope—and her cuffs. "Hold out your hands." She did so and he placed the cuffs on her wrists then took two ropes, tying an end to each of her wrists. Only when he had the ropes firmly in hand did he untie her other binding.

Quickly he pulled her arms up, running the ropes over the top of the four-poster. Tying one rope off on one corner and the other rope on the other corner, he then knelt and spread her feet, using the rest of each rope to secure her ankles, which he first bound in their cuffs. Once she was secure, he knelt on the bed behind her, moving in close to her, but not touching—he only waited. He doubted he'd have to wait long and he was not disappointed.

Her arms stretched to the corners of the bed, she was even more aware of his belt tightly wrapped around her waist. She could see herself in the mirror in this position—the long pier mirror that hung on the wall—the only one in the room. Her waist was tiny — pulled in sharply by the belt. Just below it hung the second strap, also tight against her skin. She could see where the belt disappeared down between her legs to the vibrators below.

Just then the one in her pussy started to vibrate and she wanted so much to come. When he knelt behind her, she waited for the touch of his hands on her - anywhere. She could feel him, right behind her. Why didn't he touch her? Biting her lip, she tried to be patient, but the tension grew too much. She could just see his outline in the mirror and he knelt silently, his outline framing her own. She squirmed around, trying to see behind her. "Sir? Oh, Sir, please...do something!"

"So my slave doesn't like just being still? Drinking in her own beauty all spread out for her master? Feeling the wonderful helplessness of being tied? Knowing she has been invaded in her pussy and in her ass. An invasion put there by her master...an invasion he controls."

His words sent shivers through her and her breathing grew heavy. She could not take in a deep breath, and the shallow breaths only increased her need. He controlled her — and she reveled in it.

Slowly she became aware that her ass was vibrating. It had started so slowly it was a full minute before she realized it had been going on for quite some time. Through eyes heavy with her passion, she watched her body in the mirror as if it were something that belonged to someone else. Something apart from her. Her lips parted and a low moan came from them as the vibrator in her pussy now started its throbbing inside her.

Her head fell back and he was there to catch her. He knelt up on the bed, supporting her head with his chest and she could see the two of them reflected back at her. "What a nice couple they make," she thought abstractedly. She watched as he reached around, kneading her breasts and toying with her nipples. He pinched them and she saw her body arch and heard her own gasp of surprise.

She floated in a haze of pleasure, supported only by the ropes and him behind her. The vibrations increased and she saw the woman in the mirror writhing with an obvious need. She saw his hand dip lower on her body, touch her mound, then push through her hair and part her lips to apply pressure to her clit.

And the world exploded. Wave after wave caused her to dance in the ropes as her orgasm ripped through her body. All her senses shut down save those between her legs—and from them came a wonderful throbbing that cascaded over her and around her and through her.

She had no memory of it ending—only that the dance was glorious. When reality came back to her, she was lying on the bed, his belt gone from her waist. Only the ropes hanging on the corners of the bed and the dimly felt vibrators in her ass and pussy told her it had not been a dream.

The bed gave a little under her and Sarah felt him sit next to her, his hand rubbing along her back. Reveling in his caress as it dipped along the rills and hollows of her body, she allowed him to turn her over to face him and saw his smile—the one that always made her stomach give that little flip.

This time was no different, in spite of her euphoria. Raising herself on one arm, she smiled back, her eyes lazily drifting along the contours of his shape. But when she looked at his shaft, still stiff and hard, she frowned a bit. How was it fair that she felt this wonderful lightness, while her Master was still shackled to the earth? Moving more on instinct than anything else, her head followed her gaze as her hands reached out to caress him.

But his hand on hers stopped her. "No, slave. Not like that." He stood and motioned for her to lie crosswise on the bed. She did so and he reached under her, pulling her body head first toward him until her head hung just off the edge. There was no fear of her falling; her shoulders still rested firmly on the bed.

He now moved forward, straddling her head with his legs. Leaning forward, his hands supporting him, he bent down, his thick shaft coming closer and closer to her mouth. Eagerly she opened for him, wanting to give him pleasure. As he touched her lips, her tongue snaked out, licking and caressing the purple tip of his cock.

What a difference a week had made. Last week he had possessed her mouth and she moved from toleration to an attitude of indifference. But now she wanted to make love to him with every ounce of energy she had. Her hands stretched up, encircling his engorged cock and cupping his balls as her mouth took in more and more of him. The more he bent down, the more of his cock filled her. She gagged and he pulled out a bit, but she guided him back in—opening her throat to let him past. Wider she stretched until her nose was buried in his balls, her mouth and throat filled with the wonder of his musky scent.

Slowly at first, then faster as passion ruled his actions, he pumped into her mouth. Her lips squeezed around him, making the opening tight against him. Higher and higher he climbed as her hands worked back to his ass, kneading his cheeks. And when her finger dipped between those cheeks and pressed against his asshole, he exploded; his seed bursting forth in a fitful stream down her throat.

His come filled her throat and mouth and for a few moments she could not breathe. He seemed to know, however, and just as she was about to panic, he pulled out of her, letting the air into her lungs again. In her position, she could not help him to the bed, but watched as he fell sideways along the width. Scooting down, she finished the job of cleaning him, letting her warm tongue send shivers of pleasure through his body.

They lay together for some time, the vibrators inside her quiet now, her face resting beside his now-soft cock which lay cradled in her hands. Neither felt the need to move—both floated in a wonderful haze as the afternoon wore away.

* * * * *

He stirred first, climbing off the bed and untying the ropes from the bedposts. Sarah lay as she had fallen asleep; on her stomach, just being lazy, watching and enjoying Phillip's actions as his arms reached up. She so liked the way his chest muscles rippled as he struggled with a stubborn knot. He was so tall, the cleanup did not require him to stretch much, yet Sarah enjoyed watching him pad around the room in his nakedness as he coiled the rope and set it on the chair.

It had been a wonderful afternoon, in Phillip's opinion — and he had not really pushed any of her limits. As he helped her to let out more and more of the slut buried deep inside her, the sex was getting better and better. He thoroughly enjoyed the role of puppeteer to her puppet. She had been so deliciously beautiful dancing in the ropes as she gave her orgasms to him. The way her breasts hung heavy and jiggled as she came, the way every muscle in her body tensed when she was right on the edge, how she came hard with her entire body, holding nothing back from her own pleasure. Oh, yes, she had come a long way in only a week. He knew now he could take her much further.

But time for a little more training. The ropes all coiled, he turned again to her prone form as she lay watching him. "Roll over, slave."

She dutifully rolled to her back, still watching him.

"Arms up." She put her arms over her head and she felt him lock them, first together, and then to the short chain attached to the head of the bed.

"Spread your legs." Those words always gave her a small thrill. Always he had treated her well, but she was beginning to love this command, with its nastier connotation. Slowly she spread them, aware again of the devices still imbedded inside her.

Once her ankles were fastened and she was spread and helpless, he stood and looked at her, ready again, for he could see her moist pussy glistening. She lay there, still watching him, wondering what more he had in mind. When he took the few steps to the chair and put on his shirt, she almost cried out in protest. He couldn't leave her here like this!

But he had—twice the week before. She bit her lip to keep from crying out as he reached not only for his pants, but for a clean pair of shorts as well. Only when he was fully dressed did he approach the bed again.

"Remember, you are my toy. I can play with you, or not…as I see fit. When I am done, you see that I clean up my toy after use, storing her until I am ready to use her again."

His words sent shivers down her spine. She was an object— a thing. She had no choices, no opinions. And if she did, they didn't matter. He was done with her for now and he'd set her aside for use later on. The thought brought her very close to a climax.

He leaned over her now, reaching down to remove the vibrator from her vagina. His almost impersonal manner affected her and she bit back the temptation to raise her hips to his hand as the fingers of one hand pushed her outer lips apart while the fingers of his other hand reached inside her and pulled out the vibrator. Almost she would have thought herself in a gynecologist's office, his manner was so businesslike.

Reaching deep into her crack, he found the butt plug and removed it in like manner. Without saying another word, he took the mechanical toys to the bathroom and she heard the water run. After a moment, he returned, drying the objects with a towel. He put them away in a drawer and then used a damp cloth he had to wipe her no-longer-private areas. He could've been washing his car, for all the emotion he showed. A small whimper escaped her throat.

Finished, he toweled her dry, having even cleaned out her pussy juices. The room was darkening in the late afternoon sun, but she could still see him clearly. Taking the washcloth and the towel back to the bathroom, he emerged and left the bedroom without even a glance in her direction.

And now she writhed on the bed, pulling on her bindings, trying to get release. Anything to take away the great need that had built up at his treatment of her. She whimpered and twisted her body, but he did not come back – and she could not come.

It was a long time before her need faded. Every time she would start to relax, the memory of his manner toward her would resurface and send her back up again. She lost count of the number of times she hovered on the brink, only to fall backward again without reaching that last and most glorious point.

Oh, but she needed to come! She would have fucked a Coke bottle at that point, she was so horny. And then she laughed. Right out loud. "What language!" she thought to herself. It was a word she never used—not even in anger. She laughed again, thoroughly enjoying her predicament.

She settled in to just take pleasure in the fact that she was bound and could go nowhere. The clock on the dresser ticked away the time, but she paid it no mind. She would lie here for eternity if that was what he wanted. Stretching against her bindings from time to time, she reveled in her helplessness.

Soon a delicious odor wafted into the room and her stomach growled in response. Whatever he was cooking for dinner, it smelled wonderful. Breathing deeply, she waited for him to release her.

And if he expected her to sit at his feet again while he ate? And then eat from his plate when he was done? Then she would do so—the idea no longer disturbed her. In fact, it was beginning to feel like her rightful place. She stretched in her bindings. Just as this was a wonderful place to be. Set aside like a toy on a shelf—just waiting to be used again.

She grinned in the darkness, knowing her thoughts had gotten her wet again. She heard his step and instinctively tried to straighten up, but of course, bound as she was, there was little she could do to make herself more presentable.

"Turn your head away, slave," he instructed her kindly and she closed her eyes and turned her head. A sudden light filled the room from the small bedside lamp and she waited till her eyes adjusted before opening them and looking at him.

"You have been very good this afternoon, my slave. Are you hungry?"

Sarah's stomach answered for her and they both laughed. Phillip unlocked her wrists and helped her to sit and then he freed her ankles. "I hope you like Chinese," he said as they walked back to the kitchen, him in front and her behind, as always.

"Yes, Sir, I do," she replied, surprised to discover a wok on the stove and a home-made meal of Chinese food on the table.

"Then take your place at my side." He much preferred her sitting at the table, but knew this discipline was good for the both of them this weekend.

She knelt and bowed her head as he said grace, then leaned back on her heels as he placed his napkin. But he had no paper this time; to her surprise, he started a conversation with her as if she were sitting at the table, not kneeling at his side.

"So, my slave, what did you think about this afternoon when you were on your 'shelf'?"

Grinning at the imagery, the very same imagery she had thought of, she replied, "I didn't really think of much, Master. I mostly just enjoyed being put there by you."

He paused in his eating, sparing a glance at her before finishing the bite. "You enjoy being used in such a manner?"

"Yes, Sir," she answered, amazed at herself to discover such a truth. For in the light of his question, she realized how preposterous it sounded. How could she like such treatment after years of demanding respect from men? But he did respect her—that was just it. He had not mistreated her—he had opened a new door for her. "Yes, Sir," she answered more firmly.

He smiled inwardly. Her training was progressing very well. When they had first met, he had seen the restlessness in her and had wondered at its source. Through their conversations on their early dates, on occasion he steered their talk to matters regarding her sexual convictions and had determined that a dominant male might be just what she needed. And the more they dated, the more he hoped he'd been correct—his heart was becoming involved.

But there was only one way to be sure—and so when the opportunity came last weekend, he'd seized it—he tested her and found her willing. This weekend, he tested her further. He knew well his own need to dominate. Independent women made great friends—but he hated when a woman wanted to tell him how to please her in the bedroom. There he wanted the most intimate trust a lover could give to him—and he would settle for nothing less.

And out of the bedroom? He liked spirited women who knew their own minds. To find one who would be willing to bow to his dictates at home and yet be independent in public was his dream. And until today, he was sure it would remain a dream only. While it was true he was a church-going man, it was only while he was shopping for her that he considered bringing her out and testing her in public so soon. But he might as well find out now. Could she function as an equal companion when in company, and function as his slave when in private? His heart had been soaring all day to know that she could—and better than he'd ever dreamed.

She enjoyed having her limits tested, although he realized she did not fully understand that was what they were doing. In continually testing her, he was also training her. First he needed to find the walls then work on breaking them down and submitting her will to his. She was doing beautifully.

His dinner finished, he stood reaching his hand down to her. Puzzled, she put her hand in his and he raised her up, gesturing to his seat. She sat, a little discomfited to find herself in his chair. He bowed and offered her a fresh napkin, which he then fanned open and draped it over her naked lap. He gave her a fresh set of chopsticks and was pleased to discover she knew how to use them. Pulling out the chair she usually occupied, he sat while she ate before him.

At first she was shy and knew she was blushing to be treated in such a manner. But his easy smile and banter as she ate relaxed her and soon she was enjoying his companionship as she always had.

Dinner done, he helped her clear. "You wash tonight, slave." Dutifully, she filled the sink with soapy water and began the chore. He dried, but had fallen silent. In quiet peacefulness, the two worked to clean the kitchen and do the dishes.

She was on the second to last pot when he put down his towel. So busy was she in scrubbing a tough spot, she did not notice him take off his shirt. Not until he stepped behind her, his body touching hers, did he get her attention. His hands rested on her shoulders a moment, then followed her arms, all the way down into the soapy water. Her breath caught and her knees weakened a bit as she felt his fingers entwining with hers.

Gently he took each of her hands and, with her holding the scrubber, he guided her hands, slowly cleaning the pot together. Around and around the rim he guided her, then deep into the pot itself; his hands sensuous in the slippery water. The pot clean, he helped her to lift it and rinse it, his hands caressing hers, his head dipping to kiss her neck.

Only the wok was left and she lifted it into the water. Again his hands encircled hers as she washed around and around the pot, her eyes following the movement of their hands, her body unconsciously moving as she became more and more aroused. He set her hands deep in the water and lifted the wok, rinsing it and setting it in the drainer to dry. Reaching into the dirty water, he pulled the plug, letting it go. Then soaping his hands with fresh soap, he lathered them. Full of suds, he took her hands in his again, washing the grease and old soap from them.

Her head fell back on his shoulder as he washed her hands. Never before had washing dishes been erotic to her. Now she would remember this moment every time she so much as rinsed a dish at home. He turned on the tap and rinsed her hands, setting them back in the sink when they were clean.

Running his wet hands up her arms, he watched the goose bumps rise on her skin all the way to her shoulders. "Spread your legs for me, slave."

She shivered at his words and moved her legs apart for him.

"Lean into the sink and present yourself to me."

Trembling, she leaned forward until her elbows were almost touching the bottom of the sink. Her ass was high and she knew how open she was for him.

"Looks like my slave likes this position," he remarked. "Your pussy lips are already open, inviting me in."

Her breath quickened as he stepped up to her again and bent down to whisper in her ear. "I am going to take you here, slave. I am going to use you right here at the sink."

A small cry escaped her—the thought increased her desire. Once again he was enjoying her as a thing, an object—and she wanted it more than anything.

He savored the moment; running his hands down her back, he spread her cheeks, exposing her ass to him. He would not be gentle this time. She wanted use, she'd get used. He let out the animal he usually kept caged inside.

Grabbing her hips, he paused only briefly at the entrance to her pussy before plunging deep inside, pulling her hips back to take him fully. Pulling out almost all the way, he paused again before slamming into her once more.

She cried out at his sudden roughness. Contrasted to their dishwashing, it was unexpected. After only two thrusts, however, her body responded, accepting his powerful thrusts and wanting more. She lost count of the number of times he pulled out only to slam into her body, using it roughly.

And then he pulled out completely, setting his hard cock against her ass hole. Well lubricated, he knew it would slide in easily if she could relax enough. He pushed and was rewarded by her immediate loosening of her sphincter muscles. She wanted this as much as he did.

Once again, he took her all at once, forcing himself into her, forcing her to give way to him. She cried out, her passion rising as he pumped into her ass, his balls hitting against her pussy.

"Oh, Master! Master! I'm going to come!" she yelled.

"Then come for me, slave. Come like the slut I want you to be."

The use of the word sent her over the edge. She was a slut—his slut—and she was proud of it. Her orgasm rocked her body as she slammed her hips back, impaling herself on the cock her pussy had craved all afternoon. In moments, her reward came as his hot seed filled her ass and his groans echoed her own. Together they climbed, together they reached the summit and together they relaxed and came down.

Phillip rested his hands on the edge of the sink as he fought for breath. Only once he was soft did he pull out of her. Sarah still leaned heavily into the sink, her chest heaving against the cold stainless steel. His juice leaked out of her ass and dribbled down her crack to pool with her own.

Regaining his composure, he stood and helped her to do so. Neither were steady on their feet and they stood for several moments, wrapped in each other's arms, enjoying the close embrace as their hearts slowed. Phillip kissed the top of her head and brushed the hair from her eyes. She looked up at him with such trust and innocence she stirred deep feelings of protection in him. For a moment, he worried about her—she so obviously needed what he had to give her, what would happen if another Master walked into her life—one who might not have her best interests in mind, but only be interested in his own pleasure?

Gently he bent and kissed her soft lips, wanting to give her safety—and he wanted to give it to her for a long time. He took her hand.

"Come with me, I want to show you something." His voice was still husky with desire. Going to the living room, he pointed to the floor by the couch where he wanted her to kneel. Once she had done so did he go into the bedroom, returning after a moment with a long, thin box. He sat down on the couch next to where she knelt and opened it.

Inside was a long strip of leather, about an inch and a half wide. There was a metal buckle at one end and a D-ring in the center. A small lock was nestled at one end of the box. "Do you know what this is?" he asked her.

She shook her head no—but the sight of it gave her goose bumps.

"It's a collar," he explained. "People who demonstrate they can be good slaves to their Masters are given a collar to wear that shows their status. Should another Master walk in here right now, he would see you collarless and assume you were available. A collared slave belongs to the Master who collared her. Does this make sense?"

She nodded. "Yes, Master. It does. A collar is like a ring to the outside world—a symbol that shows ownership."

His cheeks dimpled as he smiled. "Yes." He paused then caught her eye, his demeanor letting her know how serious this was. "Someday I will ask you to wear my collar, Sarah. I want you to be my slave." He closed the box. "But not yet. You are not ready for such a commitment. However, you need to understand my intentions. When I deem you ready, I intend to collar you."

Her breath quickened. She understood the seriousness of his intent. And he was right, she was not yet ready for such a commitment. She barely knew *what* she wanted, this was all so new.

He put the box on the table. "I only want you to know what it is, so you will understand as you read this week."

Her brow furrowed. "Am I going to be doing some reading this week?"

He laughed as he stood. "Yes, slave, you are. Come with me."

He led the way over to the corner of the room, where his computer was. "If you give me your email address, I will send you some sites I want you to study this week."

She gave it to him, sort of surprised that they hadn't exchanged emails earlier. She watched as he typed it in and sent her a list of websites.

Done, he turned to her. "You are not to stray from these sites. Each one has links to other pages, but I do not want you to go there yet. Are you willing to do this for me this week?"

It was the first time he had directly requested anything from her during time they weren't together. But looking at websites wasn't a big issue—she spent more time than she'd admit surfing the web. Having that surfing guided by his choices for her was actually erotic. She nodded. "Yes, Sir. I will learn what you wish me to learn this week."

He led her back to the couch where they reclined, she spooned against him, wrapped in his arms; he softly caressing her, enjoying the feel of her skin next to his.

For a while they just lay together, basking in each other's presence. But soon, the pillow talk began, even if they were still only on the couch. They discussed the day's events and the happenings in the world, talking their way to bedtime. When both were yawning more often than not, he stood up and took her by the hand, leading her to the bedroom.

"Come, slave—you must leave early in the morning if you are to make it to work on time."

The thought crossed her mind that she did not know what he did for a living. He had already been here when she arrived on Friday—and it sounded as if he'd be here when she left tomorrow morning. If she weren't so tired, she might ask him about it. But a yawn interrupted her thoughts and she snuggled under the covers and into his arms.

* * * * *

Morning came too soon. The radio woke them both. "Stay, slave and take a few more minutes." She didn't need to be told twice. Dimly she was aware that he got up and went into the bathroom. When the alarm went off again ten minutes later, she had to roll over to hit the snooze button. As she rolled back, intending to ignore the morning for a little longer, he reentered the bedroom.

"Oh, no, you don't, slave. Up you go!" With a graceful flourish, he pulled the covers off the bed. Even as she protested, he was there with the key to unlock her cuffs. "Go—take your shower and breakfast will be ready by the time you get out."

As it did every work morning, the shock of the water hitting her face brought her to full consciousness. Quickly she showered and dressed, feeling odd in her work clothes. She was so used to her nudity while in the house that to walk around in it fully dressed seemed almost wrong. The thought made her wet and she knew she'd better get a hold of herself; she had to make it through the day on the one pair of panties she'd brought.

Tea and toast was ready for her when she went to find him. "Oh, thank you, Master. And I'm glad you didn't make a big breakfast. On weekdays, I generally don't eat till mid-morning."

He laughed. "I suspected as much. The professional woman on the go. You look wonderful." She turned around for him, modeling her slacks, turtleneck and sweater.

"It's kind of you to say, so, Master—but Versace would think otherwise, I'm sure."

Ten minutes later she was ready to leave; he held her bag in his hand and stood at the door, watching her slip on her sensible shoes. After a weekend spent barefoot most of the time, the constriction on her feet felt awkward. He walked her to her car, put her bag in the back seat and turned to her.

And now she hesitated. Somehow a "thanks for a great weekend" seemed inane. But how did one say goodbye without sounding maudlin? He stepped forward as she reached for the door handle, his hand on hers, turning her around to face him. His eyes smoldered and she did not want to look away. Bending down, he kissed her deeply, his tongue reaching in through her parted lips to caress her. She opened to him, work totally forgotten.

And then he pulled away. Abruptly, in the middle of the kiss. "There, slave," he said, "that's for you to remember me by while you're away." With an insouciant smile, he swatted her on the behind. "Now, go to work."

Her heart pounding, she slid into her seat and he shut the door. Numbly, she started the car, automatically putting it into gear and driving out of the driveway. She was over half way to work before she began to set aside her thoughts of him and think about her week ahead.

Sarah's journal

The week between

Monday

In the history of passionate kisses, that one *has* to go down as being in the top five. No, the top three. And the number one kiss of my life.

Does he know what that does to me? To have his tongue possess me in such a way? His hands on my waist, holding firmly onto me so that I have nowhere to go? He must know. He manipulates me too well for it to be an accident.

I know I don't often write in this journal; I see the last entry was several months ago—and concerned a major point in my life that now seems minor. But I suppose that's the way with me. I only write here when things are getting intense in life and I need a moment to stop and think about them and I do that better with a pen in my hand.

And things are definitely getting intense between Phillip and me. He is incredible. For two weeks I've been trying to determine just what it is that turns me on so much about him— and I think I'm getting closer to an answer.

He asked me to look at some websites this week—and to keep an open mind. I sat down Monday night when I got home, to just take a quick glance at a few of them while dinner was on the stove. To make a long story short, I burned dinner and only explored one site most of the night. And it wasn't even a particularly exotic or exciting site!

It was a medical site apparently written by women for women that went into great detail about women's genitalia and every possible thing that could be associated with it. There was so much information there that I never learned in health class! I've seen some of the porno pictures of naked women before, and always thought, "Well, I don't look like that." But I'd never really looked at myself before. I knew I had a clit—but had little knowledge about it. After seeing those pictures on that site and then examining myself in a mirror, well, let's just say I can't believe I've missed out on so much.

One of the places I spent a lot of time was in the "fantasies" section of that site. It really explained a little better to me why I like it when Phillip ties me up and calls me 'slave.' Even writing those words causes a flutter in my stomach. There's a part of me that still doesn't believe I voluntarily did what I did on both of these last two weekends. And even while that part of me watches in disbelief, my mind readily accepts the fact that I will go back again this Friday for more of the same treatment.

At least I know now that I'm not alone—or abnormal in my submissiveness. It sounds like many women would like to experience what I have experienced with Phillip. That gives me a great deal of comfort, believe me.

Tuesday

One of the girls at work mentioned today that a bunch of them were going to the movies on Friday night—did I want to come along? I told her I had plans and she asked if I had a date. I told her yes and then changed the subject. But it got me to thinking. If I spend every weekend with Phillip, what does that do to the rest of my social life? Not that I have a very busy one—but I do have some close friends. I don't want to give them up—but I want to be with him as well. It is something we will need to discuss, and soon.

Tonight I went to the next site on his list and found the definitions of some words that have lately become a very important part of my vocabulary. The site was more from the point of view of someone who is an online submissive or dominant, but was helpful nonetheless. I definitely know now I am not alone in this need/desire to please.

That need has been haunting me, I must say. How could I, who have striven for independence all my life, just suddenly toss it aside and say "Yes, I'll be your slave"? It just hasn't made sense to me. Phillip's words about something missing were dead on—but I'm still struggling with the need to command in the workplace vs. the need to submit to him.

And at first, I was submitting only for the sex. Which was terrific. Incredible and terrific. Out of this world and terrific. Did I mention that sex with Phillip is terrific?

But after this past weekend, when he asked me to submit in other ways, the eating after him and from his plate, wearing clothes out in public that he chose for me…made me realize I want to submit to him in many more ways. There's a comfort in making no decisions, in having only one job to do: to please him in any way he wishes. But there's also a danger that I'll lose myself. The independent me that I like so much. Is there a way to have both?

I suppose I do at the moment—have both, that is. During the week, I'm a normal, well-adjusted, independent working career woman. And on the weekends I'm a sex slave.

Okay, I'm back. Can't believe I actually wrote that last paragraph. Laughed so hard I had to go to the bathroom. The fact that it's the truth just heightens the absurdity.

<u>Wednesday</u>

—another day, another website. I keep checking my email to see if Phillip might actually send me a note, but there has been nothing so far. And while I know I could just email him by using that 'reply' button, I think I'd better not. If he wants correspondence, he'll start it. He's the master after all.

Holy cow! I found it! On the next website on his list, I found this quote by a slave that keeps a log: "*What I really, really want is to fly out of myself and visit that place where time doesn't exist and the spirit can roam among the stars. Being literally tied to the earth, holds my body so my soul can soar.*"

That's it! I have always wanted to get to that place, and, until I met Phillip, have never achieved it. And yet, with him, I've been there twice over the past two weekends.

I really like this page. There are lots of other pages to the site, including a page of links. But Phillip asked me to stay only on the sites themselves and not to stray off them. I have no trouble with that—there's so much information here on these three sites alone that I know I haven't yet discovered it all.

I also liked this quote that was from her master: "*I want control of a woman's body the same way a conductor wants control over an orchestra. Her body is my instrument, the whip my baton. Just as an orchestra cannot make music without the conductor, just so a slave cannot make glorious music without her master.*" That really explains to me why Phillip likes to do what HE does. And that is an important part of this exploration for me. Not only do I need to know what's in it for me, but I need to know what's in it for him.

One of the things that first caught my attention regarding Phillip was the latent power I felt emanating from him. It's soft, gentle, always present, yet I got the feeling the waters ran deep. And that first night, when he asked for permission to tie me up—I looked into his eyes and saw the absence of a power trip. Now I understand why. He doesn't do this to lord it over me, but to release the emotions in me that I've hidden for so long. He does it to release the "glorious music" in me. Wow.

But I'm still curious about the collar…

Thursday

Two sites tonight—the last two he listed. The first one I really liked and I did in fact, print out the list to take to him—since I suspect that's why he included it. It's a checklist of activities. Some of the things on there, well, let's just say never in my wildest dreams did I ever even imagine them! Others look intriguing, some we've already done. It should provoke some discussion.

Especially 'cause of the last site.

This last place was a story archive. Apparently lots of people have fantasies about Dominance and submission and write stories about either their adventures or their dreams. The story Phillip had me read involves a slave who needs even to ask permission to go to the bathroom, and when she finally gets the courage to ask, is punished for her "sin" because her master had told her he wasn't going to let her go until the morning. That's going WAY too far. I mean, come on…give the woman a bit of credit for having a brain! Sorry, if *that's* what Phillip has in mind, I'm so done with it.

Tomorrow is Friday and we shall meet again. I cannot wait—in spite of the one story and my other concern (about my friends)—the thought of seeing him soon already has my heart pounding. Truth to tell, I'm falling in love.

Addendum, late Thursday night: I can't believe I forgot to mention—besides the websites, Phillip asked me to shave for him. All of me. I've been thinking about it all week and had decided to wait till tonight so it would be "freshly" done for tomorrow night. Good thing, though, that I did that right after work and before I read that story—not sure I want to follow orders after reading that!

But it feels weird. I just put on my nightgown and it's so smooth down there. Silky, but in a different way from when my mound was covered. I am very aware of my sex at the moment. Don't know HOW I'm going to make it through the day tomorrow!

Addendum, Friday morning: BLAST! Got my period in the night. Will still go to Phillip's, but will probably be home tonight. Will take enough supplies to last the weekend though, just in case.

Chapter 6
Bindings

Pulling into his driveway Friday evening, Sarah threw the gear into park and turned off the engine with a vengeance. It had been a lousy day. She leaned back against the seat, taking several deep breaths, trying to put it all behind her. Finally, she just unbuckled and got out of the car, slamming the door behind her in an attempt to trap her troubles in the car. The last thing she wanted was to let work interfere with her planned weekend.

Grabbing her bag from the trunk of the car, she stalked up the path, stopping half way to get a hold of herself. "No," she told herself. "You are to leave it in the car. So scoot—all you problems and stresses of the day—go away!" With an effort of will, she straightened her shoulders, squared her chin and forced a smile to her face. Advancing to the door like an actor in a bad play, she didn't notice that he was already waiting on the porch.

"Are you all right?" Concern was etched in his face.

"Yes, of course," she replied, fake smile in place and determined to put the day out of her mind. "Just fine!"

"Then come on in." He reached for her bag and stepped aside, letting her enter the house first. But his eyes showed he was not convinced everything was "just fine."

She paused in the hall, waiting for him to tell her where they were going next. Last week she'd done a playful little striptease for him—did he want that again? She doubted it would turn her on in her present mood, but it would be easy to keep that smile plastered on and tease him.

Except, he simply set her bag down in the hall and took her hand, leading her to the couch. Sitting down, he patted the cushion next to him and she sat, folding one leg under her and facing him.

"Did you have a good week?" he asked her, tucking a stray lock of hair behind her ear.

"Yes," she replied, a little relieved that they weren't going to get right into hot and heavy sex this time. Last Friday they'd both needed the release. This week, she had her period and she doubted he'd even want her to stay. Plus, there were those other issues...

"Okay, Sarah, what is it?" He sat back, facing her, his eyes stern. When she hesitated, he took her hand in his. "You need to be honest with me, Sarah. I'm not blind; I can see something is wrong. As your master, I have a right to know."

She put her head down, embarrassed to tell him about her period; unsure how to ask about how far he expected his Master-dom to go. Instead she twisted her fingers together, searching for words.

Patiently he waited, but she was silent for so long, he finally reached out and gently pulled up her chin—his own stomach lurching. "Or have you decided you do not want a master?" he asked quietly.

"No!" Her eyes went wide at the thought. "No! It has nothing to do with you, I mean, well...not like that, I mean." She shook her head at her own folly and the words came tumbling out. "It's just that, well, I got my period yesterday and I know you won't want me to stay, and it's already been a lousy day 'cause I had to fire someone at work, and having to leave will be the icing on the cake. But if you think I'm going to ask for permission to go to the bathroom, you've got another think coming! I can think for myself and am not going to be punished just because I had an extra drink!"

His laugh filled the small house; she'd gone from embarrassed to angry to indignant all in the space of a few seconds. "I see the dam broke—now, don't you feel better?"

After a moment, she grudgingly smiled and as he gazed fondly at her, her smile grew. "All right," she grinned at him. "I do feel a little better."

"Shall we deal with those issues one at a time?" When she nodded, he continued. "Now, first of all, why would having your period affect whether I let you stay or go?"

"I doubt you really want to have sex with me at this particular moment—I can get pretty messy." Her cheeks turned red at the admission. She never discussed her menses with anyone, except for her mother and her doctor, of course. Certainly she did not discuss them with anyone she was dating—or trying to impress.

"And did you bring napkins with you? Or do you use tampons?"

His frank use of the terminology shocked her and it showed on her face. He laughed again. "I have sisters—several of them. They used the euphemism that 'their little friend' had come calling."

Now it was her turn to laugh out loud. "My mother used exactly the same phrase! So I can tell you I use napkins and you'll know what I mean?" She shook her head in amazement. "Next you'll be telling me you actually went to the store and bought them for your sisters!"

"I did."

She looked to see if he was kidding, but there was only honesty in his eyes. She shook her head again; her father and brother wouldn't have done such a wonderful thing for all the money in the world.

"You know, we can still have sex, even if you have your period." He reached out and dealt with that stray hair again.

"Yes, I know, but I can't imagine it would be very pleasant—or sexy." She made a face.

"There are other parts of your body that can be equally aroused. If you're willing to stay, I think we could explore those parts instead this weekend."

A slow grin crossed her face. He wanted her to stay. "Yes, Sir. I would like that." She gratefully slipped into her role.

He leaned over and kissed her. It was a simple kiss, yet she melted into it as if a huge stress had left her. And, of course, it had.

Sitting back again, he let his fingers drift across her mouth and come to rest on her cheek. "So tell me about the next part. Who did you have to fire?"

She shuddered. "It wasn't a good time, I'm afraid. The company is downsizing and one person had to be cut from my team. I had to make the decision as to whom. I suppose I ought to be glad my supervisors didn't make the decision for me, 'cause they would've chosen someone else. But they trust me to run my team the way I need to run it. Even so, I hated having to be the one to tell her that she was being let go."

She bit her lip to keep from crying. It had been an awful scene—she'd never fired anyone before and she fervently hoped she'd never have to do it again. He gathered her into his arms and just held her until she regained her composure.

"I'm glad it wasn't easy for you," he told her. "That sort of thing should never be easy." He looked down at her face, now upturned and listening to him. "I'm glad you are not callous," he said quietly.

They sat for several moments more before she pushed herself up—ready to tackle the third point her outburst had raised. "About that story you had me read…"

He grinned. "I thought that might push a few buttons with you."

She nodded. "Oh, it did that all right. Every time I turned around today I've been either thinking about the firing or about that woman chained to the end of the bed." Her nose wrinkled. "Not that being chained to the bed is such a bad thing," she admitted. "But just the way he treated her!"

"So if I told you that you were going to be chained to the bed all night, so to be careful about what you drank, and then you ignored my command..." His voice trailed off and he looked at her appraisingly.

"Well, first off, I doubt that I'd ignore your command. But let's say I had." She stood and paced the room. "Let's imagine I forgot, or maybe I didn't realize I'd drunk quite as much as I did. You chain me to the bed and I go to sleep." She paused and looked at him frankly. "We'll ignore the fact that the master and his friend just had to have a loud conversation in the doorway of the room where she was sleeping—they could've shown just a little consideration there! That was just plain rude." She sniffed at the idea. But then she cocked her head to one side, thinking out loud.

"Wait, I think that's it right there! He demanded obedience from her—and respect of his wishes. But he showed none towards her! Not once did he ever accept the fact that she should also be respected. Never did he accept the fact that she had a brain. It wasn't an issue of whether she did what she was told or not that bothers me—it was his attitude toward her!"

"Excellent!" He grinned from ear to ear. He stood and put his arms around her. "I promise to always respect you, my slave." Bending down, he kissed her in passion this time and she returned his love. More of the day's stresses melted away and her shoulders slumped down as the weights were lifted by the touch of his lips on hers.

"So if I tell you that you're going to be chained to the bed all night and that you should be careful about what you drink..." he murmured into her hair.

"Then I will obey your commands and expect to be punished if I do not meet them, Master." She looked up at him, a hunger growing inside her. "I agree to that, because you respect me and I know you will never punish me gratuitously, as that master did."

His hands drifted downward, brushing against her still-covered breasts; breasts that were much more tender at this time of the month. Their lips met again, open and soft. When his tongue entered her mouth, she pressed herself toward him, letting him know his possession of her was complete. How could she have forgotten the sweet taste of his tongue as it encircled hers and left her breathless?

"How hungry are you?" he asked, pulling out of the kiss.

"I could eat," she answered, suddenly remembering she'd skipped lunch because of an upset stomach. Now, relaxing in his arms, she felt a small gnawing in her stomach and grinned. "Yes, I definitely could eat."

"Come on, then, my slave. There's a great Chinese restaurant not far away."

They shared a pleasant dinner in a perfectly charming place only a few miles away from his cottage. About half way through the meal, she finally brought up the last remaining topic that she felt they needed to discuss. And it was good they weren't in the house. Out here in the real world, she felt more comfortable asking him about her friends.

"So are you saying you'd like me to meet your friends?" he asked.

"Yes—I guess that's part of it. I'm torn, that's the problem. I want to spend time with you and with them." She put her chopsticks down in exasperation. "How do married people do it? We are not the first couple to have this problem!"

He laughed. "And we won't be the last. I also have friends I haven't seen because of the time we spend together."

She hadn't considered that. But of course he had friends. "So we just have to find a way to introduce you to my friends and me to your friends! Gee, that sounds so simple." She laughed, relieved. Why had she thought he might want to prevent her from seeing her friends? Because she'd been reading too many of those silly domination stories in the newspaper, that was why. The general press had no idea what it was talking about when they reported such things, she decided. They only reported the extreme cases, not the normal, everyday folk who chose such a lifestyle.

"Then how about next Friday?" she ventured. "Would you be willing to meet my group next weekend? I only ask because Beth is having a housewarming party and I'd really like to go."

He chuckled. "So there was an ulterior motive to this all along, hmm? Very well. I will meet your friends on Friday night and you will meet mine on Saturday. Sound good?"

She nodded. A fair solution. They finished their meal and returned home. It was funny how his little cottage was quickly getting the feeling of belonging for her. Because night had fallen while they were eating, the house was dark when they arrived.

As he had their very first night in the cottage, he bid her remain at the door while he went in and turned on a light. Feeling the familiar tingle of anticipation, she waited patiently for his return. He wasn't long. The light blossomed in the open doorway and he was right there, holding out his hand. Taking it, she let him lead her over the threshold once more.

Once again he stopped her in the hallway, standing behind her, her fingers still entwined with his. Only the small table lamp was lit, casting a romantic glow over the otherwise mundane hall. Stepping behind her, he pulled her arm back and up, bending it at the elbow. "Give me your other hand, slave," he murmured in her ear.

Obediently she put her other arm behind her and he took that hand as well, bending her arm up until her forearms were bent cross-wise across her back. "Hold onto your elbows," he instructed. She reached further and felt her breasts strain against her bra. Because dinner had followed so closely upon her arrival, she had not yet changed out of her work clothes. She still wore the deep red button-up blouse and black slacks she'd worn to work that morning.

Phillip's fingers now trailed along her collarbone, pulling her thick, straight hair back and out of his way. Nuzzling against her neck, he reached around her to the front of her blouse and slowly unbuttoned each button. Pulling it free of her slacks, he let it hang open in front for a moment while he paid particular attention to one of her ears. She sighed and felt herself sway as his tongue circled and dipped into the hollow and his breath sighed in her ear.

His hands steadied her and he pulled the blouse off her shoulders, letting it rest on her clasped arms. Then he stepped close to her again and this time let her lean into him as he reached around to release her breasts from their confines. Sliding a finger under her breast, he teased it a moment in the bra. Then carefully, as if he were handling a most precious object, he pulled her soft breast up and out of the cup, letting it hang down over the binding. He did the same with the other and she was glad for his support behind her. His slow undressing of her made her feel more naked than when she wore nothing.

"Go and take care of your monthly visitor, slave," he whispered in her ear. "Come back to me wearing nothing but your panties."

It didn't take long in the bathroom to refresh herself and strip for him. He was waiting on the couch. Several candles lit around the room gave a pleasant, comforting glow. Remembering his preference, she knelt in front of him, her hands behind her back, her posture straight. The first time she knelt to him each weekend brought a special thrill to her. There was both a comfort and an excitement. As if she were settling into a comfortable pair of shoes that she was to wear to an amusement park. What wonders would he show her next? Her ankle and wrist cuffs sat out in the open; at his nod, she put them on, locking them in place.

He brought out the small box he'd shown her the week before. Opening it, he again showed her the leather collar with its small lock. His voice was quiet. "I showed you this last week and told you I would ask you to wear it when you were ready. In the restaurant I was not entirely truthful with you." He looked at her apologetically and she simply waited, sure he'd told her as much as she could hear in public. Now he was telling her the rest.

He ran his finger along the leather band. "I would be happy to meet your friends, that is not an issue. In fact, I like the fact that you want to introduce me to them — that you'd share that part of your life with me." He smiled and her stomach fluttered. Oh, how her friends would tease her, for finding such a handsome man!

"But my friends..." His eyes held hers and she saw them turn serious — very serious. He was rushing things, and he knew from past experience that this was dangerous. But Sarah was right about their friends. His would understand his absence from their number if he told them he was training a new slave — in fact, several of them already knew. Yes, it was possible to meet her friends and put off meeting his own, but Sarah was an intelligent woman and would soon begin asking why. Better for her to understand up front. "My friends are different, Sarah. My friends will know you are my slave."

It took a moment for his words to register. He had used her name, signaling that he wasn't playing. As things stood right now, no one but the two of them knew of their relationship. Sarah had no one to talk to about it — everyone she knew would think her insane for giving up her freedom to anyone else. And when she introduced him to her small group on Friday night, none of them would know or need to know that they had anything other than the girlfriend/boyfriend thing going on.

But Phillip's friends *would* know. There would be other people that she would meet, socialize with, talk to, who would know their secret. Unbidden, a blush crept up her neck and into her cheeks. She looked at him, uncertain.

"Among my circle, there are protocols to be followed. A collared slave has certain protections that an uncollared one does not. Don't worry," he hastily added, seeing her look of alarm. "None of my closest friends would try anything underhanded. But in the larger circle of Doms...well, let's just say that, like 'normal' life, not everyone is to be trusted. If you accept my collar, you are under my protection."

Again he paused. When he didn't go on, she spoke up. "So if I accept your collar, you will protect me from all unwanted advances?" He nodded. "And by accepting your collar, then I become your property, don't I?"

He nodded again. "Yes. You become my property. You have no rights, no opinions, but what I give you or allow you to express. While you wear my collar, you are my slave."

And there was the crux of the matter. Accepting his collar meant this relationship had gone beyond the bedroom fling she wanted three weeks ago. It had blossomed in a way Sarah had never dreamed, not even when with her husband.

Phillip had never asked about him—and Sarah had told him only the barest of facts, not wanting Phillip to think she was comparing the two of them. Indeed, there was no comparison. Where Tom had been short, Phillip was tall. Where Tom was gentle, Phillip was firm. Where Tom was passive, Phillip was dominant. Very dominant. Wonderfully dominant. Sarah knew her reply.

"I am already your slave, am I not?" He smiled at her, but there was little mirth in his eyes. She sat back on her heels and searched for the words she wanted. "You have given me two wonderful weekends filled with love—and lust. A whole new world has been opened to me because I said 'yes' to you when you asked me on the beach if I would do anything you commanded. I do not want to stop exploring this world with you. I understand that accepting your collar involves a commitment on both our parts. It is a commitment I would like to give. Yes, Master. I would like to wear your collar."

He smiled in earnest now. He had been right about her! She wanted this as much as he did.

"Then turn around, slave." She did so without standing up. The leather had warmed from his touch as they talked. It was stiff, not yet broken in—like her, she thought. Time would make them both pliable. There was a soft 'snick' as the lock closed tight and the sound made her shiver.

Sarah put her hands up to explore her newest binding. The D-ring in front was colder to her touch than the leather. Gently she tugged at it to see if it would come loose. It did not. She ran her fingers around the back, where it was locked under her hair. The lock hung there and she tugged on that, hard. It did not open. The collar was firmly fastened onto her.

"Turn around and let me see, my slave." Still kneeling, she turned back to face him. Phillip reached out and looped his finger through the D-ring, pulling her to him. Bending down and holding her, he kissed her—a deep, long, passionate kiss. She felt the rush between her legs at the way he could so easily control her now. Oh, yes…she liked this collar very much.

"It is getting late, my slave," he murmured. "And you have had a long day. Come." Keeping his finger hooked through her collar, he led her into the bedroom.

She had no choice but to follow—and the yearning deep in her loins spread, making her heart beat hard. Controlled, submissive, a slave following her master, she followed him as he brought her into the bedroom and sat her in the chair.

He picked up a chain he had on the nightstand and held it up for her to see. It wasn't long, but there were three equal parts to it. The way he held it, the chain formed a "Y." She sat patiently as he tilted her chin up and attached one end to the D-ring in her collar. The other two ends rested their coldness in the cleavage of her breasts and she resisted the urge to flinch. The ends fell just at a level with her nipples.

But it was not her breasts he was interested in. Taking one of the remaining ends of the chain in one hand and her wrist in the other, he fastened the chain to her wrist cuff. In a moment, both her hands were connected, via the chain, to her collar. He smiled at her so bound and she experimented with the limited movement she now had.

She could touch her breasts, play with them if he wanted her to, and she could raise her arms a little ways above her head. But if she tried to go up too far, the chain bit into her chin, even with her head back as far as it could go. She also had limited side-to-side movement. Definitely an interesting position to be in. If she relaxed completely, her hands hung in their cuffs and Sarah felt very much like a puppy dog begging for attention.

He put on some soft, romantic music, lit several candles around the room and turned off the electric lights. She was getting aroused just watching him pad around the room in his stocking feet, and when he started his striptease for her, she squirmed a bit in the chair. Watching him undress always made that warmth bloom between her legs.

Unbuttoning his shirt, Phillip left it tucked into his pants, the front of it hanging open. She could see his chest, covered with fine dark hair—and she longed to run her fingers over it. Unbuttoning his sleeves, he rolled them back, taking his time, never looking anywhere but at her. Her breath quickened.

Phillip loved undressing for her; her face was so wonderfully expressive. With each garment he removed, her lips would part, her breath would quicken, her eyes would grow heavy with desire. Yes, she was an appreciative audience and her rapt attention appealed to his vanity. With a deft movement, he unbuckled his belt, and unbuttoned his pants, then slowly unzipped them. His shirt was in the way, however, and she could not see what she wanted to. Her eyes were glued to his movements and he obliged by unbuttoning the last of his shirt buttons and pulling aside the edges. Only a small part of his underwear could be seen; very tight underwear, revealing nothing. Unaware that she was even doing it, she began to play with her nipples.

The sight of her arousal increased his own. He stripped off the shirt and throwing it into the corner, advanced to stand directly in front of her. Sarah's eyes were glued to his crotch, so he slowly opened his pants, sliding them down to his knees. His hardening cock was barely restrained by the tight fabric and he saw the longing in her eyes. She pulled harder on her nipples now—her own urge building.

Deftly he kicked off his pants then slowly brought out his cock. The tip glistened with pre-come—he wanted her now—

and wanted her badly. Her need was as great and she opened her mouth willingly, wanting to be filled.

He put his hands on her head and guided himself into her mouth. She relaxed her throat muscles and he went deep inside her all in one thrust. Her hands, chained as they were, were in a perfect position to caress his balls, and she made good use of them. He pulled out and entered her deeply again as one of her hands reached up between the crack of his ass, feeling for the hole that was there.

He felt her chains brush against his balls and the touch fueled his desire. She was his slave—his toy. Willingly she wore his collar—willingly she gave herself to him. Her trust and her desire to please him sent him over the edge and he came quickly, filling her mouth with his seed. Satisfied, he watched as she struggled a moment to swallow all that he had so quickly given her. Concentrating, her throat constricted once, twice, and she smiled up at him, licking from her lips the few drops that had fallen there.

Kneeling before her, Phillip raised her arms and licked a few drops of his come off her breasts, then continued licking and kissing their wonderful softness, pulling a nipple deep into his mouth. She gasped and he gently pushed her back till she was reclining in the chair and he lay half on top of her. One hand dipped down, over the top of her panties and she moaned— menses or not, she was still in need.

Rubbing through her panties and sucking on her nipples, kneading her breasts, her own hands unable to contribute; his hands played her and she came. Not wildly, not with fireworks tonight; instead it was a long, slow rumble that took its own sweet time passing through her body. With a final shudder, she opened her eyes and smiled at him.

"Did my slave have a pleasant experience?" he asked her, grinning.

"Your slave did, my master. And did my master have a pleasant experience as well?" she asked, feeling better than she had all day.

"Mmmm...a very nice experience. Thank you, slave." He stood and held out a hand to her.

"You're very welcome, Master. And thank you!" she added as she got awkwardly to her feet. Without the use of her arms to steady herself, she was grateful for his balancing touch.

"Time for bed now, I think, slave. Do you need to use the bathroom?" He bent down, cleaning up his discarded clothes.

"No, Sir—I'm fine." She hesitated. He'd given no indication of removing the chain—which he had locked into place with small locks similar to the ones on her cuffs and collar.

"Then into bed with you!" He blew out all the candles but the one next to his side of the bed and pulled down the covers. She got in, but did not lie down. "Is something the matter, slave?" he asked her.

"Ummm...these chains. Is it your intention that I should wear them all night long?" She wasn't sure how she felt about this.

"Yes, my slave, it is. You sleep with your arms tucked under you anyway—and this is my desire."

It was another test—another limit he was pushing. She could see that now. Ducking her head a moment to hide the smile, she considered. It was true, she did sleep this way. But that was her choice. Could she sleep the same way she had for dozens of years when it was *not* her choice?

"Yes, Sir." She slid under the covers and snuggled beside him. It was funny. She never even thought of using her hands on herself when she was with him. But the moment she couldn't, she wanted to.

He gave her breast an affectionate squeeze. "I like it when you submit to me," he admitted. "You give me your trust—you give me your body. That creates a bond stronger than any other."

She nodded, sleep starting to steal over her already. He was right—it had been a long day and she was more tired than she realized. "I do trust you, Master Phillip," she said sleepily. "I trust you with my heart."

He held her for several minutes, listening to her breathing as sleep took her. There was something wonderful about having a woman fall asleep in your arms and he gently kissed the top of her head where it rested on his shoulder. His finger ran along the chain he had placed on her—the chain she had accepted from him. He could not see her collar, but knowing it was there spread warmth through him. "I trust you with my heart, too, Sarah," he whispered before he too, fell asleep.

Chapter 7
Enslavement

Waking, Sarah went to stretch her arms over her head as she had every morning she could ever remember. Except this morning her arms were brought up short and a chain grated along her chin.

Her eyes flew open and she remembered the bindings he'd put on her the night before. A quick look to her side showed an empty bed—the clock read 8:30. How had she slept so late? Tilting her head up, she rubbed her eyes, listening. No sounds came from the kitchen or the bath. She needed to use the facilities, but with her arms bound so, she could not remove her panties before soaking them and the pad she wore.

"Master?" she called tentatively. When there was no answer, not even a paper rustle, she called again, louder. "Master!"

She heard his footsteps coming up from the basement then she heard the sound of logs dropped on the hearth. But there was no need for her to call again—Phillip appeared in the doorway, brushing the dirt off his hands. "Morning, sleepyhead-slave!" He came over and sat beside her on the bed and fingered her chains. "You seem to have slept just fine with these on. Apparently you two are a match." He grinned.

She smiled back, but there was little time for niceties. "Please, Master—I need to be released so that I can use the bathroom."

He laughed, pulling out a set of keys. He found the right one, unlocked her and released the chain from one of her wrists. "Don't get up just yet, though," he cautioned. "I don't want those muscles to cramp on you." He kneaded her arm, both above and below the elbow, and she smiled as the muscles relaxed. Once he was satisfied the arm wouldn't bother her, he released the other one and did the same. Only when she'd been divested of all cuffs and chains did he let her up. The collar remained.

"Take your shower while you're in there," he called after her. She yelled an affirmative response and he went out to the kitchen to prepare their breakfast.

She let the hot water run on her arms a little longer than usual as she flexed and stretched them out. There was a mild soreness in her right shoulder, but it would fade as the day went on. And her period was done. Overnight there had been but a little spotting. She decided it would be safe to go panty-less. And that way she could show him she'd shaved for him. There was no hair on her mound or her pussy. And what had grown back, she took care of quickly with the razor she'd brought just for this purpose.

Carefully she dried the collar as best she could. Its presence around her neck was meant to be permanent, apparently. Well, permanent while she was here. Wouldn't she just be a sight walking into work on Monday morning wearing a collar locked around her neck? She grinned and went into the bedroom to change.

Her cuffs were not on the bed, nor was the bed made. Quickly she righted the sheets and comforter, glancing to see if he'd put her cuffs out elsewhere. No, he must have something different in mind, she thought to herself. Draping the towels over the rack, she brushed out her hair as the striped sunlight beamed through the blinds to paint her body. For a moment, she dallied in the light, standing on tiptoe to let one of the rays of sunshine warm her nipples. It was going to be a glorious day.

He was waiting for her in the kitchen—she smelled the bacon when she came out of the bathroom, so she knew right where he was. "Anything I can do to help?" she asked.

"Pour the orange juice," he nodded toward the fridge, not looking at her. But when he turned around and saw her shaved pussy, he smiled. With only a small suggestion from him, she had gone ahead and fulfilled his wish. Phillip was grateful for the small confirmation that Sarah enjoyed his gentle guidance. She turned from the refrigerator, the orange juice pitcher in her hands, her pussy stark below. He could feast his eyes on such a sight all day. Instead, he turned back to the task at hand. Time later to tell her how much she pleased him. Still, he said nothing.

Sarah poured the juice and in short order, two places were set at the table and breakfast was ready. She was relieved she didn't have to kneel through his breakfast and wait for him. She would do it; that was no longer an issue. If he asked it of her, she would quickly comply. Eventually, Phillip knew, Sarah would beg to be allowed to kneel as he ate. But it had to come from her deep-seated need to serve — it could not be imposed from above. Such an attitude could be trained, however, if she was open-minded enough to accept it, and Phillip was secure in the knowledge that her training was successfully begun in that regard.

Over breakfast, they discussed the day's activities. He needed to go out for a bit and run a few errands and if she wanted to join him, he would be happy to have her along. She nodded, just happy to spend the day with him, even if sex wasn't a part of it.

"Remember, however," Phillip warned her, "you are my slave for the entire weekend — even if we are out in public. I may not call you 'slave,' but that does not change our relationship." It was important that she understood fully that this was a lifestyle choice — not a game that they played.

Sarah nodded. Church the weekend before had been the same. Seeing her agreement, Phillip continued. "And you will wear what I give you to wear."

That sounded ominous. But he had already shown her his excellent taste in clothes, so she just smiled her acquiescence and the conversation moved on.

Dishes were done and the kitchen cleaned when he led her back into the bedroom to dress for their outing. With her period done, she would be able to wear the special undergarment he had bought this week for her. Bringing the box to her, he set it on the bed. "Stand before me, slave."

She did so, putting her hands behind her back and spreading her legs as he had taught her. Her reward was a satisfied smile from him. Now her shaved pussy was right there in front of him and he ran a finger along her mound, then his hand cupped her sex. "Very good, slave. You have done as I requested."

A shiver went through her at that. She had done as he had requested. On her own time, with him not near, acting only on a suggestion from him, she had shaved herself because she wanted only to please him. Her juices flowed into his hand and he slipped a finger inside her, pulling her forward so he could kiss the smooth skin that lay bare to his touch.

She whimpered a bit and stepped forward, feeling his lips brush along her smooth mound, his fingers now moving up along the thin valley to her ass. One finger slipped inside her anus with ease, as Phillip used her own lubricant. He pushed her back a bit then slid to his knees, letting his tongue flick along her pussy, one hand holding her lips open; the other beginning to pump his finger in and out of her ass.

Phillip had claimed her pussy three weeks ago—first with his mouth, then with his cock. Now he reasserted that claim over her naked skin, he was a master in more ways than one.

Sarah closed her eyes and the sensations he created washed over her; she cried out as his teeth gently pulled on her clit. The intensity grew and she swayed where she stood, her mouth slightly open, her breath shallow and fast. Small whimpers came from her throat and she fought to remain upright. Still his tongue darted over and around her clit until, with a deep thrust of his finger and a sharp pull with his teeth, she came all over his face. Her juices squirted out into his mouth, carried by the contractions of her orgasm.

When she was finished and her body had slowed its writhing, he pulled away, leaving her standing there, swaying;

her legs still spread but her knees locked, her arms gripping each elbow behind her back.

When Phillip returned, he had cleaned up and carried a warm washcloth to wash her. "Is my slave content?" he asked, already knowing the answer. She murmured her thanks to him, still basking in the afterglow even as her heart settled into its normal rhythm.

"Now, where were we?" Grinning like the Cheshire cat, Phillip turned his attention to the box behind him; reaching in he took out a two-strap contraption of hard steel. "Do you know what this is, slave?" He held it for her to better see. One strap of steel formed a horizontal circle, the other was U-shaped and depended from the first. A steel clasp with a place for a lock connected the two straps on one side, a weld connected them on the other. The strap that hung down also had a hole, more of a slit really. She shook her head no. She had no idea what it was.

"Watch." He undid the clasp and the lower steel belt came loose as did the two sides of the horizontal circle. She could see now that there was a small hinge at the back of the circle near the weld. He put the steel around her waist and snapped the waistband shut. It was a snug fit, but not tight. A glimmer of understanding came to her and when he reached between her legs and brought up the other loop of steel, she was sure. He snapped it into place and quickly put a lock on it, effectively locking her into a chastity belt.

He laughed at her look of utter surprise and shock. She did not know such things even still existed! Her hands explored it, trying the lock, pulling at the steel bands. It didn't budge. No matter how horny she got, she wouldn't be able to touch herself. Grabbing the waistband, she tried moving the bar between her legs, hoping to make it rub. No such luck.

The fact that he had just given her a wonderful orgasm mattered little. And of course, the more she realized her predicament, the hornier she got and the wider his grin got. "No, slave," he told her. "You are mine and you are going out in public. No one will touch you with this on!"

"Oh, like anyone would've touched me anyway." She laughed and took a few experimental steps. At first it felt like a two-by-four was between her legs, not an inch of steel. But after a few turns around the room she felt more comfortable. Yes, she could wear this in public and no one would know. That thought caused a sudden wetness between her legs and she looked down in panic. But it was not her menses, it was her arousal. Now there was lubricant between her legs the belt became, while not comfortable, at least not unpleasant.

"Stand before me slave." His command brought her to heel and she returned to her position. "Turn around." She did so and she felt his fingers checking her, making sure the belt was not causing her any problems. It wasn't. "Raise your arms." She did so and the belt rose up, pressing against her sex, but not giving her the rubbing she needed. "Keep them up," he commanded as her arms began to sink down.

He encircled her body with a fine damask and bone corset and began the laborious task of lacing it up. Once fitted to her, he would only need to loosen the laces to remove it from her body. But this first time, it needed to be done the long way in order to get a proper fit. He eyed her build appreciatively as he laced. She was not petite—he preferred a woman with a little meat on her bones, as his father used to say—nor was she plump. Healthy and wholesome in a Renaissance sort of way. Just enough of a figure to make a corset sexy.

Sarah had never worn a corset before. Phillip gave her permission to lower her arms and she helped him by holding up the top as he laced up the back. Made of white damask and bone, it was a proper Victorian garment. The smell of her sex pervaded the room and she blushed. A medieval chastity belt and a Victorian corset. Was there any clothing ever made that was more restrictive?

He finished the lacing, then set to tightening them down. For this part, he instructed her to hold onto the pole of the canopy bed and to hold her breath. Bit-by-bit the laces tightened and her body was confined in a steel cage beneath and a bone cage above.

When he was finished, Phillip moved her in front of the mirror so that she could see herself. Gently he pulled her hair back so she had a clear view of her collar, its D-ring centered on her neck. The corset pushed her breasts up and gave her cleavage she never thought she would have. She was pushed up so far, one could practically rest a cup on her chest! Her nipples, hidden from view by the top of the corset, were squashed flat by the pressure, which had achieved this shelf-effect with her breasts by pushing in, not only from the sides, but from the front as well.

From her newly shaped breasts, the line of her body continued downward in a graceful inward sweep to her now compressed waistline. It wasn't any tighter than the crotch rope had been the week before, but it was infinitely more attractive. A flare at the bottom of the corset allowed for her hipbone, although even there, the contraction of her body continued. The corset stopped just above where her mound began—her denuded mound.

Her shaven pubic area now gleamed with the silver band that glimmered below the corset. If she looked hard enough, she could see the small bump at the waistline caused by the horizontal steel belt, but the lower belt shone in the sunlight streaming in from the window. She twisted this way and that, examining her new undergarments.

"Of course, my slave cannot yet go out in public in such clothing..." He was rooting around in the closet and Sarah missed the "yet" in his sentence. He came out holding a long, flowing, flowered skirt and a bright red peasant blouse. "Medieval, Victorian, the 60's," she laughed.

She slipped on the blouse, leaving it untied for the moment, while she tried on the skirt. It had an elastic waist, which wasn't stretched much since her waist was cinched so tightly. He gave her a pair of sandals to wear and tied her top loosely, letting one side fall off her shoulder. She resisted the urge to pull it up.

Turning her again so she could see, she had to admit she liked the look.

Because of the corset and the loose tie of her blouse, her cleavage was very apparent. Bending over was not an option for her, and she was glad. But those taller than she — and Master stood right behind her now — would have an eyeful. She glanced up at him and his grin let her know that was his intent. And with the chastity belt on, she was safe as well — not that she expected anything to happen along those lines. She was dressed as an almost slut, not completely slutty.

"Let's go, slave." He headed out of the room and her hand flew to her collar. Did he really mean for her to wear this out in public too? She tried to run along behind him, but the corset winded her quickly and she realized the clothing had another purpose — to keep her in her place. Fingering the collar, she met him at the door where he waited for her.

"Is there a problem, slave?" he asked.

Her hesitation lasted only a moment. "No, Sir — there is no problem." With her head held high, she walked through the door and he grinned. Oh, yes, her spirit was coming along very nicely.

* * * * *

Their first stop was at the grocery store. She stayed put as he turned off the engine, then came around and opened her door. With the stiffness of the corset, she needed the hand he extended in order to stand up. Smiling, he tucked her hand under his arm and they walked into the market.

After a while, the corset began to feel almost comfortable — once she learned how to relax into it and stop trying to fight it. She pushed the cart as he selected the items he needed. It wasn't until they got to the produce department that she was reminded of her purpose as his slave.

He sauntered over to the cucumbers and she dutifully followed with the cart. He had already selected several other fresh vegetables for salad, so at first she thought nothing of his ambling. But then he hefted a rather large cucumber in his hand and looked at her, appraisingly. "What?" she asked, then understood as his gaze dropped below her waist and his grin turned decidedly naughty.

"Sir!" She was shocked — surely he didn't think she could take all of that? She glanced around to see if anyone had noticed his look and her outburst. But the department was empty except for one old man squeezing the melons and he paid them no mind.

"Well, based on that reaction," he told her, "then this is definitely the vegetable I need." And he placed it in the cart. Her face burned all the way to the checkout counter, sure that everyone knew what she did. Her dress covered the chastity belt, and only she could feel the slickness that had gathered there, although to her own nose, the aroma of her own sex grew strong and she was sure everyone knew.

Grateful they were leaving, she followed him out of the store and would've helped him with the bags, but her corset prevented her from bending down to get them out of the cart. Instead, he unlocked her door and helped her into the car, then loaded the bags into the back himself.

Their next stop was at a rather large hardware store. That wicked look was in his eye again and warily she followed him in. He went straight to the part of the store that sold chain. Critically he looked over the various weights and types of chain. "Hold out your arm," he instructed her.

With a glance to check that no one was in the aisle, she held out her right arm. He draped a short length of chain over it from one of the many rolls on display. "No, not right." He let that one go and tried a different one. This time he wrapped the cold steel around her wrist. She moved closer to him to shield his actions from a passing customer. "Sir," she whispered in warning.

"Yes, my dear?" His grin was naughty and it was obvious he enjoyed her uneasiness. He shook his head. "No, this one's not right either." He let the chain drop and she sighed.

A few steps further down the aisle and he found the right one. "Ah, here it is. Hold out your arm again." She did so and he draped a heavy chain over her wrist, one with large steel links. Because of the air conditioning, the metal was chilly against her skin and she flinched a bit as the weight dropped onto her outstretched arm. "Yep! This is the one." He grinned at her and looked for someone to cut the length he would need.

A salesman procured, Phillip then made a show of trying to decide how much he needed. Finally he looked at Sarah and took her hand, pulling her forward a bit. "I need as much as six times her height. Can you use her as a guide?"

The clerk looked a little startled and Sarah's cheeks burned red. "Yes, sir, I believe I can," the salesclerk replied. "If you would stand here, Ma'am?"

Keeping her panic under control, Sarah stood beside the huge roll of chain. The clerk unrolled a length and held it to the top of Sarah's head, letting it unspool until the chain reached the floor. Then he stepped on it to keep it still and pulled the next length up until it was level with her head. He repeated the process until he had a length that was six times her height.

Wound and paid for, Phillip took her hand and led her to another part of the store where he chose several clips and locks. Then off to the checkout to pay for these little purchases and they were out the door. She could barely walk, she was so horny by this time.

She had felt humiliated in the store, and yet, she had liked it. His requests were odd in the salesman's eye, yet perfectly innocent. Like the purchase of the cucumber. Innocent to all except Sarah, who knew his mind and guessed at his intentions. She squirmed in her seat as they drove home.

She helped to carry in the bags of groceries; the chain was far too heavy for her to lift. Indeed, she saw his muscles strain a bit under the load, her heart quickening at the sight. Oh, but he was strong! And how his chest rippled under his shirt as he mounted the steps to the house.

The windows were open and a breeze blew the kitchen curtains as she put away the vegetables—even the cursed cucumber. The day was a warm one and her blouse stuck to her back a bit—the corset made her sweat a bit more than usual. She heard the chain hit the floor in the dungeon—she really should stop thinking of it as that word—he didn't exactly torture her in there. Her thoughts turned to the cucumber she'd just put in the fridge—well, he hadn't yet anyway.

By the time he joined her, his shirt was also sticking to his back and he peeled it off right there in the kitchen. He grabbed a bottle of water from the fridge and downed it in one long gulp. She watched, her knees getting weak at the sight of those muscles now bared.

He finished the water and turned to her with lust in his eyes. Her stomach fluttered. He advanced and pulled on the string that held her blouse up. Pushing it off her shoulders and arms, it fell to her waist. Now he turned her around and inspected the laces of her corset, giving an experimental tug on a few of them.

"Hmmm...seems to have come loose as you've worn it, my slave. We can't have that, now can we?" He tugged at the laces, tightening them down. "No, these definitely aren't tight enough." With a single move, he pulled down her skirt and blouse together, leaving them in a pool at her feet. She gasped and out of habit, covered her mound with her hands.

He took her hands and placed them on the edge of the kitchen sink. "That's enough of that," he told her. "Now take a deep breath." She did and in a quick motion, he tightened her laces tighter than they had been before. But still they were not tight enough to suit him. He slapped her bare bottom—hard. She gasped and he pulled again. Tying them off, he turned her around.

She teetered a moment, practically unable to breathe. The corset was tightly laced around her waist and she couldn't get in a deep breath at all. He steadied her, running his hands along her corset, feeling her new figure. "Yes," he murmured into her ear, "I like this sort of bondage, don't you?" He bent down and ran his tongue over the tops of her breasts, rounded from the corset's forcing. She put her arms around his shoulders to steady herself, afraid she would fall.

He put one arm around her waist to steady her, letting his other hand dip down to run along her chastity belt. He felt the wetness and was satisfied. She was ready to come, but the belt prevented it. And would continue to prevent it, until he wanted her to come. Her body was his to play with; she would come when he allowed and not one moment sooner.

Hooking his finger through the ring in her collar, Phillip led her into the dungeon. His lust mirrored in her eyes, her need growing ever stronger; she followed willingly. Once inside, he positioned her before the tall cage and stepped behind her. Taking a leather belt from the table, he instructed her to put her hands behind her back, palm to palm.

She did so and he fastened them together with the short belt. A second belt went below her elbows, pulling them together almost until they touched. A third belt above her elbows completed the binding of her arms.

Now Phillip turned her body to face him. With a twist of the key, her chastity belt came free and she willingly spread her legs so he could remove it. But that was not what he had in mind. Gently he lowered the bar between her legs and checked—there was no chafing, her constant state of arousal had seen to that. Letting the bottom section hang loose, he went back to the table and selected two small vibrators. Kneeling again before her, he slipped one into her pussy.

Sarah tried to push her hips forward to give him better access, her body craving his touch, but he only put his hand on her stomach and held her still. He pulled the vibrator from her pussy and trailed it up and down along her passage a few times as he built the tension inside her. But instead of letting her come, he brought the vibrator back along her crack and slipped it inside her ass. She moaned and bent over further and Phillip grinned to see the effect his playing caused.

Taking up the second vibrator, he turned the dial to high and did the same thing. First a plunge into her pussy to get it wet, then trailing it along between her lips and over her clit. Over and over her clit. She couldn't breathe. If she'd had breath enough, she would've begged for release, but speech was beyond her now. With a quick motion, he plunged the vibrator deep into her pussy, then brought up the lower part of the chastity belt, fastening it and locking it in place once more.

Now she did have her voice and she cried out in protest. The twin vibrators pushed her to the edge, but the belt prevented her from reaching an orgasm. Her knees gave out and he guided her to the floor. With more leather straps, he bound her ankles, then her knees. As a final touch, he pulled her feet toward her bound hands, tying them all together in a hogtie. There was only one thing missing.

He knelt down beside her as she writhed on the floor. "Slave," he said softly. "You must trust me. Do you?"

She nodded—she was already beginning to float.

Deftly he placed a medium-sized ball gag into her mouth, fastening it behind her head. She flailed her head about, trying to dislodge it, but it wouldn't budge. She was totally helpless. The vibrators had invaded her pussy and ass, the gag invaded her mouth. The belt prevented her from coming and she moaned loudly.

He now made himself comfortable on the floor, watching her squirm. He had grown very hard when he put the gag in her, knowing she was now entirely his. Unzipping his pants, he pulled out his cock, rubbing his hand over its velvety softness. She saw him, hard and ready and wanted to shout to him, 'Take me—get me out of this mess and take me hard!' But she was gagged and helpless. She was not her own person any more, she was his slave. He wanted her bound like this, wanted her gagged. Her moans turned to whimpers as her need continued to taunt her.

"Do you want this, slave?" he asked softly, holding up his cock for her to see. Pre-come hung at the very tip and she wanted nothing more than to lick it off. She nodded. Yes, she wanted him desperately.

He stood and stripped, pulling a chair over in front of her. Reaching down, he pulled her up so she was balanced on her knees. Taking out the ball gag, he bent his head down to hers. "Tell me, my slave. Tell me what it is you want. Beg me for it."

She was almost in tears. He had humiliated her in the store then bound her tighter than she'd ever been bound, gagged her and now wanted her further reduced. "Beg me," he repeated.

Humiliated and aroused, she let go of her pride. "Please, Sir, oh, please. Let me suck your cock—let me please you." The pleading need was evident in her tone and in the desperation that filled her eyes.

"And is that what you really want, slave?" His hand was on her head, holding her up as his eyes held hers.

"I want to come, Sir—I want to come and I want to please you!" The tears trickled down her face at her own dilemma; torn between the desire to please and the desire to be pleased.

He smiled. "Then please me, slave, so that I might please you." He guided her head to his cock and she opened her mouth, taking him in eagerly. Never had her passion been as great as it was now. She sucked him hard, wanting more than anything to feel him explode in her mouth. Her chest was bound so tightly, she could not get a deep breath, so she sucked his cock with her mouth while grabbing short breaths as often as she could.

At first, she gazed only on his cock, concentrating. But then she chanced to glance up and saw him watching her—his slave, servicing him. She could not look away and sucked him all the harder as the vibrators buzzed inside her. For the first time, she saw his climax come rather than just feel it. She saw it in his eyes, locked on hers as her mouth covered him. But then his eyes lost focus, closing as he groaned and his body convulsed.

The warm, sticky liquid streamed down her throat and still she continued to suck him, lick him—want him. She held him inside her mouth, swallowing his come as his body shook and she kissed his shaft as it grew soft, still licking along it, her need pushing her on. Finally, he sighed and relaxed, his eyes meeting hers again; except that where she had expected to see satisfaction and contentment, she saw he still smoldered. He put his hands on her shoulders and moved her aside, laying her down on the floor again. Was he done with his toy?

Bending, he replaced her gag, then left the room without a word. She screamed in protest. He promised! Again she wriggled on the floor, this time trying to get free. How long he was gone, she had no idea; her body was turned away from the door and she did not see his return until she felt his hands on her body. And so she did not see what he held in his hand.

He first unlashed her feet from her hands, letting them straighten. Still bound tightly together, she could not spread them for him; could not give him the access she wanted him to have. For a moment, he simply caressed her body, wiping away the drool that had dripped down her chin, running his hands along her.

She whimpered at his examination of her. He was toying with her, she understood that. And she was his to play with—that's what being his slave meant. But her body cried out for release. There was no denying that the gag had excited her; he had taken away the ability for her to spit it out and use a safe-word. Even though the drool embarrassed her and made her feel dependent, the total lack of control caused waves of arousal to course through her.

"I like you like this, slave," he told her. "Helpless. Unable to talk to me, unable to move...unable to come." His hand continued to caress her. "My pet. To do my will; to come on my command." He brushed a stray hair out of her face. "You can't come at the moment, because I have not given you permission, you know that, don't you?"

She didn't know any such thing. What did he mean? She couldn't come because she couldn't get the friction she needed.

"It's true. You have given yourself to me, submitted your will to mine, even if your conscious mind has not yet admitted it. Would you like proof?"

She nodded—and thought maybe he was thinking a little too highly of himself. Her submission was strictly voluntary. He got only as much as she was willing to give.

"You feel you cannot come, but in truth, you have not come because I have not given you permission. You are a good slave, and you wait for me to allow it. I can prove it." He held her eyes, his hands no longer touching her. "Come, slave. Come for me now."

Her body executed his command with a vengeance. In spite of what her mind told her, in spite of what she thought, her body acted on its own and fulfilled his order. An explosion ripped through her and she screamed into the gag. Wave after wave of tension built and released, making her body dance on the floor. Gasping for breath, breath she could not have because of the corset and gag, she gave her body to her climax, relaxing into it.

After an eternity, a moment, she slowed and her body lay still. He leaned down, his mouth next to her ear. "Come again, slave. Come because your master wishes it."

And she did. Her body writhed with her climax and tears streamed down her face. She had never known such intensity— or such humiliation. Her body betrayed her—it was not hers any longer—it belonged to him. The orgasm passed and she lay whimpering on the floor. He leaned down to her ear again.

"Now you see your body is mine. It is my plaything and dances when I want it to. And I want it to dance again, slave. I want to see you come one more time. Come again, slave."

And her body did. She was completely betrayed and she cried. The climax was smaller this time as her body was exhausted — as was her will. She could not fight — did not wish to. The climax ended and her body continued to shudder as she sobbed into the gag.

He smiled. She was enslaved.

* * * * *

She awoke from dreams of being captive. The dreams faded in the space of a few heartbeats, but their reality continued. She remembered her body's betrayal and turned her face into the pillow in shame.

Only then did she realize her nudity. The bindings were gone; the corset a memory; the vibrators also gone; the belt, however, was still fixed firmly around her. She rolled over to inspect it and a chain brought her up short. Her collar was leashed to the headboard. With a bitter sigh, she fell back on the pillows and thought about what had happened.

When it came right down to it, she hadn't minded the playing in the stores. In fact, the naughtiness of it had pushed her a long way into her arousal in the first place. She liked the feel of the corset; the binding of her body into a different shape excited her. Knowing that women had worn the things for ages past gave her a connection to them she'd never expected. They, too, had been slaves of their husbands — but her slavery was different.

Wasn't it? Their submission to their husbands had come with the force of law; her own was voluntary — and he wasn't even her husband. She had to smile at that. Those women would've been totally shocked at her behavior. And she could walk away any time she wanted. Ruefully, she pulled on her chain. Well, almost anytime. No, her servitude was in a different category than theirs had been. She ran her hands over her breasts, feeling small divots in her skin from the stays of the corset. They would fade as the day progressed, but now they reminded her of the rigidity of the garment. She would wear it again—and enjoy it.

Her hand drifted lower to finger the chastity belt. This was a garment she wasn't sure she liked. It wasn't so much the fact that she couldn't touch herself as what it symbolized. It was fun at first, but the fact that it was still on her irritated her a little. And, she was surprised to discover, thrilled her a little. She weighed the two feelings as if she had a scale before her she could set them in. She was irritated because he felt he had to lord it over her; control a part of her he already controlled. And she was thrilled because he was showing her he controlled her—and could control that part of her as long as he kept the key. She grinned—okay, it didn't make sense. Wearing it was irritating, but thrilling as well; she'd just have to accept that for now.

But then her thoughts turned darker as she finally confronted his actions in the dungeon. His actions and her reactions. There was no doubt in her mind of his absolute mastery of the situation—and of her. But how did she feel about that? And how had it changed their relationship?

Because it had. And that was the reality she had to face. There was the underlying knowledge now that she had taken an irreversible step. No matter what her conscious mind decided, no matter what she thought about a particular activity, there was always the reality that her body would submit. Always. She had crossed the line from playing at being submissive, to being a slave.

And it shamed her. If he walked in here right now and commanded her to do something, anything, she knew she would do it. No matter how demeaning, no matter how her mind rebelled, her heart and her body would submit. And he knew it.

That brought the tears back to her eyes. He knew he had broken that barrier—it was what he wanted all along. He wanted to show her the slut inside herself—the slave that wanted to serve—and he had. She had denied that part of her existed; he had known the truth and brought it out and forced her to look at it.

Phillip walked into the room to discover her tear-stained face and was surprised when her hands covered herself as he entered. She turned away from him, unable to bear the fact that he knew her deepest, darkest secret. Something was seriously wrong. Had he pushed her too far?

Concerned, he sat on the side of the bed and turned her over to face him. His thumb dried the tears on her cheek and he bent down to kiss them. He kissed her forehead, her nose, her lips. Gently, softly, letting her know how he cared for her. Leaning on one arm, he stayed close to her, brushing her hair from her face, murmuring soft words of comfort until she could look at him. Only then did he ask the question that weighed so heavily on his heart.

"What is it, Sarah, have I hurt you?" His voice was tight. He would never forgive himself if he had damaged her in any way. In so many ways she was so strong, that he had forgotten how fragile her psyche could be.

Sniffling, she shook her head. "No, Sir. It's just that, oh, Phillip—I cannot believe what I am, deep down inside. I mean, I've always known that side of me to be there, but never thought, never dreamed…I mean, I never thought I'd share it with anyone—ever. But I did, with you." She paused to wipe her nose. "And I'm glad I did, really I am."

Her eyes met his and Phillip saw the painful vulnerability she could no longer mask. Relief flooded his heart. With his guidance, she had peeled away all the layers of pretense that she had so carefully build up over the years and had faced the darkest parts of herself. But what made his heart sing, was that she had emerged whole and complete.

She still hiccupped and sniffled, so he gathered in his arms again, lying down beside her, his hands gently rubbing her shoulders to ease her tension.

Her breathing steadied as he caressed her; he was not some monster come to lord it over her—he was still the man she had fallen in love with. That was another reality to face. After several moments, she looked into his eyes, unsure what she would find.

The love and care she had for him reflected back at her. "I love you, Sarah," he told her softly. And her lip trembled again. He took her into his arms and kissed her lips. "I will protect you always."

And she knew it was true.

Chapter 8
Exposures

The birds were singing when they awoke the next morning — the sun beaming in through the open window. Sarah sighed and stretched, no bindings held her this morning. Well, only the bindings around her heart.

Phillip, too, stretched and the two shared a look. Their coupling of the night before had been romantic and intense. He had removed her chain and the chastity belt and then made love to her as if it were their first time. All she wore was her collar and every time he looked at it, he'd grown hard and they'd made love again.

The sunlight fell on them as they gazed at each other. His hand reached out and brushed that ever-errant strand of hair from her face; she smiled at his tenderness. His fingers trailed along the curve of her cheek, down to her chin, then continued down her neck to her collar. She raised her head, giving him her vulnerability as his finger hooked the D-ring and gave a little tug.

That was all the invitation she needed to cuddle in close to him. Still basking in the afterglow of last night's lovemaking, she ran her hands over his satiny smooth chest, absently kissing him and nuzzling her nose up under his chin. His hand stroked her dark hair and the two of them rested together, both loathe to break the spell cast by an evening of lovemaking followed by a most glorious morning.

Phillip stirred first, unlocking the slave's collar she wore around her neck. "Come on, my lovely slave. We need to get ready for church." He patted her rear end and slid out of the bed.

With a grin, she watched him pad across the room towards the bath. "Yes, Sir," she assented, while snuggling under the covers again. He grinned and went to use the facilities.

Sarah basked in the warmth of the sun as the morning light fell across the bed. Was it her imagination, or did the sun actually shine brighter here than it did in her city apartment? She rolled over and closed her eyes.

Returning quietly, he whisked the covers off her in one fell swoop. "Your turn!" he announced. She shrieked and sat up, making a feeble attempt to catch the sheets before they eluded her grasp. But he was too fast for her.

"Yes, Sir," she said again, a bit of sarcasm in her voice and a grin on her face. She made short work of her toilette and decided possession was nine-tenths, so she would take her shower first, while she was there. By the time she got back into the bedroom, the bed was made and her clothes laid out for her. He swatted her again on the rear on his way into the shower and she squealed and stuck her tongue out at him.

The clothes were the same that she'd worn to church the week before: a navy blue suit with white piping, stockings—not pantyhose—garters, and the sheer bra. She wrinkled her nose as she gazed at them. These people would think she had nothing else to wear. But then again, she hadn't expected such an elegant gift in the first place. The designer name on the suit was evidence that this outfit had cost him a pretty penny—and she still didn't know what he did for a living.

She was dressed and ready when he emerged from his shower. Sitting on the edge of the bed as he dressed—he favored white shirts and dark pants—they talked of small things. He finished tying his tie, and she held up his suit coat for him to slip his arms into, then stood next to him, admiring the couple she saw reflected back in the long mirror.

There remained but one small matter before they left. Silently, he took another small box off his dresser and handed it to her.

"Master, you really shouldn't be spending so much money on me!" Mindful of the suit she was wearing, bought by his money, she opened the box. Inside was a thin leather strap. She looked at him in confusion.

"You cannot wear my collar out in public—society has not progressed that far," he explained. "So I give you this to wear instead." He took the box from her and removed the leather strap. "Turn around, slave," he instructed.

She did so, lifting her hair out of his way. He placed the leather against the skin of her neck, tying it neatly in the back. The ends hung down only an inch or two and were hidden under her hair. Turning back to the mirror, she examined the choker. Nondescript, plain brown leather that wouldn't raise anyone's suspicions. But she would know—and that was his point. She was to wear a sign of her slavery out in public.

Smiling, she slipped her arm through his and they headed out to church.

* * * * *

Phillip liked to sit about three-quarters of the way up the aisle, on the left. Acutely aware of the glances that were sent in her direction, Sarah took her seat beside him. The service began; in moments the congregation was forgotten as she lost herself in the beauty of the weekly ceremonies. Only afterward, as they greeted parishioners as the two of them made their way out did she become aware that not all the glances shot towards them were friendly ones.

He took her to a different restaurant for a more formal brunch this week. Set in buffet style, the two filled their plates and settled themselves at a cozy corner table.

"So you left some broken hearts in that church today, I see," Sarah commented, sipping her orange juice.

He looked puzzled. "What broken hearts?"

She set the glass down. Did he really not know? "There were a few women who…well, let's just say, I'm glad looks can't really kill, or I'd be dead." When he frowned, still not understanding, she put on a patient look and explained. "I think there are women in your church that had hoped to 'catch' you — and bringing me to church twice in two weeks has them a tad…upset."

The light dawned in his eyes. "Oh, you must mean Mrs. Finch and her daughter Emily!" He laughed. "Mrs. Finch is always trying to find a husband for Emily. She's a sweet girl; we dated a few times. But she's very much under her mother's thumb."

Sarah smiled. Those two had certainly been chief among the unhappy faces. She tried to picture tall, strong and handsome Phillip with mousy-looking Emily. A sudden picture popped into her imagination of Emily bound and gagged, submitting to her Master. So real did it seem that she choked on her toast.

He helped her to a glass of water and raised her arm over her head until she could signal that she was fine. Waving the waiter away, he waited until she regained her composure before questioning her, "What happened?"

She grinned weakly at him and told him the image that had invaded her thoughts. He grinned right back at her and looked off, considering the picture. "Hmm…" he teased. "I see the two of you lying on the floor, bound and gagged together."

"You would! Isn't that every man's fantasy? To have several women serve him at one time?"

His eyes grew serious. "And if it is?"

She frowned as she considered his implication. Making love to another woman was not something she had ever considered — well, not considered for herself. Two of her friends were lesbians and it had made no impact on her friendship with them at all. Whatever happened behind closed doors was none of her business.

Phillip watched her consider this new thought. Broadening her horizons was a part of what he wanted her to experience. Each step of her training took mental preparation as well as physical. Sarah had given him an opening to introduce this idea to her—was she yet willing to perform it? He ate his breakfast and observed her reactions.

How did she feel about him having two women at one time? Sarah fiddled with her fork as she delved for the root issue. Could she share him? Was that the question? No, the real question was, did she even have the right to demand his solo allegiance to her? If she was his slave, did she have the right to tell him no?

"I don't think I'm ready to do that, Sir," she finally answered, her voice low in the crowded restaurant. "I mean, I'm not asking you for a commitment or anything...what you do during the week is your business." She hurriedly sipped her water. "But on the weekends, when I am your...slave," she whispered the word, "I'm not ready to share you."

He smiled, almost in relief. She was about to learn the most important lesson he had to teach her: that Master/slave relationships involved a sharing of power. Reaching across the table, he took her hand.

"Sarah," he began, knowing that when he used her name, she recognized the seriousness of what he was about to say, "you *do* have a commitment from me—you wear my collar." Her hand flew to her throat to feel the small leather choker. "That commitment goes both ways," he continued. "You serve me with your submission, but I also have a responsibility to serve you—not only by protecting you, but also in respecting your wishes." He paused and let that sink in.

"So you're not angry that I really don't want to have another woman around yet?"

He laughed. "Of course not! But I noticed you used the word 'yet.' Does that mean someday you might say yes?" His eyes twinkled as he further planted the idea in her head.

Sarah grinned. "I know what word I used—and I meant it." She grew serious. "I know that as the Master you have the right to command me. But you're saying that what you really want is more of the exchange of power you had me read about as opposed to a suppression of my wants and desires?"

"Exactly. Sarah, I am falling more in love with you each day. You're witty and intelligent and a wonderfully independent woman. And on top of all that, you are willing, each weekend, to set all that aside and kneel before me as my slave. That is a wonderful gift you give me—and I treasure it deeply."

Sarah felt her breath catch in her throat. He was so earnest—the deeply held power she'd glimpsed on several occasions was so evident she was surprised everyone in the restaurant didn't turn around and bow down to him. Had they been home, back at his cottage, she would have dropped to her knees in submission. He wanted her. He was in love with her. The passion of his words made her head swim.

"I have fallen in love with you, Phillip," she murmured, her eyes filling with tears. "You make me complete." He had seen the side of her that she kept hidden and, instead of being shocked by it, had embraced it and let it come forth.

He raised her hand to his lips and kissed it, lingering, his eyes never leaving her face. She turned her palm to him, resting it on his cheek. They might have sat there for another hour if the waiter had not chosen that particular moment to bring the check.

Grinning broadly, Phillip paid the bill and the two went home.

* * * * *

Once back at the cottage, Phillip opened the door and stood back for her to enter first. He always did that, she realized. He held the door for her at the store, in church—he always got the car door for her. Always. He treated her like a lady every moment.

Inside, the two headed to the bedroom to change and get more comfortable. For Phillip that meant taking off his suitcoat and tie, for Sarah that meant divesting herself of all her clothes and putting on her cuffs and collar. She stood by the closet and neatly rehung the jacket and skirt of her suit. Before taking off her undergarments, she glanced at him — last week he had wanted those left on. But Phillip had left the room, so she sat on the side of the bed to undo her garters and roll down the stockings.

Retrieving her cuffs from the bedside table, Sarah clicked them into place, smiling as she always did at the snick the locks made as they closed, securing the straps of leather around her wrists and ankles. She fumbled at the public 'collar' but could not get it untied. Instead she picked up the larger collar he had given her to wear in the house and went out to find him.

She found him in the dungeon, sorting through some things on the table. Hearing her step, he turned to see her framed by the door; her nakedness took his breath — as it did every time. Ample breasts that gave a man something to hold in his hands, a delicious little curve from her waist to her hips, her naked mound shaved just for him; she was a combination of innocent and siren. Phillip knew he was grinning like an idiot as he gestured for her to kneel.

"Let me help you with those collars, my slave." He liked saying those words. Not only did they reinforce her position, but the term was quickly becoming an endearment. She bowed her head to him and pulled her hair out of the way and he noticed how easily she moved now. Quite a difference from a few weeks ago when she was afraid of her nudity.

He removed the small leather strap and held his hand out for her larger collar. She handed it to him without hesitation and his heart was glad. She wanted this as much as he did. Placing it around her neck, Phillip waited while she again lifted her hair so he could lock it in place.

There was something arousing about this particular 'snick' she decided. The collar was filled with symbolism and her body responded to it with a very definite physical reaction. Immediately she felt the familiar soft moistening gather between her legs.

Holding out his hand to her, Phillip helped her to her feet. "I thought we might go for a walk this afternoon, slave. You haven't seen much of my property except for the house."

She laughed. "A walk sounds wonderful—it's a beautiful day for a walk in the woods. 'Cept I didn't bring any jeans with me." All she had with her were the clothes she had worn to work on Friday and the work clothes she intended to wear on Monday.

He just smiled and raised an eyebrow. His meaning sunk in and she gasped. "Oh, no…I can't go walking in the woods in my birthday suit!"

"Not even if I commanded it?" he pushed.

She opened and closed her mouth several times, trying to frame an answer. Finally she gave up and just glared at him, perplexed and unsure.

His hand came up and gently he lifted her chin. With a swift move, he attached a leash to her collar. Drawing his hand back, he ran the chain through his fingers, keeping a firm grip on the leather handle.

She looked down in shock. A leash!?! What did he think she was? Her eyes were pulled over to the small cage she'd spent some time in their first weekend together. Covered now in a blue cloth, pushed up against the wall, it posed no threat. He had treated her like a favored pet then; it was the same way he was treating her now.

Gently he pulled on the leash and she moved toward him, uncertainty wrinkling her features. His arms slid around her and he let the chain fall between them as he took her in his arms. Letting his hands wander over her back, he bent down to capture her mouth in a kiss, pushing his tongue against her lips until she relaxed and let him enter.

She loved the feel of his tongue as it danced over hers. Not able to help herself, she leaned into him, opening her mouth, inviting him deeper. Her hands squeezed the muscles of his arms, thrilling in the hard-packed strength under her fingertips. One of his hands drifted lower, caressing her lower cheeks. Her stomach fluttered in response.

His lips moved from her mouth to her hair, nuzzling along to find her ear. "Will my slave wear my leash?" he murmured in her ear.

"Oh, yes," she replied. "If wearing your leash leads to kisses like this, I will not fret about a length of chain." She turned her head and he possessed her mouth again.

For several moments they hung suspended in time, each of them aware only of the other. Their souls touched and when they at last withdrew, their eyes twinkled with happiness.

"Come with me, my slave," he told her, his eyes bright with mischief. Catching the leash in his hand, he stepped around her, leading her by the chain connected to her collar.

The glint of mischief caught her curiosity and she went willingly. Did he really intend to take her outside dressed in nothing but her cuffs?

It seemed he did. Through the rooms they went to the back of the kitchen. He opened the door and a breeze wafted in, smelling of sunshine and warmth. She thought how ironic it was that she had been to his cottage several times now and had never even looked out the back door. Well, it wasn't as if her mind—and her body—hadn't been occupied elsewhere. Now she saw that a small deck formed an unroofed porch at the back entrance to the house. He stepped through the door and her chain went taut as she halted.

Yes, his house was out in the woods. Yes, she had gotten used to walking around inside completely naked. But outside?

He gave a small tug and she took a step forward, pausing again on the doorsill.

Phillip watched her as she cautiously poked her head out of the door, her arms covering herself—one across her breasts and one covering her mound. She probably wasn't even aware that she was doing it. He gave her time—he wanted to push her limits, but only if she wanted them pushed. Some Masters didn't care about their slave's feelings; he'd seen several examples of that in his time—indeed, when he first started, he had made similar mistakes.

But he was older now and had learned a great deal. He also knew that this slave was different from any other he had played with. This one had captured his heart. The others came and went and he let them go. Sarah had touched something deep inside him; he hoped she would decide to stay for a very long time.

Had Sarah looked at him, she would have seen the tenderness in his eyes as he watched her. But she was so caught up in her own sense of modesty and propriety, that she missed the softening of his gaze as it fell on her.

"There is no one here but us," he reassured her. "I own 80 acres of land and the cottage sits in the middle of it." He gave an encouraging tug on her leash.

Tentatively she took a step forward, then another. The door closed behind her and she jumped as it slammed. He grinned an apology. "Gotta get that fixed one of these days." He looked at her, standing stricken like a deer caught in the headlights. "Put your hands down, slave."

She looked down—when had she covered herself? With an effort, she lowered the hand from her bosom, then the hand that covered her mound. Swallowing hard, she willed them down to her sides, then looked at him, feeling more vulnerable than ever.

"Walk now, around the edge of the deck."

With a width of ten feet and a length about the same, it was a short walk. He stood in the center and rotated as she tiptoed around the edge, letting her hand run along the railing to keep it from the urge to cover any part of her. Biting her lip, she kept glancing nervously toward the woods whose border wasn't very far away. She came back to her starting point and stopped.

"What are you feeling, slave?"

She looked quickly up at him—what did he mean? His concern for her shone in his face and her look softened. "Sir?" she asked.

"What are you feeling? I have put a leash on you, pulled you out into a much more public place than you have been, and you're naked. What are you feeling?"

He wanted honesty—she'd learned that lesson before. Problem was, she had been concentrating on actually being out here and hadn't let herself feel anything. Taking a deep breath to relax a bit, she thought out loud.

"First of all, I'm all right, Sir. I'm a little nervous and scared, but you're here and I trust you and that you won't let anything come out of the woods and hurt me—or worse, see me." She grinned as she realized what she had said. "Yes, it's true, right now I'm just worried that someone will drive up the drive or come out of the woods and see me naked."

"And you don't want others to see you naked?"

She wrinkled her nose at him. He was always putting new naughty thoughts into her head. Turning the tables, she asked, "Do you want others to see me naked?"

But he was ready for her. "This isn't about me, slave, it's about you and what you want." He paused, then repeated the question, a little more insistently, "Do you want others to see you naked?"

Blast him! Now she had to try and think it through. And, of course, that was precisely what he wanted her to do. He could tell her his preference, but then she would agree to shed her clothes in front of others just to please him. He wanted her to shed those clothes because *she* wanted to. While he suspected the exhibitionist inside her, he wanted to give her time to discover it on her own. The bond between them would be stronger because of her own journey of discovery.

"Walk for me again, slave. And this time imagine the woods filled with eyes. Do you want them to see you naked?"

She glanced again at the woods; before, she had been afraid someone might really be there. Now, knowing there was no one, she filled it with imaginary people and took a step along the wall of the house. Still biting her lip, her eyes strayed out to the woods again as she made her circuit, but her hand did not graze the railing and her posture was straighter. Once again she came to her beginning and stopped.

"Now, slave, what are you feeling?"

She grinned and put her head down, a blush creeping up into her cheeks. "Not so nervous, this time."

"And would you like people to see you naked?"

Her blush deepened. "Yes," she whispered.

He stepped toward her, pulling her chin up again, gazing with pride into those eyes. "Then I shall be sure that some day you are displayed for others to appreciate."

Her breath caught—did he mean that? A part of her thrilled at the thought, a part of her recoiled. She felt his kiss on her forehead.

"But just not today, I think. You have done well, my slave. Inside with you now."

For just a moment she hesitated. He said he would show her his land—and all she had seen was the deck and the backyard. Trying unsuccessfully to hide her disappointment, she turned and went back into the kitchen.

"Wait here," he instructed. Dropping her leash, he went over to a closet in the corner of the kitchen. Reaching in, he pulled out an old pair of overalls. "These'll do, I think," he told her, holding them open for her to step into.

"You're not going to make me walk naked through the woods?" she asked him, not sure if she was more disappointed or relieved.

He laughed. "No. There are way too many brambles and places that might tear that lovely skin of yours. Button up and I'll get you some shoes."

Relaxing completely now, she closed the front of the overalls and pulled the attached belt tightly around her waist. The legs were far too long, so she rolled up the ends to just above her ankles. Long-sleeved, it would be warm to walk in, but wearing it was much better than going without.

A few moments later, he returned with an unopened package of socks and another shoebox. "Sir!" she exclaimed. "You didn't!"

"Of course I did," he laughed. "And you would have had a new pair of jeans for here as well, but I couldn't find the style I wanted in your size." He opened the package of socks. "Apparently ladies' work socks come only in packages."

She took a pair out, leaving the other three, and sat on the floor to put them on. Except that her cuffs were in the way. Jingling the keys, he dropped them down to her and she removed both sets of cuffs. He showed her the sneakers and she reached up to take the laced one while he set up the other shoe. Shod, she ran in place and tried them out. "Perfect!" she announced.

"Let's see if you still say that after I've hiked you all over the property." Taking hold of her chain, he unclasped it from her collar and hung it on a hook beside the door. "Don't think my slave is going to run off—and it isn't safe to have you wear it out in the woods."

His words touched her. That very first night when he had asked her to come home with him, she had looked for signs of a power-hungry male. She had not found them then and hadn't in the several times she'd looked since. He really cared about her—the power exchange they discussed earlier was obviously a belief he held deeply. Contentedly, she followed him out the door, careful not to let it slam this time.

* * * * *

True to his word, he hiked her all over the property. Most of it was covered with woods, but several sections had obviously been only recently planted. He explained that he had bought the land from an older farmer who wasn't able to farm as much as he used to. Phillip was buying up the pieces as the man sold them and returning the land to a more natural state, reforesting it as he purchased it.

The afternoon was waning by the time they returned to the cottage. Hot and sweaty, she couldn't wait to get back inside and shed the heavy overalls. "I need a shower!" she proclaimed.

"Yes, slave, that you do," chuckled Phillip. He caught a whiff of his own sweat and grinned. "Apparently, so do I. Come, slave."

He stripped off his shirt and dropped it over the railing. The sun beat down upon the back deck and the sweat glistened on his chest, his rippling muscles shining in the light. For several moments, Sarah simply stood and looked her fill—his handsomeness took her breath away. His dark hair was damp and clung to his neck, coiling up in little curls that plastered against his skin. When he turned and smiled at her appreciative stare, his dimples made her heart skip a beat. How was it possible that this gorgeous creature could be hers?

Crossing the deck in two cat-like strides, he reached for her, his eyes never leaving hers. Almost in a trance, she felt his fingers unbuttoning the overalls as she gazed at him, her heart in her throat as she realized their possession was mutual. She submitted to him and he wanted her submission. There could not be one without the other. Two sides of one coin. He belonged to her as much as she belonged to him.

His hands pushed the coveralls from her shoulders and she helped him take them off the rest of the way, her newfound understanding making her giddy. Tottering, she giggled as she tipped sideways, her foot snagged in the heavy fabric and he caught her with an arm around the waist. Scooping her up, he kissed her soundly in the sunlight.

She kissed him back, her arms going around his neck and embracing him. This close to him, she could smell his sweat mixed with her own odor of perspiration and arousal. Their pungency threatened to be overwhelming in the hot sun. She broke from the kiss, wrinkling her nose.

"I think Master needs a shower even more than I do!"

He laughed and stepped to the door. "Open the door, slave. My hands seem to be filled with a saucy slave who needs a washing."

Laughing together, she managed to get the door unlatched and with a little trial and error, he carried her into the house. So much for Hollywood 'over the threshold' scenes. Apparently they didn't have screen doors that opened outward!

Once in the bathroom, he deposited her next to the shower, reached in to turn on the water, then gestured for her to enter first. It was a large space with no tub; its three tile walls and clear glass entrance was certainly big enough for two people. She stepped into the water and he followed her, closing the shower door behind him.

Steam began to rise as he took the soap in his hand, rubbing it to make a handful of lather. "Turn around," he told her and she faced the cascading water. Slowly, his hands scrubbed her back, one hand holding the soap, the other slippery with lather. Sarah put her hands on the tile wall before her to steady her suddenly rubbery knees.

He let his hands drift lazily over her back and bottom — was there anything finer than a well-shaped ass? He lingered there a moment before stepping closer and bringing his hands around her sides and up to her neck. She still wore his collar and the leather had turned dark with the moisture. It would have to come off to dry later, but for now, the sight of the dark mark of ownership against her white skin made him hard and he knew he would take her here.

With more purpose, Phillip's hands now lathered her breasts and she leaned back against him. Not since she was a baby had anyone washed her; his hands sliding along her body aroused her in a way she never thought possible. When he dipped to wash between her legs, she spread them wide, giving him all the access he wanted.

And then he was kneeling behind her, soaping her legs, lifting each one in turn to wash her feet. There was something humbling about his actions that touched her. She was the slave, yet he washed her as if he were the servant. Standing again, he turned her to face him and raised each of her arms, letting the soap cover each one.

Gently moving her back to stand completely under the running water, he watched as the water flowed over her curves. She tilted her head back, getting her hair wet and feeling the warmth spread over her face. He held her in his arms, and she relaxed into them, letting the water carry her away.

His cock pushed against her and she stood, taking the soap from him. Silently, she moved from under the waterfall and circled around behind him. He turned to face her as she now imitated his movements of before; working up a lather on her hands, she started on his chest, running her fingers through the fine hair, over his shoulders, down each arm, around to his back. He was tall and they both chuckled as he had to stoop down so she could reach the back of his neck.

Skipping over his midsection, she soaped each leg, kneeling in the water to do so. She wanted to return the honor to him; carefully she washed each foot. Only then did she turn her attention to the part of his anatomy that stared her in the face.

Getting plenty of lather on her hands, she set the soap down and cupped his balls. Rubbing the lather all over them, she trailed her fingers between his legs and up the crack to his ass. He helped her by spreading his legs and giving her permission. She accepted the invitation and pushed her soapy fingers deep into the crevice, cleaning him. The other hand now soaped his cock, already standing stiff and erect. Over and over she rubbed the soap, admiring the veins pulsing life to the glistening head. Finished, she stood and nodded for him to rinse.

Obediently, he stepped back and let the water cascade over his body. Smoothing the hair from his eyes, he pulled her under the waterfall with him. Far from dowsing his desire, the heat of the water fueled his need. Their clean bodies entwined and he kissed her, the water running over his face to splash against their kiss. With a sudden movement, he lifted her and she wrapped her legs around his waist. So ready was she, that he entered her in one swift motion, burying himself deeply in the warmth of her smooth pussy.

Turning, he leaned her back against the tile wall and rode her, his desire at its peak. Over and over he thrust into her, the water spilling down into the valley made by their joining. The shower walls amplified her passion as his force made her moan and explode. Her head fell back against the tiles as wave after wave of passion careened through her fevered body.

Sarah's pussy contracted around him as he held her in his arms, urging him, driving him; he couldn't hold back. His groans echoed hers, loud in the glass and tile shower and his seed shot up inside her. Together their bodies moved as one as their orgasms peaked—together their bodies slowed as the passion waned.

Phillip and Sarah rested, panting, their gazes searching deep into one another's souls. It seemed all the secrets of the universe were contained within their spirits. He kissed her again; if he could keep this moment forever, he would. She wrapped her arms around his neck gently receiving his kiss.

The water chose that particular moment, however, to go chill. With a cry, he jumped back as the cold water hit his back and he put her down quickly. Reaching to turn the water off, they both started laughing.

"Well, apparently the hot water tank here has just the right amount of hot water in it, Master," she giggled.

"Apparently," his face twisted in a wry grin. He opened the doors and they both grabbed for their towels, goose bumps pimpling their skin. She fingered her hair. "Guess I'll have to wait to wash this," she said.

"Are you telling me I'll have to shower you again later, slave?" he teased her.

She put on a mock innocent expression. "Only if my master wants a clean slave!"

He laughed. "It will take some time before that tank gets hot again." He padded out to the bedroom and she followed him, both of them clad in their towels. He looked back and saw the dark line of her collar. "Come here, slave." She complied without hesitation. Picking up the key from his dresser top, he unlocked the collar around her neck. "Put this in the sun so it can dry."

The late afternoon sun still shone through the kitchen window, so she took it out there and set it on the sill to dry. Their dirty clothes still lay on the deck outside—all except his pants, which he had removed in the bathroom. Clad in her towel, she went out to retrieve them. When she turned around, he stood naked in the doorway, watching her. He didn't need to tell her what he wanted. Holding the clothes she had just picked up in one hand, she undid the towel, letting it fall. She raised her bundle over her head and pirouetted, showing off her nudity to the world.

It wasn't easy, but she wanted to do it. She wanted to show him she was willing to expand her horizons—as long as it was safe to do so, anyway. Having traipsed all over the property, she understood just how alone the two of them were. If the deer wanted to see her naked, that was fine with her.

Yes, she was coming along nicely, he thought to himself.

* * * * *

The two of them made dinner, ate, cleaned up and chatted about small things—all their normal activities; with one exception: Phillip stayed nude the entire evening. She was used to him wearing clothes while she wasn't, and to see him walking around in his birthday suit gave her an odd feeling. Not until they snuggled on the couch, candles lit against the dark of night, did she finally have words to ask him about it.

"I have to admit, Sir, it feels odd to have you undressed."

He brushed a kiss onto her forehead. "Why, slave? Don't you like seeing me nude?"

"Oh, I like it very much, don't mistake me," she smiled up at him. "It's just...well, my nudity is a part of my slavery. When you're dressed and I'm not, then that serves as a very powerful signal as to who's in charge. When we're both not wearing anything, that levels the playing field, so to speak. Does that make sense?"

"It does. Can I take from your comments that you don't like the playing field leveled?"

She had to consider that. "My husband and I had a level field—a normal one by what society says, I suppose. It was wonderful. We were very much in love and that was what we both needed." She sighed. "But he's gone now, and since I've met you, I've realized that all fields do not need to look the same. I keep coming back because I like the field we've been playing on."

He continued her analogy, ignoring for the moment her comment about her husband. "So even though my nakedness arouses you, you want the symbolism of me being clothed and you being naked on the field."

She nodded. "Yes. At first it bothered me a little, didn't seem quite fair somehow. But now the symbolism is important to me. Maybe later it won't be, but for now, I like it very much."

"And what we talked of before—your being naked in front of others?"

She made a face. "In several ways, that excites me, but terrifies me at the same time."

"But would you?"

Her blush reached all the way to her toes. "Yes," she whispered. "Yes, if you were there, I think I would."

He kissed the top of her head. "Then it shall happen soon."

The hour had grown late and she yawned. "Bedtime for you, slave," he told her and they uncurled from the couch. Taking her hand, he led her to the bathroom. For most of the day, she had been uncollared and uncuffed. It had been pleasant, but she found there was a part of her that missed those marks of ownership. She shivered as she thought about how enslaved her heart had become.

He mistook her shiver and covered her with the bedclothes, pulling her close to his own warmth. Snuggling in against him, she breathed in his scent—clean and wonderful—and hers. Sarah wrapped her arms around the man she was learning to call "Master" and hugged him tightly.

"Sarah," he said, and her heart jumped to hear him use her name. "You mentioned your husband earlier. Do you realize in all our time together, that was the first time you spoke of him?"

She smiled up at him. "I don't often speak of him, I guess. To anybody." She fell silent, remembering his look, his smile, his love of life.

"You miss him still, don't you."

It was not a question, just a simple statement of fact. She did miss him. Terribly sometimes. Even here, in Phillip's arms, the loss was overwhelming and tears burned in her eyes. She nodded, not trusting her voice.

"It's all right, you know. He was a part of your life for a very long time; when he died a piece of you died with him. You were very lucky to have had such a wonderful partner."

His words washed over her and her tears fell, turning to sobs. She missed her husband terribly, but if he were here, she never would have met Phillip. This exploration would never have occurred. And her heart would never have found a second love.

She quieted herself, sniffling a few times. Reaching over to his nightstand, he grabbed several tissues for her and she blew her nose and dried her eyes.

"Phillip, thank you. I haven't had anyone to talk to about it—and it means a lot to me that you understand. But know this, with him gone, I have to move on and make what I can of the rest of my life. I'm no Miss Haversham to sit and mope around because my true love is gone."

She threw the tissues into the basket. "I am twice blessed in my life. First him, now you. I don't know what I did to deserve two such wonderful men, but I thank the powers that sent you both to me."

Caressing his cheek, she lifted her tear-stained face to his and he kissed her deeply. If she would love him with half as much love as she showed for her deceased husband, then he would be a happy man. Entwined in each other's arms, they fell into a comfortable silence, and from there, into sleep.

* * * * *

The morning was a bit of a rush for her to get her shower, eat breakfast and get out the door. Again, he was up and had toast ready for her when she emerged from the bedroom, dressed in her work clothes and her mind already beginning to leave the weekend behind.

"I've sent you some more websites to visit, slave," he told her and she grinned at the appellation. "Email me details of Friday night—although if it's possible, you should come here so we only need to take one car." That was the practical side of his nature talking, she realized.

"I can't wait to see where you're sending me this week, Master," she teased. "Last week's web adventures were pretty good. I could probably spend hours just exploring more on those sites."

"Go ahead—I only sent you a few this time around." He kissed her and opened the car door for her. "Have a good week."

She got in and rolled down the window—putting her face out so he could kiss her again. Laughing, he obliged. Then standing aside, he waved to her as she drove down the drive and back into her normal world.

Phillip's Journal
the week between weekends three and four

<u>Monday</u>

I still am having a hard time realizing I may have found the woman of my dreams. I've thought this before, with Tamara and with Anne. But both times, they tired of 'the game.' Neither one ever seemed to see it the way I do—as a lifestyle choice.

Other Doms have found willing submissives. Until now, I've found women only willing to explore until it got hard. Then they bailed. So far, Sarah's been wonderful in letting herself explore a world that, I know, is very foreign to her. I have to keep reminding myself to be patient and not push too fast. That's what I did with Tamara—I pushed her into doing things she wasn't ready for and she was right to leave me. I know, I brooded about it then, but I've since realized the fault was with me that time.

So I've brought Sarah along slowly. I have to admit, that first night was just for the sex. In our dates, she seemed pretty normal, but there was a restless quality about her, as if she needed something and didn't know what it was. I knew she was a widow—and I'm not exactly one to complain about someone having sexual experience. But bondage is a whole different 'playing field' as she called it. And so is submission. So I gave her the option of an 'audition' to find out what she'd do.

When she showed up that second weekend, I knew this was a relationship I wanted to pursue. That first day, I pushed her pretty hard, punishing her for small infractions, putting her in a cage. But she came back anyway. I admired her for that. And yes, I was ready for her. Although truth be told, I wasn't at all sure she'd show up.

Gotta call the group today—tell them Saturday's at my place and let them know she's ready to meet them. Will have to remember to tell Will to keep it calm, though. He and Jill can really get rocking sometimes—and Sarah is definitely not ready for that. No, a simple gathering at the house for munchies with some easy play afterward, I think.

Tuesday

Saturday's set. Have warned Will and Jill (told Jill she could have at least found someone named 'Jack' for her master instead of someone who makes their names sound like something out of a bad fairy tale). He's agreed to keep her in line—and himself as well.

Got Sarah's email late—the computer's acting up again. She'll meet me at the cottage, but we have to be at her friend's housewarming not too long after. I'll have her clothes all laid out for her so she can do a quick change and freshen up before we have to dash off again.

Wednesday

Found the perfect outfits for her for the weekend. It's funny, I never cared for shopping for myself—suppose that's why most of my shirts are white and my pants are black or brown. And none of the other girls I dated liked for me to buy them clothes. Said my style wasn't their style—and again, we're back to the lifestyle thing.

I suppose I haven't been totally upfront with Sarah on that. Initially I set this relationship up as only a weekend kind of thing for my benefit as well as hers. No rushing into things anymore. If this turns into a 24/7 kind of deal...well...I'm getting to like the idea more and more. But it's only been a month, two if you count from our first meeting in the grocery store. Way too early to know if I want to negotiate her moving in with me—even if it is as my slave.

Thursday

Weather's turned nasty — looks like rain all the rest of the week and into the weekend. Don't have much time to write today.

Friday

Went shopping for me today — didn't buy anything. Sarah seems to like my white shirts, and a good thing, too. Nothing out there for a man my age — all stuff my father would wear, or stuff for the kids.

She'll be here soon — and I find myself growing excited at the thought. Yes, sexually excited as well as just plain old can't-wait-to-see-the-girl-I-love excited. Have already cleaned the place up and gotten the clothes out for her. Now it's just puttering around until 6:00.

Have also been thinking about the lifestyle topic. Will see how she takes meeting the group before I think any further along those lines. Not that I need their approval, but I do want to be able to show her off. She did all right last weekend when I put her out on the deck, but I could tell the thought of being naked before them scares her — a lot. Will have to ease her into it, I suspect. Maybe I'll let Will and Jill loose just a bit and let her just watch?

Go putter, Phillip. You'll drive yourself batty if you keep mulling things over like this. Although writing about her is almost as much fun as seeing her…

Chapter 9
Her friends

Sarah had to admit she was a little nervous about letting him choose the clothes she was to wear to Beth's housewarming. Beth had been her best friend since high school, her maid of honor at her wedding, her confidant in all things. Well, she had been — until now.

Several times over the past few weeks she'd tried to tell Beth what she'd discovered with Phillip, but the words got stuck in her throat every time. Beth was so wrapped up in closing on her first house, Sarah was fairly sure she hadn't realized that Sarah hadn't been very forthcoming about the time she spent with her new love.

Beth had, however, been pestering to meet him and tonight it would happen. Sarah was glad there would be lots of people around; she wasn't sure she wanted her friend buttonholing her lover and forcing him to spill secrets. A mental image popped into her head as she drove to Phillip's: him backed into a corner by a woman half his size, jabbing her finger in his chest and demanding to know just what his intentions were.

She laughed out loud, imagining his answer, "Well, my dear woman, I intend to make your friend into my sex slave." No, Beth would definitely not understand.

Phillip heard her car in the drive — she was going to have to have that engine tuned up soon. Knowing they didn't have much time, he had the door open as she came up to the porch. Bending down, he gave her a quick kiss and a swat on the rear end. "Move it, slave — neither of us likes to be late."

She grinned and stuck her tongue out at him, stripping as she hurried to the bedroom. By the time she reached the bed, she had a wad of work clothes in her hand and was down to her pantyhose. Dropping the pile onto the floor beside the bed, she pulled off her stockings and dropped those on top.

"Mmm...what a nice view, slave." He leaned against the doorjamb watching the tornado fly about the room, brushing her hair, pulling off her earrings, and generally looking a little frazzled. The clothes he had picked out for the evening lay on the bed and to help, he scooped up her work clothes from the floor. Unwilling to look away for long, he stood in front of the closet as he hung up her suit and watched the show.

A long-sleeved denim shirt and jeans lay side-by-side for her to wear. Picking up the blue shirt, she looked for a bra, but a chuckle from the corner clued her in: there was none. She looked up to see him wearing a silly grin. With a resigned shake of her head, she held the shirt against the light and felt relief — it was not see-through. Sliding her arms through the sleeves, she pulled it close to button it; the feel of the material on her breasts made her catch her breath. It had been years since she had gone braless; doing so tonight would make her feel very mischievous indeed.

She picked up the jeans and looked around for the panties, already knowing there were none. No socks either, but the pair of sandals she'd worn to the store waited beside the bed. Sketching a bow, she called out, "As my Master wishes!" pulled on the jeans and zipped them up.

The arousal was immediate. The roughness of the material rubbed against her pussy and made her feel wanton and sexy. A slow smile spread across her face.

Moving beside her Phillip took her in his arms. "I want nothing between us tonight, but a bit of fabric. Every time you move, you will think of me and of your desire. I find that very erotic." Bending down, he kissed her, long and lingering, until he felt her relax completely. Only then did he break away.

Oh, but he knew how to make the cares of the week fade and disappear, she thought to herself. He held out his hand and she saw the little leather collar lying across his palm. There was a question in his eyes—a challenge. With a smile, she turned and lifted her hair so he could fasten it around her neck.

He was glad her back was to him—he couldn't contain his grin. Tonight was a test—could she be his slave in front of her friends? So far, she had worn what he chose and had accepted his collar. It was enough. He would not test her further.

* * * * *

The car slid through the darkening evening as they sped toward Beth's new house. Sarah tried to fill him in on a few of the people he would meet tonight.

"There's Tasha, she's the tall, blonde and beautiful one of the group. And Paul is the tallest male." She looked at Phillip with a critical glint in her eye. "Although you might be taller yet. Just don't ask him if he played basketball in school. He didn't— and he hates being asked."

Phillip nodded. "Understood perfectly. I get asked the same question—and before you ask, no, I didn't either."

Smiling, she continued her litany. "Martha and Christine are a couple, but no one ever makes a big thing over it. Their sex lives are none of our concern. That's pretty much how I feel about our sex life as well. What happens at the cottage is none of their business."

She hadn't intended to sound so bossy about it, although as she said it, she realized she was being awfully demanding for someone who was trying to see herself as a slave. Maybe she didn't really have it in her, to totally submit. Being submissive in private was easy—but in public was a whole different question.

Phillip did not comment on her vehemence, but he noted it. Truthfully, he was ambivalent about others knowing as well. The rest of the world saw only their public faces, but wasn't that true of every relationship? Even 'normal' ones? Once a couple went home and shut the doors, society really didn't want to know. Perhaps someday both he and Sarah might wish for others to know and understand their choices, but the time was not yet right—for either of them.

'Course it would be different with his friends. The people she would meet tomorrow night already knew about their lifestyle, since they lived similar lives themselves. But he kept quiet about that for now. Tonight was her night and he was going to meet her friends.

"And of course, there's Beth—she's been my best friend since grade school, so be ready for her. Sometimes she thinks she's my mother." Sarah's apologetic look made Phillip laugh.

"So I need to charm Beth, bond with Paul, ignore Martha and Christine's love for one another, and ogle Tasha—do I have that right?"

Now it was Sarah who laughed outright. "Yep. That about does it!"

"So are poor Paul and I the only males in this group?"

She laughed. "I doubt you'll be the only two tonight. Beth and Paul are an off-again, on-again couple. At the moment, they're on, so I'm sure he'll be there. No family, because she's a transplant here like me. When I found a good job here, she followed me—and we've both done well. Martha and Christine, Paul and Beth, and Tasha: those are the only ones I'll know at the party, but there will be lots of others."

"There it is—that's the place." She pointed to a small, stucco house nestled in among the other houses on the block. There was no room in the driveway, so Phillip pulled alongside the curb opposite, parked and handed Sarah out of the car. Retrieving a bottle of champagne from the back, they crossed the street, arm in arm.

Beth greeted them at the door, her words of welcome for them both, but her eyes for Phillip—appraising eyes, he realized. She was shorter than Sarah, plumper, but with sparkling brown eyes that missed nothing. Bending down, he kissed her cheek as Sarah had done and presented the bottle of champagne.

"For the new homeowner—congratulations." He bowed, his smile genuine—his first impression of her was favorable.

"Come on in and meet some of the others," Beth invited. "It's very informal tonight—I'm barely unpacked. I expect people will be coming and going all night."

They entered the tiny house and Sarah noted how perfect it was for a single woman. Beth showed them around the downstairs—then took them up and showed off the two bedrooms and bath. Already her own stamp was being made on the place—Sarah noted several objects that had been Beth's for years scattered about the rooms.

And so they passed the next two hours. Mostly Sarah stayed at Phillip's side. At first he thought it was because she didn't want him to feel uncomfortable, but when the other three girls she'd spoken of walked in together, Sarah's relaxation was immediate. It was as if she had been holding her breath all night and now that they were here, she could breathe again. She dragged him over to meet the trio, who, it turned out, all lived near each other and so had brought only one car.

Initially, Phillip thought it was just a matter of a girl showing off her new boyfriend. But as the night progressed, he realized his new slave was tremendously shy. Even with her friends, she tended to be the listener—actively enjoying the conversation, but rarely adding to it. Because Beth was the hostess, she flitted from room to room, group to group. But Sarah stayed put, pleasantly enjoying the company of those who were nearby.

Several times, Phillip's arm wrapped around her during the night—almost casually each time. The touch of his hand on her waist gave her a warm feeling inside. She hated big parties like this, too many people one didn't know and not really an atmosphere that provided for anything other than small talk. And she'd never mastered that skill; talking of the weather or the latest football game or someone's hair loss just never interested her.

At last the evening was winding down; the acquaintances were gone and only the close friends remained. They settled down around the dining room table, telling old stories on one another, filling Phillip's ear with tales of humor and woe. He took a liking to them—all of them were transplants to the area and they all watched out for one another. He was glad to know that Sarah had such loyal friends.

But even here she did no more than add an occasional comment or two. Paul and Beth were the storytellers, Tasha added forgotten details; apparently the memory of the group—getting the fine points right. Martha and Christine—Phillip was already thinking of them as one entity—added a few stories of their own. Sarah and he seemed to be the audience and that was fine with him. Seeing how she behaved when surrounded by her friends, gave him new insight into her personality.

Kissing Beth at the door as they left, Sarah again tucked her hand into the crook of Phillip's arm. But not until they were in the car and about a block away did she let out an explosive sigh.

"Been holding that in a while?" Phillip asked.

"Sorry," she apologized. "Didn't realize it till just now, but yes, I suppose I have."

"Nervous about me?"

"Some. Big groups of people aren't my 'thing.'" She turned to face him in the car, twisting her body so she could sit comfortably yet talk directly to him. "Thank you for this, Phillip. I knew I had to go because Beth's my best friend, but I really wasn't looking forward to it. Then, when you agreed to go, I knew there'd be at least one person there I could talk to."

"I hadn't realized how shy you are."

She bowed her head, and the same shy smile he had seen all night played about her lips. "My secret is out. I just never know what to say to people! If I can get them talking about themselves, then I'm okay—all I have to do is stand there and listen to them." She sighed again.

"It's that submissive side of you, expressing itself in a socially acceptable way."

For a moment, she watched the scenery, considering. "Yes," she finally agreed. "Yes, I think you're right. I can be a take-charge kind of person in situations where I'm comfortable, like at work. It's my job to command others and I enjoy it there. But elsewhere, I'd rather not. Listening to people has always been my preferred option, instead of telling the stories like Beth." She laughed. "That's probably why we're such good friends—she's the talker and I'm the listener."

He flashed a smile at her as they turned onto his road. "We can't all be talkers—and you'll find that among my friends tomorrow, I tend to be a listener as well."

"Will there be a lot of people there?"

"You mean 'here'," he told her as he turned up the drive.

"Here? Your friends are coming to the cottage?"

He nodded and parked. She was so excited, she didn't wait for him to come around and get the door for her. "That's wonderful. It's always so much easier to meet people when I have a role to play. Being hostess, like Beth was tonight gives me something to do and say when I don't know what else to do."

He laughed at her enthusiasm—and decided to let it slide that she hadn't let him get her door. It was a small thing, but an act of chivalry he enjoyed. Instead, he caught her hand and led her to the porch, stopping in the moonlight just before the steps.

"It's too beautiful a night to go in just yet, don't you think?" he murmured as he pulled her close.

Her stomach fluttered as she tilted her head up to look at him. Pale moonlight glowed on his face, illuminating his eyes, dark with desire. He kissed her, gently at first, then with an increasing pressure as the animal within him struggled for freedom. His tongue touched her lips and she parted them, wanting to taste him. When his hand pulled her shirt from her pants, she helped, still locked in his embrace, wanting to feel his hands on her bare, braless breasts.

With a growl, he pushed up her shirt and engulfed a breast in his massive hand, squeezing it hard. His other hand still wrapped around her, grabbed her ass, crushing her to him. Her mind was being overwhelmed and she let go, giving her body to him, wanting him.

He stepped away from her, almost thrusting her away from him. "Undress for me, slave. Undress now, in the moonlight and show me your naked body."

She could not refuse. Her eyes locked on his, she rapidly undid the buttons on her shirt, her breasts rising and falling with her quickened breath. She flung the shirt away, then ripped off the pants.

"Stand as you were taught." The animal banged against the bars of its cage.

She spread her legs to the night air and put her arms behind her, clasping her hands and thrusting out her breasts. Moonlight streamed down and made her luminescent in the darkness. Proudly, she stood naked before him, eager for his touch.

With an oath, Phillip stripped his clothes from his body and in two strides covered the distance between them. Grabbing her, the pent up animal broke the bars of his cage. He put his hand between her legs, her wetness was proof of her own desire to be used. Hooking his finger through the small leather collar, he pulled her toward the porch and cast her at the steps.

Sarah barely caught herself as she fell. Quickly she turned to stare at the man she thought she knew. Lust snarled his features as his face twisted with his need. Sarah had compared him to a lion — but the creature before her now was no playful cub. This was the hunter bringing down his prey. Only once had she caught a glimpse of this animal — and it had frightened her then. Now it was loose and she wanted it, her breath ragged, a whimper in her throat. Phillip's hand rubbed his cock as it grew hard and thick and Sarah knew the animal would not rest until it had been sated. Lying on the steps, she spread her legs in the moonlight, inviting the beast to consume her.

And he did. With another oath, Phillip flung himself on top of her, entering her in one movement. She cried out as his cock stretched her, pushing relentlessly to bury itself inside her. He pulled out and, growling, thrust in again, taking her hard. Each thrust drove her need deeper and she dug her fingers into his shoulders, her nails making small marks in his skin.

Again and again he drove into her until she thought she would rip in two. Her hips rose to meet each thrust, her mind screaming her need. And then his movements changed—his ascent matched hers. Both of them moaned and growled into the night as he fucked her on the steps of the porch, their passion joining in loud crescendos as they crested together. An owl's screech echoed their screams as the two of them rode the night, two animals mating.

Stunned, she lay without moving, her body spent, the warmth from him spreading along her. Was she more amazed at him—or at herself for responding to his animal? Her body continued to quiver as small aftershocks pulsed through her.

It took Phillip longer to recover; he waited until the animal faded back and returned to its cage. Once it was safely out of the way, he rolled off her, unable to meet her eyes. What must she think of him? Master or no, he had been tremendously rough with her.

Sarah saw the misery in his eyes. Sitting up, she touched his cheek and pulled his chin up until he looked at her. Then she smiled and he understood that she was not hurt. Why, the little vixen liked it! As comprehension dawned, he sat on the porch, amazed that he'd found a woman who just might be able to handle the wild beast he could not always contain.

There was no need for words between them. Sarah stood and retrieved their clothes from their far-flung places in front of the cottage and returning, entered when he held the door for her. Watching her, Phillip grew hard again, although the animal stayed where it was.

Sarah dumped the clothes in the corner of the bedroom and as he came up behind her, she felt the evidence of his growing need press into her back. She turned to face him, one hand caressing his cock as she watched him, waiting for instructions. How would he use her a second time tonight?

Answering her unspoken question, Phillip put his hands on her shoulders. "Kneel, slave," he said softly and she knew what he desired.

Obediently she kneeled before him. Patiently she waited for permission before touching him. "Now, slave, suck me. Take me in your mouth."

His voice was rough and she realized the cage was not locked. The animal that drove him was still very much present. With his come still leaking from between her legs, she took his cock in her mouth, using her hands to knead the stones in his balls. Staying only on the tip, she flicked her tongue over and around it, trying to set the animal loose again.

He came out with a vengeance. Roaring, Phillip thrust himself deep inside her mouth, gagging her. He retreated only long enough for her to recover and thrust in again. Her own juices mingled with his come and dripped down her thigh as he grabbed her head and guided her motions. Relaxing, she let him control her and was rewarded with the familiar salty taste filling her mouth. She swallowed much of it at once, licking the rest from him as his motions slowed, then cleaning her face and swallowing the rest of it as he watched.

If he weren't so exhausted from two orgasms so close together, the sight of her kneeling on the floor eating his come would have made him hard again. As it was, he barely made it to the side of the bed before his knees gave way. "Come here, slave," he commanded, his voice husky.

He was only a few steps away and it was easier to crawl on all fours than to stand and then kneel again. Seeing her crawl over to him gave him another rush—my god, what this woman did to him. He hooked a finger through her collar again, pulling her up close to him. "Do you like being my slave, Sarah? Even when I use you so roughly?"

Her head tilted to the side and she smiled up at him. "Yes, Master Phillip. I like being your slave, especially when you use me so roughly."

"Then come up here, slave. Come to bed now."

She climbed into the bed beside him, tenderly covering them both with the blankets. The animal inside him slept now, and it wouldn't be long before he did as well.

"Good night, Master," she whispered in his ear. "Thank you."

But if he heard, he gave no indication. He had fallen asleep. Snuggling in next to him, her body tired from the stress of the day and his use of her outside, she soon followed him in slumber.

Chapter 10
His friends

The two of them spent the next morning cleaning the cottage. Not that it needed cleaning, but as Sarah's mother would have said, it wasn't 'company clean.' Phillip's domain was the kitchen and he prepared several trays of veggies, tucking them away in the fridge till later. Sarah discovered he also was a baker–the cheesecake he created looked wonderful.

"The secret, slave, is letting it stay in the oven with the door ajar until the oven is completely cooled." She had come in from dusting and vacuuming and now stood peering into the open oven door, the heat warming her naked body. "Then you don't get cracks in the top."

"Is that how they do it?" she exclaimed. "I've only baked a few in my life and figured the cracks came because I didn't have a fancy oven like one of the pros." She shook her head at his talents.

He laughed. "Well, I'm no pro, but my aunt used to bake the best cheesecakes in the city and she passed on her tips to me."

Sometimes he looked like such a little boy, she wanted to go over and hug him. This was one of those moments. It was a cloudy day outside and the kitchen light was on to dispel the gloom. Maybe it was hearing him talk of his aunt, or maybe it was a reflection of the light, but there was a gleam in his eye that belied the existence of the animal she had experienced last night. She hid her smile. And they said women were complicated.

"While it's cooling, let's eat lunch—then we have some furniture to move."

It didn't take long to make and consume several tuna fish sandwiches. Since that first weekend together, Sarah had discovered the canned seafood was his favorite lunch. Sometimes he liked it spread over crackers, sometimes on bread—but always tuna fish. Knowing it was better for her than the nachos and hot dog she usually ate at home, she was beginning to favor the plain fare herself.

"How many people will be here tonight?" she asked, munching on a pilfered carrot stick.

"Only eight, including us. A small gathering."

Part of her was relieved, part panicked. She preferred smaller groups, but that meant nowhere to hide. Nowhere but in her role as his hostess.

He saw the look in her eye and guessed which way her thoughts were headed. Reaching over the table, he took her hand. "You'll do fine. Especially after I train you this afternoon. There are very specific 'rules,' if you will, for a slave in the presence of other masters."

"Other masters?" Butterflies flew in and settled in her stomach—as if she weren't already nervous enough.

He nodded, finishing off his lunch. "Yes, slave, other masters. I told you my friends were different from yours." He pushed his chair back and watched her digest the information along with her tuna.

"I know you did...Master." She stressed the last word, grinning. Swallowing the last of her drink, she stood to clear the plates. "I think I just put it out of my mind, however." She stopped and turned around. "But you'll teach me? So that I know what to do?"

"That's important to you, isn't it? Knowing what to do, what to say."

She nodded and came back for the glasses, clearing the rest of the lunch stuff as well. "It is." She grimaced and there was no mirth in her eyes. "I don't play the fool well. That's probably why I'm not a very good storyteller. Being the center of attention and then messing up is one of my worst nightmares."

He stood and kissed her on the top of her head. "Well, then, slave. Since tonight you will definitely be the center of attention, we'll just have to make sure you don't 'mess up'."

Her nerves calmed somewhat at that. Of course she was going to be examined tonight—just as he'd been given a thorough going over the night before. But if he was going to show her the ropes, figuratively speaking, then maybe it wouldn't be too bad.

In the living room, he began pushing furniture this way and that, and she helped, creating a rather large space against the short side of the room. Finally, he was satisfied and he led her into the bedroom. She now wore the wider collar she actually preferred. Symbolic as they both were, this one's presence around her neck was a more physical reminder of her status—a status she increasingly enjoyed.

"Time to put you on the shelf, slave." A thrill ran through her—he was finished with her for now. Of course, as soon as she knew that, desire peeked its head out. But she said nothing, simply holding out her hands and legs in turn so he could attach her wrist and ankle cuffs, locking them into place on her limbs. Locking wrist to wrist and ankle to ankle, he had her lie down on the bed. Taking up the "Y" chain she had worn the weekend before, he fastened her arms to her neck and bid her roll over.

She complied, awkwardly, but with his help, got onto her stomach. He now fastened a length of chain from the headboard to her D-ring—then fastened her ankles with another short length of chain to the footboard.

"Sleep if you can, slave," he told her on his way out the door. "Tonight will be a long night for you."

The directions sounded ominous, but he was gone and she did not call him back. She recalled the words he had spoken a while ago—after a particularly erotic evening. Phillip had warned her then that someday she'd meet other masters—

apparently 'someday' was today. And now he expected her to sleep?

Sarah's mind tossed from one topic to the next as she lay still, chained to the bed. Wait! He hadn't trained her at all yet. Was her role as a submissive hostess different from that of a normal hostess? She was sure there must be protocols she should follow. But she was on the shelf and her master did not expect to hear a sound from her.

There was a certain excitement at being thus treated and she had already accepted the fact that her body fell first to his control and then her mind. Every handling of her took her to new places inside herself—a journey of discovery that stretched her boundaries and taught her insights about her personality she never before considered.

Take what he said last night, for example. That her shyness was just another form of submissiveness. That had rankled for a bit, but the more she thought about it, the more she realized he was right. Long ago, she had accepted her nature as being the 'quiet type' and had not delved any deeper than that. But Phillip was not satisfied with only surface reflections. His observation made her see that she had always been the observer—she watched people, and when they needed something, she was there. In fact, Beth had commented on it several times—how Sarah always seemed to know what people needed without being told.

Sarah also thought about how she always gave in to Beth's desires when the two of them planned an evening. Even with her husband, if Sarah wanted one thing, but her partner wanted something different, she usually caved in. Of course, with Tom, it was more equal—he acquiesced to her as often as she gave in to him. But not with Beth.

A sudden thought occurred to her and her jaw dropped open. Could Beth be a Dominatrix? Was it possible? She thought about her friend's relationship with Paul—he was so easy going, could he be...No. Her mind would not go there.

What about Phillip's friends tonight? If there were masters coming, would there also be slaves? What would they look like? Her mind conjured Hollywood images of slave harems. No, she decided. Phillip's living room didn't look any more like the stereotypical harem than his dungeon looked like the stereotypical dungeon. Try as she might, she had no idea what his friends would be like.

In spite of herself, she knew that her thoughts, along with her helpless position, were working their magic on her. Her thoughts continued to swirl as desire ached between her legs. Like an itch she could not scratch, it remained just under the surface as finally, she fell asleep.

*   *   *   *   *

His gentle kiss woke her. Breathing deeply, she smelled soap on him and her eyes flew open, momentarily confused — was it morning? No, the light was wrong. The party! He was releasing her, removing first her ankle cuffs, then the bindings on her wrist. She rolled over and he undid the chain from her collar.

"I checked on you several times, and you were sound asleep," he told her. "I even took my shower and dressed — you never moved."

"Cleaning is tiring work, Sir!"

He sniffed the air. "And sweaty — go take your shower and be sure to run the razor over all important parts. Your clothes will be on the bed for you," he called after her as she hurried into the bathroom.

In short order she had freshened up and taken her shower, returning to the bedroom to dress. Her black garter belt and stockings waited for her — and a black bra. Quickly she donned them, slipping into the heels he set out for her. Usually these were her church shoes, but she had to admit, they added to the overall sexy look.

She fastened the bra in place, then turned it around to pull the cups up over her breasts. Except there seemed to be something wrong with the undergarment. A huge hole was cut in each cup. Well, maybe the hole wasn't huge, but certainly as big as a quarter. Upon closer examination, she realized they had been designed that way; the hole was neatly finished off. Blushing, she understood what must go there. With another twist, she seated her nipples in the center of each hole. The exposure to the air when the surrounding breast was covered caused the nipples to stand straight out. His intention, no doubt, she thought.

But there were no more clothes on the bed. Surely he did not mean to make her greet his guests looking so wanton. Hearing his step, she called out to him, "Master, I don't see the rest of my clothes—what else did you want me to wear?"

His hands on her waist made her jump. She hadn't realized he had entered the room. "No need to shout," he murmured into her hair as he put his arms around her and ran his fingertips over her exposed nipples. While such a fondling usually caused her to grow weak in the knees, tonight she was too nervous to settle. When she didn't relax, he turned her to face him.

"You are my property and I wish to show you off. I told you I would. Last week you said you would be willing to be naked in front of people. Are you saying now you aren't?"

She opened her mouth with the intention of saying exactly that. The sane and rational side of her raged against appearing in public like this—even if it were only for six people other than themselves. Yes, she said last week that she wanted to do this—someday. Not now! How could she? But even as the rational side railed inside her head, the wanton side of her wanted this—and not only wanted it, but was pleased that he was proud of her and wanted to show her off. The wanton got the words out first: "I can do this, Master—for you."

"Good." He bent down and kissed her. "Let me fasten your collar." She obediently lifted her hair and raised her neck, lowering her shoulders as he wrapped it around and fastened it, the snick of the lock sending shivers through her for an entirely different reason than normal. This was no game tonight; this was for real and she was scared.

He attached the heavy chain leash to the D-ring and had just finished putting on her ankle cuffs when there was a knocking at the door. He checked his watch. "Figures. That'll be Aleshia and Anton—she's always early." He stood and started for the door. "Finish putting on your cuffs, then sit there till I come for you."

She suddenly wanted to sit here all night. With trembling fingers, she attached the cuffs, having to make several attempts in her nervousness to close the locks. By the time she was done, she was sure everyone was here. Still, she sat on the edge of the bed, balefully watching the door as if her doom were about to enter.

But it was only Phillip. His manner was brusque. "Stand, slave." She did so, her hands at her side, opening and closing, clenching the air in her fear.

"Sir...you didn't, I mean, there wasn't time for training this afternoon. I don't know what to do—or say to them."

He nodded. "You do what I tell you to do—and nothing more, slave. Understood?"

Her lip trembling, she nodded.

"And as to what to say, I've given that some thought and have come up with a way to calm your anxieties." He turned her by the shoulders and she felt his hand press something against her mouth. The bit! Automatically, her mouth opened and he seated it quickly, drawing her hair back and letting the straps hold her mane away from her face. She heard the snick of a lock close and realized her mouth was bound. He had indeed taken care of the problem: she could not speak to the guests tonight.

He pulled her arms back and fastened her wrist cuffs to one another. With her shoulders now pulled back a bit, the bra cut into her breasts slightly and pushed her nipples out for all to see.

In spite of her fear, or maybe because of it, she felt a gush of fluid between her legs.

Turning her to face him, he gave her one last instruction, "Just do what I tell you to do, slave. I will not let you come to harm."

She nodded, her butterflies showing in the whites of her eyes. With pride, he pulled on her leash and she followed him out the door.

This whole evening was so out of her purview, she had given up trying to imagine it earlier. There were just too many unknowns. But now reality spread itself before her as she entered the brightly-lit living room.

Three couples sat ranged around the room. Two men sat in the chairs she and Phillip had put against the front wall earlier. She was struck, not so much by their appearance as their bearing. Both sat with the same ease and grace she'd seen in Phillip—a natural grace that emanated power. A woman sat on the floor beside each of them.

On the couch opposite, reclined a beautiful woman, her black hair pulled away from her face in a soft bun that accentuated her rather sharp features. She also had that aura of power. Beside her, a man knelt on the floor. Sarah's eyes grew wide at that. She was just beginning to understand her own need for submission—why on earth would a man want to submit to a woman?

And then her gaze fell on the space that had been empty when Phillip had put her "on the shelf." It was empty no longer. At the far end of the room, lit with all the spotlights from the track lighting above, was the tall cage. Black iron bars gleamed in the soft light, its open door just waiting for someone to cross its threshold. She almost cried as she realized who that someone would be and what her master had meant when he had told her she would be on display.

"May I present my new slave, Sarah Jackson-Parker," he announced and a shock went through her being — he told them her name. How could he expose her like that? But then rational thought took hold. What else did she expect him to say? Didn't she introduce him the night before by his whole name? It was what normal people did. Except she did not feel normal. Not at all.

She trembled and he knew it. Moving his hand up her leash, he pulled her forward. While he stood in the center of the room, he guided her so that she was forced to make a full circle around the room.

"Meet my fellow Masters and Mistress, slave." He knew this was hard for her, yet she was enduring it beautifully. Her steps were tentative and slow, but he was patient. Once she had made a full circuit, he pulled her into a second one, this time pulling up on her chain and making her stop before the first master.

"This is Master William, slave. Bow to him." He had not warned her of this, wanting to test her resolve. In future meetings with his friends, he would test her much more severely. But tonight it would be enough just for her to acknowledge their presence.

She didn't want to meet them. It was hard enough being displayed so wantonly, her nipples standing out straight, her freshly-shaven mound glimmering in its nakedness. She wished he would just put her in the blasted cage and be done with it. Her mind could slink off then, pretend she wasn't really here, wasn't really mostly naked before so many strange eyes.

But he had given her a command — and she didn't want to embarrass him by not obeying. So she turned, keeping her eyes downcast so she wouldn't have to see Master William looking at her, and bowed from the waist, her legs pressed tightly together.

"Look at me, slave Sarah." Master William's voice held the same raw power as Phillip's. She didn't want to look, but found her gaze drifting upward until her eyes met his. His eyes looked at her kindly, with no trace of the lewdness she expected to find. He smiled at her and her face softened.

"This is my slave." He gestured to the woman beside him who knelt in a very familiar position. She was clothed, Sarah noted, in comfortable jeans and a pullover sweater, a pretty leather collar around her neck. Short, wavy hair neatly framed her pert face. "Her name is Jillean." His hand brushed the top of his slave's head. "Jill, say hello to slave Sarah."

The woman stood with the practiced ease of one who had been rising from such a low level for years. Sarah watched her face and saw a welcoming calmness in the woman's deep brown eyes. The slave put her hands on Sarah's shoulders and leaned forward to kiss her on the cheek.

The tender understanding in the gesture touched her and tears formed in Sarah's eyes. As Jill pulled away and returned to her former position, Sarah wished she could thank her, except the bit prevented her. But a nod from the now-kneeling slave made her realize the slave understood.

Phillip was also touched by Master William's gesture with his slave. Will and he had been friends for over a decade — in fact, the other master had been Phillip's mentor when he first admitted his need to dominate in a relationship. As Phillip pulled on Sarah's chain to take her to the next master, Will winked at him and he knew he had his mentor's approval.

"This is Master Dominic, slave. Bow to him."

Master William and Jill had done a great deal to ease her mind, so this time Sarah was able to turn and bow without hesitation. She looked up into Master Dominic's eyes, but did not find the same kindness Master William had shown her. His eyes flashed when she looked at him — was it anger? Had she done something wrong?

With a curt gesture, Master Dominic waved his hand in the general direction of the woman at his side. "This is Cora."

Sarah looked down at the slave-woman kneeling rigidly beside her master. She was dressed more provocatively than the others in the room; a short skirt barely covered her ass, the neckline of the sweater plunged about as deep as it could go and still remain fastened in the front. She also wore a collar, but one of steel. A leash attached to it, the other end held casually in Master Dominic's hand. As Cora stood, she teetered just a bit, then straightened. She did not look at Sarah—in fact, she looked at no one, just kept her gaze straight down. So Sarah saw what Cora did not—a slight narrowing of Master Dominic's eyes at her ever-so-slight lack of grace. Now Sarah was glad for the bit, or she would have had a few words for the man who slouched in the chair.

Sarah was not in a position to initiate anything, but if she had been, she would have given Cora a hug for being beside such a lout. First impressions were important, she knew—for her first impression of this man was not a good one. Cora barely came to her shoulder, her shoulder-length black hair hanging loosely about her face. Executing a simple bow to Sarah, Cora returned to her position.

As Phillip tugged on her leash again, she tried to catch his glance to signal a question to him, but he studiously avoided her eye. Master Dominic and he had had several disagreements on both how to train a slave and how to keep one—and that was the reason he had invited him tonight. Part of him was vain enough to want Sarah to see what life could be like if he wasn't such a nice guy.

"Lady Aleshia, this is my new slave."

Sarah stopped before the woman and bowed as she had to each of the men. Like the Masters, she was simply dressed in jeans and a casual shirt, but Sarah could easily imagine her in latex, thigh high boots and all. Red nail polish gleamed on the tips of her fingers as she idly played with her slave's hair.

"And this is my slave, Anton."

Anton stood...and stood...and stood. Sarah's eyes traveled up and up as the slave towered over her. The man must stand at least six foot six! She had no idea how tall the other masters were, as they had remained seated. Gazing back and forth between Phillip and the slave, she realized he had several inches on her own master. She saw he also wore a simple leather collar that looked quite attractive on him.

The male slave bent down and kissed the opposite cheek that Jill had welcomed. Like the other slaves, he did not speak, but as he pulled away, he grinned and dimples graced his cheeks. In spite of the bit in her mouth, Sarah found herself answering his smile with one of her own.

Some of her tension melted away as Phillip pulled again on her leash, taking her to the cage. Lightly she stepped inside, turning to face the front. Phillip swung the door shut and turned the key.

For a moment, Sarah relaxed. She made it. She had crossed the room and gotten into the cage where she expected she would remain for the rest of the evening. Nothing to do, and with the bit in her mouth, nothing to say. No way to mess things up. Quietly, she sighed.

Her relief was short-lived. Phillip was not quite done with her. He wanted her on display—all of her. Stooping down beside the cage, he reached in and took hold of her ankle, gently tugging it. She shifted her weight in confusion—what was he doing? Her ankle touched the cold iron of the bars and sent a shiver through her as she heard the familiar "snick." Locked in place, her legs were spread a bit and suddenly she realized his intention.

There was no way to tell him no, to beg him not to show her to all these people. His hands were at her other leg now and she moved it out of a habit of obeisance rather than out of a desire to do so. Her ankles, locked in place, spread her and the scent of her sex drifted up and filled her nose. They would all know!

Desperately she tried to see him to let him know with her eyes, but he had disappeared behind her. She felt his hands around her wrists as he pulled them back to fasten against the bars at the rear of the cage. Ever so slightly, she was pulled off balance, her arms forcing her breasts into the confines of her open bra. In spite of herself, she knew her nipples had hardened even as more juices gathered in the folds between her legs. No! She didn't want to show herself to all these strangers!

Coming around front now, he reached in and took her leash. "You're doing well, slave," he murmured so only she could hear. Draping the leash over one of the crossbars, he let it dangle outside the cage. Stepping to the wall, his hand slid over the light switch, plunging the room into darkness. Except for the lights focused on her cage.

Tears formed in her eyes at her humiliation. How could he do this to her? How did he have the heart to display her so openly, so wantonly? Every part of her wanted to slam her legs shut and she squirmed in her bindings, her eyes pleading for release.

He did not give it to her. In the soft light from above, her beauty was incredible. It was a beauty she did not even realize she had, but he would teach her. He wanted to teach her so much about herself that she had yet to discover. Patiently, he waited, as did all the others. They all knew that, if she were a true submissive, it would be only a matter of time.

She wanted to see him—she wanted to look into his eyes and know he took pity on her. But he stayed in the darkness while the glare of the lights shone down upon her. Her nipples stood out in the light, bright against the darkness of the fabric that surrounded them. Down below, her mound glistened with sweat; the black stockings focused their attention on her sex. No one spoke, but she could not ignore their presence—a shift here, a small noise there. She knew they watched her. A moan escaped her and she writhed in the bindings. Wanting to hide, she strained to get loose so they could not see her. If only he would turn the lights off.

Her struggles grew wilder as her emotions bordered on panic; she tried to convince herself she didn't really want this, even as evidence mounted that her body did. She couldn't want this. To want to be naked in front of people said all sorts of things about her. Things she didn't want to admit. Things that she should be ashamed of. So why did being put on such display make her so excited?

The leash fell from the door and its sudden weight on her collar brought her up short. The collar. It was his collar. It anchored her mind and the struggles slowed. He had called her his slut once before. Not "a" slut—"his" slut. His slave. His to do with as he wanted. To be put on display before his friends, if he so desired. She had given him that right when she'd accepted the collar this evening. She had given him control.

Sarah's struggles stopped. Drool had fallen onto her breasts, leaving darker black streaks against the black fabric. Several wisps of hair had come loose and had fallen in her eyes. Tears streaked her face, but no more fell as she came to accept her place. Slowly, with great effort at first, then with more assurance, she raised her head and held her chin high.

Phillip grinned and his heart soared. Bending, he lit a candle and passed the light from candle to candle around the room as the others joined him to spread the brightness. The masters all expressed their congratulations to him.

He spoke quietly to Master William and Sarah saw Jill rise and leave the room. She returned a moment later with a small towel and approached the cage. Deftly she reached between the bars and wiped the drool from Sarah's chin, neck and breasts. Smiling her thanks, Sarah watched her hand the towel to Phillip and return to her seat.

Having the candles lit made it a little easier to be in the spotlight. She was still the brightest thing in the room by far, but no longer the only point of attention. Phillip now brought out the vegetable trays he'd earlier prepared and Sarah watched them, behaving as if it were a perfectly normal get together between perfectly normal people who just happened to have a semi-nude woman chained in a cage as their decoration.

After a while, her muscles began to grow tired, but she could not move to give them rest. She thought about moaning to get Phillip's attention, but that would put the attention on her again, and she wasn't quite ready for that. So far, she was just the object of some glances now and again as they talked of normal things one talks of at a gathering of friends.

Except for Cora. The slave's eyes never looked up, never strayed from the floor. The other two slaves, Jill and Anton took part in the conversation, although Sarah noticed they always deferred to their respective "owners." In fact the more she watched, the more she learned about how slaves behave—and how each master apparently had different expectations.

Anton's attention focused on his Mistress. She never had to request a refill of her drink, never had to ask for the vegetables or cheese and crackers to be passed to her. Anton anticipated her needs flawlessly and always had them ready before Sarah had even known the Mistress would want them. Each time he served her, his eyes lit up with a merry look and Sarah understood there was a great deal of respect and love in that relationship.

Master William and Jill also showed love to one another, but it was louder and more boisterous than Lady Aleshia's and Anton's. "Will and Jill," as Phillip had called them, laughed frequently and Sarah noticed Master William usually had to tell his slave what he wanted. She would tease him and he'd playfully pinch her arm, at which she'd squeal an obviously fake cry of pain. Then they both laughed as if it had been hilariously funny. Several times Sarah grinned around the gag. A gag that was beginning to irritate her.

Cora and Master Dominic did not seem to enjoy each other at all. Most of the time he did not participate in the discussion, instead sitting off to the side, a permanent scowl on his face. When he wanted a drink, he pulled on Cora's chain and thrust the glass at her. She would dutifully perform her task, returning again to kneel stiffly at his side. Neither cracked a smile the entire evening.

Phillip kept an eye on Sarah, without being obvious about it. He kept his face mostly in the shadows as the conversation became increasingly sexual in nature. That was the usual course for these evenings. First they spent time catching up, then reminiscing, then playing. He had already talked to Will and

Lady Aleshia about what type of play he wanted for the evening—he counted on Master Dominic to leave early.

And he was not disappointed. Sarah was tiring in her cage and Phillip needed to take her out soon. But he was loathe to do so while Dominic remained. After a few words of parting, the disliked master pulled on his slave's leash and departed.

Sarah could feel the collective sigh in the room. No one commented on him, there was no gossip about him from either the remaining slaves or their owners. She wondered at that, because if her mouth had been free, she was sure she would have had a comment or two to make.

She did see, however, some very wicked grins among them all. With a long stretch, Master William stood. "Slave, what are you still doing in your clothes?" His grin belied the sternness of his voice.

"Many pardons, Master," Jill replied, pulling off her sweater with one move. She was amply endowed and Sarah tried not to stare as the woman, with absolutely no shyness whatsoever, stood and stripped off her pants, panties and all. A quick twist and her bra lay with the rest of her clothes and Jill stood before them all, naked and completely at ease.

"Got any rope?" Master William asked Phillip.

"Some," Sarah's master grinned. He jerked his head toward the dungeon. "If you'll follow me…"

Will turned to his slave. "Stay." There was a twinkle in his eye and Sarah saw the laughter in Jill's face as she dropped to the floor in a position of servitude that lasted till her master turned the corner.

Lady Aleshia stretched and Anton was right there to tend to her. "It seems my slave is the only slave left in the room still clothed," she purred.

He smiled, his dimples dark shadows in the candlelight. "With your permission, my lady…" His voice was like deep velvet and Sarah smiled behind the gag.

His Mistress nodded and Sarah watched, fixated, as the tall slave slowly peeled off his shirt revealing the fine, muscled chest it had hidden. His muscles rippled in the candle's light as he turned for them to see, though his own attention remained focused on his Mistress.

Facing her again, he undid the clasp on his belt, letting it remain in the loops of his pants. He now flicked his thumb against the snap at the top of his pants and it sprung open. Never looking anywhere but at his mistress, he unzipped his pants and let them fall.

Sarah forgot herself and strained to see him, but her bindings brought her up short and reminded her of her position as the display. With Anton facing Lady Aleshia, Sarah could only see his ass—and what a magnificent ass it was. Only once before had she seen a rear end so beautifully formed, and it had been made of marble. Even her own master's, wonderful as it was, did not compare to the masterpiece that stood before her now.

"Turn."

Anton pivoted and Sarah held her breath. The candles cast their beams softly upon his beauty. With a wisp of black hair that curled around his ear, the hard muscles of his chest and thighs, his perfect ass and his thick cock now resting at ease, he was a DaVinci model come to life. A soft moan escaped from Sarah's gag and Lady Aleshia smiled.

Phillip and Master William entered precisely at that moment and Sarah almost jumped, her breath coming back to her in a rush. Could her master see the guilt in her eyes?

But he didn't seem to be paying attention to her as he cleared the coffee table of its contents. If she had known Phillip had watched every move of hers, she would have been shocked and dismayed.

Phillip had to turn his back to her momentarily as he cleared the trays from the short table. Indeed, all this had been carefully orchestrated between and among the dominant members of the group long before any of his guests had arrived this evening. Because of the lights that were focused on the cage, Phillip knew she could not see much beyond the center of the room. Going for the rope had been a ruse to get the two of them out of the room so Anton could perform. Phillip had watched her from the other end of the room and had seen the lust forming in her eyes.

He now touched the wall switch that controlled her lights, slowly dimming them until they only gleamed, making her skin glow against the blackness of her bra and stockings, the iron bars of the cage casting dim shadows on her figure. Grasping one end of the coffee table, he motioned to Will to take the other end and they moved it to the center of the room, right in front of the cage where Sarah would have a clear view of what was about to happen.

It was a sturdy piece of furniture. Phillip had purchased it when heavy pine furniture in a faux colonial style was all the rage. Except this one was oak—much better suited to his temperament. Pine was too soft a wood and would gouge easily. He wanted something sturdier, something that could take a little beating. His taste in furniture was similar to his taste in women, he realized with a grin. With a solid oak top and four solid oak pillars for legs, joined underneath by another solid level of oak for a shelf, this table was the epitome of sturdy.

The table properly positioned, Phillip nodded to Will, who held several lengths of rope in his hand. "On the table, slave, hands over your head." His voice was a bit gruff and Sarah realized with a start that he wasn't joking around now. There was a seriousness to his manner that would brook no disobedience.

Jill sat on the table at once, her bottom near one end. She lay the length of the table and stretched her arms over her head without a shred of embarrassment. Master William spent several minutes tying first one wrist, then the other to the thick oaken legs at one end of the table.

Her knees were bent over the end—the table wasn't long enough to take her entire prostrate form. Sarah saw the woman's nipples were hard and round in the candlelight as she obeyed her master's commands. Master William passed between the cage and the table, but ignored Sarah, giving his attention to his own slave instead.

Holding her by her buttocks, Master William pulled Jill down the table until her arms were stretched as far as they could go. Her body stopped with her pussy poised just at the edge of the table. Folding her legs under the table, he tied them to the two thick table legs, taking time to spread her knees apart so her most private parts were bared to the room.

Sarah's intake of breath was quiet, but Phillip heard it. Stepping back into the shadows, he watched his slave as the others put on their show for her. Many times he would join these four as they simply got together to do mundane things—go to dinner, see a movie, go bowling. But many more times they would get together as they were now: two Masters, a Mistress and their slaves. It had been quite a while since Phillip had a slave of his own...

Jill was thoroughly tied down now and could do little more than squirm on the tabletop. Will finished the knots on her ankles and now knelt at her side—the side away from Sarah, who could not take her eyes from the sight before her. Heedlessly, her own juices flowed freely, filling the space between her labia, and spilling over to run along her thigh.

Master William took a nipple in his fingers, pinching it slowly, letting the pressure build until he forced a moan from the helpless slave woman before him. Rolling it in his fingers, he made sure it was good and hard before he turned to Lady Aleshia and nodded.

Receiving her signal, Lady Aleshia knelt between Sarah and Jill, but subtly angled herself so Sarah's view was not blocked. Now the mistress leaned forward and licked Jill's other nipple, sucking it softly into her mouth. Master William leaned down and did the same on the other side.

Sarah's breathing had become shallow and fast. She could imagine herself on that table and the two of them working on her in such a manner. The sane, rational side of her shouted to be heard, but came through her desire as only a tiny voice: *"No, this is wrong, you shouldn't want to be on display, you shouldn't want to have others touch you."* Jill's moans became louder as Lady Aleshia took her nipple in her teeth and pulled it up, stretching the buxom breast until the slave cried out. Caught up in the scene before her, Sarah's little voice was drowned out. In the darkness, she did not see Phillip's smile.

"You are mine, slave," said Master William roughly kneading Jill's breast. "Your body is mine to play with—and if I chose to let others play with you, then that is my choice, is it not, slave?"

"Yes, Master," Jill breathed, "yes, it is your choice."

Sarah could hear the desire in her voice. The woman wanted them to play with her, and she found herself wanting to watch them play with her. If Phillip had tried to take her away now, she would have fought as hard to remain as earlier she had fought to be released.

"My slave is particularly good with the flogger," Lady Aleshia said casually.

"So you have mentioned before, Lady," Will said, as if they were discussing a friend's bread recipe. "I would very much like to see it demonstrated, if you wouldn't mind?"

"Of course not." The Lady leaned back on her heels and gestured to her slave. "Phillip? May we borrow a flogger from you?"

Her master moved back into the light and Sarah's heart beat hard. Oh, how handsome he looked in the soft light—how handsome he looked in any light for that matter. But just now, the candle threw a shadow over his features as he took another step in and, for an instant, his face changed; she saw the animal that lurked within. Hungry it looked, lustful. She knew what it was like to be on the receiving end of that animal and she wanted to see it again.

"Of course, Lady Aleshia. Have your slave follow me."

"Slave—Master Phillip has many toys from which to choose. Go with him now and return with the flogger you think best to use on this needy slave."

Although the two of them sat on either side of the table, with the woman stretched between them, they chose now to ignore her while they waited. They discussed small things and Sarah wanted to scream in frustration. How could they do that to her? Take that woman so far and then just leave her there as if she were...as if she were...her mind completed the sentence: as if she were a toy for their pleasure. As if her body were just a plaything. Would she never learn?

Phillip led the way back into the room and Anton held a rather long flogger in his hand. It was one her own master had yet to use on her—the tails were thin and Phillip had told her it could pack quite a sting.

Master William's eyes glinted wickedly when he saw Anton's choice. Moving back, he leaned up against the couch and out of the way. Lady Aleshia joined him and the two watched Anton go to work.

First the slave just walked around the bound woman, letting the tails of the flogger run over her body. No one had as yet touched her between her legs, but now as he pulled the flogger up through her pussy lips, the ends glimmered with her juices. Sarah was mesmerized by the path of liquid left as the flogger trailed its cargo up the woman's body.

With a snap that made Sarah jump and the slave woman cry out, Anton flicked the flogger to land its first blow on her breasts. Then dragging the tails for a bit, he flicked it again and landed its snap in the center of Jill's sensitive nipples. She arched her back, her breasts reddening under the flogger's stings.

And now he started a rhythm, over and over, landing the flogger on her breasts, on her stomach, her thighs—everywhere but her pussy. Unceasingly he raised and lowered the instrument of her torture until her entire body was pink. Tears flowed from Jill's eyes at the sweet torment and she moaned over and over.

Anton stopped and looked to Master William, who held up his hand. Anton's arm rested at his side and Phillip stepped forward now, holding a glass of ice. Kneeling beside the sniffling woman, he took an ice cube and ran it around her lips. Jill's tongue flicked out, licking the water and Phillip let her suck on the cube a moment while he held it.

Satisfied that her mouth was no longer dry, he removed the cube, trailing it down along her chin to her neck, letting it rest a moment in the hollow of her throat before continuing to trail it to her sore breasts. Around and around he moved the ice cube, making a figure eight between her breasts as the ice brought relief, and pain of a different sort.

The ice cube all but gone, he left the small piece that remained in the dip created by Jill's navel. Standing, he gave a small bow to Master William who motioned to Anton to continue.

Sarah knew what was coming, she was prepared for it. And yet the sudden cry from the slave and the way she arched her back took Sarah by surprise. Anton's gentle blow had fallen directly on the slave's pussy and obviously sent a wave of pleasure coursing through the woman's body.

Again he let the flogger fall, and Phillip could see Sarah's pussy lips, engorged with desire, rise to meet the blow. And when the slave on the table squirmed, Sarah unconsciously repeated the motion.

"Oh, please, Master," Jill whimpered. "Please let me come." And Sarah pleaded for the same release with her eyes.

Master William signaled to Anton for one more blow — one harder than he had yet given that delicate part of the body. He landed it and Jill screamed.

"Now, slave, take her."

Anton looked to his Mistress for permission and received it. Kneeling between Jill's legs, he poised his cock before her opening. Sarah hadn't realized how hard the beating had made him, but his thick cock was certainly ready. She could almost see it pulsating in the candlelight. Steadying himself by holding the hips of his fellow slave, he drove into her in one mighty thrust.

Sarah's moan into her gag echoed that of Jill's. Oh, how she wanted to be the one on that table! Over and over, her hips moved in time with Anton's thrusts as he repeatedly took Jill's helpless body. And when Jill cried out in her orgasm, Sarah moaned with her, her own body crying out its need.

Anton came soon after, tearing his cock from her pussy, letting his warm liquid spread itself on Jill's stomach. The two of them grinned at one another as the afterglow settled down on them.

Phillip helped Master William to remove Jill's bindings while Lady Aleshia got a warm cloth and cleaned both her own slave, and Jill. Anton gave Jill a hand off the table and the two slaves went to kneel before their respective Master and Mistress.

"You have done well, my little slave," Sarah heard Master William tell Jill. "You shall serve me later when we go home. For now, I heard there was cheesecake!"

The sexual tension in the room vanished as they all laughed and turned to Phillip, who smiled and came over to the cage. For the first time since he put her in there, he addressed her.

"Ready to come out of there, slave?"

She nodded, her mind still whirling with the incredible scene she had just witnessed. Her own juices flowed freely, sticking to the sides of her thighs.

Jill approached with the towel once more and again dried Sarah's chin and breasts. Sarah knew she should be embarrassed to have the other woman touch her there, but after what she had just seen, she had little room left for embarrassment.

Lady Aleshia now approached and, reaching around behind Sarah's head, unlocked and removed the bit. Jill offered her a drink of water, and Sarah accepted it eagerly.

The two women moved away and Master William circled around to unlock an ankle. Sarah was acutely aware that from such a kneeling position, he had a clear view of her over-excited pussy. A tug at her other ankle drove the thought from her mind as she looked down to see Anton smiling up from her other side.

She flexed each ankle as Master William moved behind her to release her wrists from the cage, then released them from each other. For the first time since they had arrived, she had complete freedom of movement. Well, almost complete, she was still in the cage.

Then Phillip was before her, the others off to the side, watching. Sarah swallowed hard as she suddenly realized she was once again the center of attention. After what she had just witnessed, the cage was suddenly a safe place to be and she wasn't sure she wanted to leave it.

Phillip saw the uncertainty in her eyes and took his time with the lock. She had done beautifully all night and his heart beat hard, knowing that he had fallen the rest of the way in love with her tonight. So helpless she had looked, so frightened — and yet, she let the wanton side of her be exposed as Anton took Jill before her eyes. He knew then that she was the one he had searched for.

Opening the door, he put his hand out, expecting her to put her hand in his. But instead, she lifted her leash and set it in his hand instead. Their eyes met, and he could not speak. Did she realize what she had just done?

She did. As he had fussed over the lock, giving her time, Sarah watched him, finally understanding what he wanted of her. She had seen it tonight in the way the other slaves served and with all her heart, she wanted to give her servitude to him. His hand came out to her in a gesture of peace and, without hesitation, she placed her leash, her symbol of subservience and slavery, into his palm.

Sarah stepped out of the cage, her eyes locked on Phillip's as he gently held her leash in his hand. She felt so strong, so confident, so comfortable with him, her semi-nude state was no longer an issue. He motioned to the others and she turned to face them, unbound for the first time that evening.

"Sarah, I would like you to meet my friends." He nodded and the Mistress stepped forward, a smile of welcome on her face. "Lady Aleshia," announced Phillip as if Sarah was meeting her for the first time.

And in a sense she was, Sarah realized as the Mistress took her hands and kissed each cheek. She was not the same Sarah Jackson-Parker standing here now that she was when she walked out of the bedroom earlier tonight. There had definitely been a change inside her. She felt bigger, expanded—as if all the world could just barely contain her being.

As Master, it was Will's turn next and he also took the new slave by the hands, squeezing them in welcome as he kissed her cheeks. Sarah's eyes were radiant, newborn. He remembered the moment when he had seen the change occur for Jill. At that moment Jill had become the love of his life. Phillip had just found his.

Jill and Anton came forward together, putting their arms around her and giving her a huge hug. Laughter welled up inside her; her joy was too big to be contained. She had passed an important test tonight, and a major barrier had fallen. She could not help but laugh in the embrace of the other two as the three hugged each other, all of them wearing little or no clothing whatsoever.

Now Phillip turned to Sarah, his own joy spilling over into a grin that split across his face, deepening his dimples. "I love you, Sarah-my-slave." His eyes grew more serious at his public admission. "I will love you forever."

Her heart caught in her throat. Her tears of laughter threatened to spill as tears of pure joy. "I love you, Phillip-my-Master. I will love you forever."

Their kiss was deep and passionate. The room faded and Sarah knew only the taste of Phillip's lips, knew only the warmth of his arms as they encircled her. Sarah's scent filled Phillip's mind as his tongue eagerly entwined with hers and he forgot his guests as he reveled in the embrace of the woman he loved.

A cleared throat eventually brought the two of them back to a wider reality. Phillip's voice was husky with emotion as his hand reached up to grasp Sarah's leash where it connected to her collar. Possessively, he gripped it and growled at her, "My guests are hungry, slave. Feed them the cheesecake."

She burst out laughing and the passion of the moment calmed to a general feeling of well-being. He led her into the kitchen with the others following in their own fashion. It was short, but careful work to cut the cheesecake and serve it. Phillip took quite a bit of ribbing from the others about the fact that he used tooth floss to cut it with. But he showed Sarah how easily the floss slid through the cake and made clean pieces with neat edges.

The pieces cut, she picked up two plates and took them to the table where the others already had pulled up chairs. Biting her lip, she wasn't sure of the protocol for serving them. But Jill rescued her. "Mostly you serve Master William and Lady Aleshia first, because they're above us. Sometimes you can serve the slave, who will then, in turn, serve his or her own master. But we're an informal group—give those two pieces to the Master and Mistress."

Sarah nodded her thanks and noted that Will's face beamed with pride at Jill's instructions. She felt an answering smile as she recognized the bond between them. It was the same bond she now felt between her and Phillip.

Going back out to get more plates, Sarah glanced at the clock, then stopped in astonishment. She had figured she had been in the cage about four hours—but by the clock, it had been a little over two. Her eyes squinted at the timepiece as if her stare could make it reflect her reality instead of everyone else's.

When Phillip handed her two more plates, she added a third, taking out his plate as well as the plates for the other two slaves before returning to the kitchen one last time for her own. Glaring at the traitor clock, she picked up her own piece of the dessert and took the last chair at the table. The conversation ebbed and flowed, much as it had with her own friends the night before.

But she had to stifle a giggle at the comparison. If those friends could see her now, sitting here, mostly nude, with a naked man and a naked woman also sitting at the table, conversing as if it were the most normal thing in the world...well, they just wouldn't believe it. A brief image of Beth in Lady Aleshia's chair with Paul taking Anton's place flashed through her mind and again she dismissed it as being just too silly.

She ate her cheesecake in very small bites. Her jaw was quite sore from wearing the bit for such a long time and each mouthful reminded her of her position. She found it a soreness she wanted to savor.

The night grew late and at last it was time for the others to take their leave. Will and a now-dressed Anton helped Phillip to move the heavy cage back into the dungeon while Jill, Sarah, and Lady Aleshia moved the furniture back into place. Finished, the three of them surveyed the room and Sarah ventured a question.

"Is it permitted for me to ask questions of you?" she began tentatively.

Lady Aleshia looked puzzled. "Of course. I expect you have many questions."

Sarah smiled shyly. "Too many to even put into words, I think. But only one for right now."

The two women smiled at her and Sarah took courage. "What happened here tonight...does this happen every time you get together?"

Lady Aleshia laughed, a deep, rich laugh that did not mock, but rather, understood. "We usually plan something of the sort about once a month. Other times we do more mundane activities. Phillip has not joined us for about a month, since his attentions were elsewhere."

Sarah blushed as she understood the woman's meaning. "I did not mean to keep him from you," she stammered.

The Lady's laugh softened into a smile. "Perhaps you did not mean it, but I see it was well worth the time spent." The mirth faded from her eyes and she held Sarah in her gaze. "You will make him a fine slave, Sarah. He does not love easily. In all the years I've known him, and that has been many, he has never given his heart. Not once. Not until tonight. You treat him well."

There was a warning implicit in the Lady's words and Sarah nodded, her heart suddenly in her throat. The men's return saved her from having to respond.

"Well, you take care of your Master, slave," Will told her with a wink to let her know he approved of her. "The man needs someone to keep him honest!"

"We'll get together some time this week, just us slaves," Jill told her. "I know you're going to have loads of questions in a day or two when what happened here tonight sinks in. Master Phillip has my number."

Hugs and pecks were distributed around and the foursome took their leave. The house suddenly grew quiet in their absence. Sarah helped Phillip extinguish all the candles but one. Picking it up, he came to her and again held out his hand. A small thrill ran through him when she placed her leash in his. Silently he led them to the bedroom where he set the candle on the nightstand.

"Come here, my slave," he said softly and Sarah glided into his arms. She breathed deeply, filling her lungs with his scent as he held her close. He nestled his nose into her hair, never wanting to let go. They stood entwined in their own world for many heartbeats before Sarah broke the spell by yawning.

They both laughed, the tired laugh one has after a long, successful evening. He undid the clasp on her bra and removed it. She started to take off the stockings, but he put his hand on hers. "Let me," he murmured. "Let me service my slave tonight."

She sat on the edge of the bed as he rolled down her stockings, caressing her legs and rubbing her sore feet. The heels of her shoes weren't very high, but after being in them all night long, her toes were tired.

Her garter belt, too, he slipped off, then took her legs and gently raised them to the bed. She watched as he undressed, blew out the candle, and came to join her.

"Phillip..." she began.

"Shhh." He put a finger to her lips. "Not tonight. Tomorrow will be time enough to question. Tonight there is only our love." He kissed her then, his mouth covering hers in the darkness. His arm wrapped around her and she melted into him, letting him carry her down, wrapping her leg over his as the kiss deepened.

He would take her with tenderness tonight, the animal had gone to sleep. Slowly his hands drifted over her body, relishing her softness, her curves. Every part of her belonged to him and he wanted to touch each part, own it again, and give thanks for it. She held his head and her fingers entwined in his hair as he bent to kiss her breasts, leaving a wonderful trail of warmth behind his movements.

His hand parted her legs and she rolled onto her back, letting his fingers caress the folds hidden there. Her sex was potent from the night's activities, but he breathed it in deeply and her heart soared. It was the final goodbye to her deceased husband, who never liked her aroused odor. For a moment, she thought she saw him standing in the doorway, but she blinked and he was gone. Completely gone, she realized. Instead, she belonged to Phillip.

The realization heightened her desire—she belonged to him now. Before those had been just words, but now they were reality. She arched her back as he entered her, spreading her legs wider to take all of him inside.

Inside where it was warm and comfortable. Inside her body as he was inside her heart. Phillip bent down and kissed her as she came, much as he had the first night they made love. Her arms wrapped around him and he held her in his own, never wanting to let go. Together they rode the gentle waves of their orgasms, their bodies locked in love's embrace.

* * * * *

Several hours later Phillip awoke, chilled in the night air. He had fallen asleep on top of her, his cock still buried deep inside. But now goose bumps crawled over his arms and he shifted, reaching down to find the blankets and cover them. She barely stirred and he realized her exhaustion had been just as much mental as it had been physical. He stretched out beside her and smiled as she snuggled in next to him, not even awake enough to realize she had done so. He wrapped his arm protectively around her and went back to sleep.

Chapter 11
Questions

Sarah was having the most delicious dream. Warmth spread from her belly all the way up her body to tingle in her fingers. Rolling over in the bed, she dreamt of a warm tongue licking along the outer lips between her legs and in her dream, she spread her legs wide for the faceless stranger. A moan escaped her lips and it was that moan that woke her up.

It was no dream. She lay on her back and Phillip's head rose to greet her, a dimple in his cheeks and the devil in his eyes.

"Good morning," he said cheerfully. "Ready to get up? Or shall I continue?"

"Oh, by all means, continue!" She stretched, raising her arms over her head and yawning in her barely awake state.

"Hmmmm." He propped himself up on one arm and stared along her length. "Methinks you have forgotten your manners, slave."

She cocked an eye in his direction as his fingers toyed with her lips—pinching them and pushing them aside, but not taking her, not touching her clit. She was becoming more and more awake the more aroused he made her. "Please, Sir—please continue?" Her voice tightened as his fingers entered her, stretching her wide.

"Do you like this, my little slave? And did you like being on display last night?" His fingers began moving in and out of her, his thumb coming up to circle her clit. "Did you like being treated like a piece of property?" His fingers pressed deeply into her. "My property?"

She gasped and cried out. "Yes, oh yes, Master—I liked it. Oh, please, Sir...please let me come."

His hand withdrew and he brought his fingers to his mouth. As she watched, he licked them clean. "Yes, slave—I will make you come." His face disappeared and his tongue licked her from the depth of her slit, into her pussy and up to her clit where it made slow circles over and around her, driving her mad with desire. She arched her back, her hands clawing at the bed sheets. "Oh, Sir!! Please!"

She felt his finger dip into her pussy, then trail down between the cheeks of her rear, trailing nature's lubricant all the way down. His finger pressed on the hole, then pushed inside. She was so wet, he had no trouble entering and he began fucking her ass with his hand as his tongue now impaled her pussy.

With a cry, the tension inside burst forth and she convulsed as the orgasm wracked her body. He did not let up, but kept the pressure on her as wave after wave made her body dance for him.

Her cries quieted into whimpers and her body settled as he brought her down. She wasn't even aware of when he left her; but when her senses returned, she was covered and he was in the shower.

Phillip's first sight upon reentering the bedroom was of his slave, wantonly lying with her legs still spread under the covers, smiling at him—a smile of total and complete bliss. He could not help himself. Flinging off the thin blanket, he stretched beside her, cupping her breast in one hand and possessing her mouth with his tongue.

He had showered, but not yet brushed his teeth and she could taste herself on his lips. The taste started the fires burning again and she could not remember a time when she had felt so alive. The air was crisper, the sun shone brighter and she felt herself to be a sexual being for the first time in her life.

Wrapping her arms around him, she hugged him tightly, her love for him bursting from every pore of her being. Phillip pushed himself up to look at her, his eyes shining as he smiled; was ever a man as lucky as he? He loved her more deeply than he had ever loved before—and the most wonderful thing of all was that she loved him back.

"I love you, Sarah-my-slave."

"I love you, Phillip-my-master."

She giggled as he attacked her neck, his breath tickling. That gave him ideas and he ran his fingers over her side finding her most ticklish spots. She squealed and let her fingers do some searching of their own. Laughing and giggling, the two of them rolled around on the bed until they collapsed in each other's arms.

"Truce!" Phillip declared and Sarah's hands immediately changed to a caress. Brushing the hair from her face, he leaned in to kiss her tenderly.

"Oh, Master," she breathed when he withdrew. "Tell me why I like this so much. Tell me why I like for you to tie me up and why I want you to whip my body pink. Tell me why I liked being mostly naked and on display for strangers last night. Tell me what power you have over me that I want to give you such control of me. I am in love with you, Sir—and I no longer have any limits."

He smiled as he smoothed her hair. Propped up on one arm, he leaned his head on one hand as his fingers drifted down to play with her breast while he explained.

"I have no power at all, Sarah. You have it all, haven't you realized that yet?"

"You mean, I have power because I can walk out any time I wish. If I didn't want to participate last night, I could have told you that before you put the bit in. Even though I didn't know the specifics of what was coming, you certainly did give me enough opportunity to flee."

"And yet you didn't." His finger idly circled her nipple. "Why?"

Her cheeks colored and she rolled over to face him, trying to understand. "I didn't run because it never occurred to me. I was scared, especially when you left me in the bedroom to bring everyone in and get them settled, and again once you turned off all the lights except for the ones on my cage. That really unnerved me." Her eyes dropped. "I'm sorry I wasn't better behaved then."

"You don't need to apologize." His hand touched her chin, lifting her eyes to his. "All your life you've been conditioned to think one particular way. Over the past several weeks, you've been exploring another alternative. The two parts of you are bound, if you'll pardon the pun, to fight on occasion." He grinned. "And I can see which side won."

"Yes, you have unleashed the wanton side of me..." Her eyes flashed as she reached down to cup his soft cock in her hand. "I want to be very naughty with you. I want to be your sex slave."

She tried not to, but giggled anyway. It sounded so absurd when said out loud—and yet it was what she wanted, more than anything in the world.

He grinned, and let her play with his cock. In the early morning light, she looked so like a child eager to please, wanting to learn. So open and innocent about her own needs and desires.

"You said you don't know why you like to be tied up when I take you. Do you really not know?"

"Well, I know a psychologist would tell me it has to do with the fact that I'm feeling guilty about all this—and that being tied up allows me to believe my actions are no longer in my control. I have to admit, being tied, I do feel freer to express myself than when I'm not tied.

"But there's more to it than that, I think. There is just something wonderful about having given up control. There's something about giving you permission to bind me—about trusting you so completely — that really arouses me. And that, I think, is the real reason I like it so much."

Phillip nodded. "It's the reason I like it so much as well. For me, the arousal comes when you submit. When I push you past where you are comfortable and you submit anyway and go along with me? That is the biggest thrill of all."

"I can tell. Just thinking about it, has made you hard." Sarah's hand continued to caress his cock, now grown to almost full size. She looked at him, a pleading in her eyes. "Please, Sir. Let me do this. Let me please you and show you how much I love you?" She climbed out of the bed and knelt at the side, her nipples standing straight up in the morning air.

He didn't even need to think about it. She wanted to service him — she wanted to show her love by sucking him off. He swung his legs over the side of the bed and leaned back on his hands. "Then make me come, slave." His voice was gruffer than he meant it to be, his heart was too much in his throat.

She understood. Smiling, she leaned forward, taking his length in her mouth and drawing up, licked the underside of his shaft; leaving a thin, wet line behind. The air hit the wet spot and he grew harder as the warmth of her mouth contrasted with the coolness of the air.

Circling the tip, she drew lazy circles around it with her tongue, looking up at him with smoldering eyes.

"Slave, what are you doing to me?" he whispered.

"Teasing you, my dear master," she replied innocently. "Would you like me to stop?"

He groaned as her mouth encircled just the tip and her tongue flicked inside the slit at the end, licking the pre-come that had already formed there. He could not answer and realized she knew it.

She grinned as she withdrew, leaving her hand to rub his skin, knowing exactly what she was doing to him. For the moment, he had given his control to her and she intended to make full use of it. Pushing his cock up, she leaned down to lick his balls, sucking in first one, and then the other, rolling the stones around in her mouth. She was rewarded by another moan.

"Slave, you are tormenting me!"

"Yes, Sir, I am." She ran her tongue from his balls to his tip, then opening wide, she swallowed his cock, the gag reflex relaxed and her nose buried into his belly. She held him there as his hips thrust against her, holding on until she needed to breathe. Only then did she release him just long enough to grab a breath and impale her mouth on him once more.

He moaned out his need, unable to form words any longer. Taking pity on him, she pumped him then, her hand and her mouth bringing him the release he longed for.

He came with a vengeance. With stars and explosions inside his body, his juices burst down her throat. The hot liquid filled her mouth and she swallowed his come just as she had swallowed his cock. Squeezing his balls to help him empty, she knelt before him and accepted his gift to her.

Arms trembling from the intensity, Phillip slowly lowered himself to the bed as Sarah now licked him clean. He felt a warm cloth and realized she had left him and come back and he hadn't even noticed. Awareness of the world returned to him.

"Slave," he called, his voice raw.

She was at his side in an instant. "Yes, Master?"

"You are incredible, slave."

She grinned. "Thank you, Master." Her smile turned naughty. "If my Master has no further use for his slave at this particular time, then his slave would like to shower and get ready for church. Or did Master forget it is Sunday?"

"Master did not forget, slave. Go shower." He watched as she rose, her nudity totally natural to her now. "Slave," he called as she reached the door.

She turned. He was still lying helpless on the bed—she had taken a lot out of him this morning and didn't feel guilty at all. He deserved such a wonderful orgasm—how many had he given her? She would make every one of them as glorious if she could.

"Never mind. Take your shower."

Smiling, she left him to shower and shave for him.

He heard her humming to herself as she prepared her shower, but didn't even attempt to rise until the water turned on. The woman wore him out! Giving her control for a short time was definitely something he was going to have to do every once in a while. Standing, he walked over to his dresser, opening it and taking out a small box. He had intended to give it to her this morning, but it wasn't the time. Not with the two of them naked and him still recovering from his orgasm.

Dressing, he tucked the little box into his suit coat pocket just as she emerged from the bathroom. "Come on, slave, there isn't much time!" He admonished her, helping by getting her clothes out.

The navy suit hung in the closet and he realized he needed to get her something else for church. She had worn this one three weeks in a row. That was fine when he didn't know how long she'd be his. This week he would go shopping again. He grinned as he pulled it out and handed it to her.

"Why are you grinning, Sir? You look like you're plotting something."

"I am, slave. Always. You know that." Setting the clothes on the bed, he turned to leave. "Meet you at the car."

She watched in puzzlement. He was definitely plotting something, but there wasn't time to chase it down right now. The stockings and garter belt from last night were going to have to do for today—she would wash them out when they got back. Slipping on the sheer bra that used to make her feel so naughty going to church, now felt comfortable—especially after that bra with the holes in it the night before.

Dressed, she passed the living room on her way to the door. It looked so normal now, just as it always did. Hard to believe the things that had happened there the night before.

And yet they had. Her cheeks coloring again, she ran from the memory and out the door.

* * * * *

She greeted several parishioners by name this week and noted at least one absence. Mrs. Finch and her daughter Emily were not among the congregation today. Sarah sighed and enjoyed the service.

The weather this weekend had taken a decided turn towards winter. The leaves were turning, but not quite at peak. After church, Phillip took a different route than the one he usually took to go home. "It's a beautiful day, if cold for this time of year," he explained. "Thought we might take a drive."

It was a beautiful day for a meander through the countryside. The hills were covered with maples and oak whose turning leaves made the hillsides look as if they had purchased new clothes. Exploring a side road, Phillip and Sarah found a small lake and decided to circle it, turning and venturing down the even tinier roads that forked here and there, always keeping the lake in view. A small diner-type restaurant hugged the shore of the lake and Phillip turned in. "Hungry?"

"Absolutely!"

As always, she waited while he came around to get her door, taking his hand to pull herself out. The gravel was uneven under her heels and she took his arm gratefully as they crossed to the restaurant's door.

The interior was that of a typical lakeside diner—lots of netting and fake fish on the walls. But the tables were clean and the view was gorgeous. The summer season was mostly done, so the cottagers had all gone home, the waitress explained. They would, themselves, be open only a few more weekends before closing for the winter. The porch dining was already closed up.

They didn't mind taking seats by the big picture window. Outside, the dock spread its fingers into the lake—most of the bays empty now. With the changing leaves, the panorama was beautiful on the still lake and they both found their gaze pulled back to the view time and time again as they ate.

Phillip paid the check and asked the waitress if it would be all right for them to take a walk out on the docks.

"Sure. But it's a might chilly out there. Wind comes off the lake and all."

Thanking her, the two slipped out through a side exit and they slowly made their way along the dock. Sarah was not surprised to find that Phillip was knowledgeable about boating—and had owned several boats in the past.

"Yes," she said in answer to his question. "I've been out on the water a few times, but never in anything other than my uncle's sixteen-foot motorboat. And then we were only going up and down the canal."

His arm was around her waist as they stood at the end of the dock, looking out over the water. "I will take you sailing then, someday. Would my slave like to be out on the water, crewing for me?"

She smiled up at him. "Phillip-my-master, I would love to crew for you any time you wish."

He turned to her and his heart skipped a beat. She looked so beautiful with the wind just lifting her hair like that. The leather collar she wore in public trimmed her neck as her face turned up to him and the sunlight lit up her eyes. His hand dipped into his pocket as he stepped away from her for a moment.

"Sarah, close your eyes."

She did so, not even thinking to question his command. She heard a creak as he opened something, but did not peek.

"Open them now."

She did. In his hand was a small, velvet box. The lid was raised, revealing the diamond ring inside.

"Sarah," he murmured, "society does not recognize my collar on you and I want the world to know you are mine. Will you marry me?"

Her eyes watered and the breath caught in her throat. "Oh, Phillip! I can't believe...I mean...you really want...Yes! Yes, Phillip, I will marry you!" She could not contain herself and threw her arms around him.

He staggered back under the force of her hug, righted himself and enfolded her in his embrace. She pulled away, looking again at the ring in the box, her eyes shining with tears.

"Here, let me put it on you." He took the ring and she obediently held out her left hand. He slid it home and it rested perfectly on her finger. She trembled to see it there—a sign to the world that she was owned. Funny how she had never seen it that way before. But it was true. She belonged to one man again, although in a very different way than before. The tears spilled over as she held out her hand for him to see.

Her face was streaked with tears of joy and he knew he had made the right choice. She wanted to be owned by him—and the collar wasn't enough. She would remain true, that wasn't the issue. But with the force of law behind their union, he would be able to take her further than she ever imagined. He could not resist. Putting his hands on either side of her face, his thumbs wiped away her tears and he pulled her into a kiss. Tasting the salt on her lips from her tears, he opened his mouth to take her completely.

And here, in a public place, where undoubtedly the few patrons of the restaurant could see them, she opened to him, letting his tongue enter and possess her again. She pressed herself into him, giving her soul up to his kiss and her body to his hands.

He did not let go of her face as he withdrew, instead, he rested his forehead on hers. "I love you, Sarah-my-slave."

"And I love you, Phillip-my-master."

Arm in arm, the ring twinkling on her finger, the collar snug about her neck, Sarah and Phillip walked back to the car and to a new life together.

About the author:

For many years, Diana Hunter confined herself to mainstream writings. Her interest in the world of dominance and submission, dormant for years, bloomed when she met a man who was willing to let her explore the submissive side of her personality. In her academic approach to learning about the lifestyle, she discovered hundreds of short stories that existed on the topic, but none of them seemed to express her view of a d/s relationship. Challenged by a friend to write a better one, she wrote her first BDSM novel, *Secret Submission*, published by Ellora's Cave Publishing.

Diana welcomes mail from readers. You can write to her c/o Ellora's Cave Publishing at P.O. Box 787, Hudson, Ohio 44236-0787.

Why an electronic book?

We live in the Information Age — an exciting time in the history of human civilization in which technology rules supreme and continues to progress in leaps and bounds every minute of every hour of every day. For a multitude of reasons, more and more avid literary fans are opting to purchase e-books instead of paperbacks. The question to those not yet initiated to the world of electronic reading is simply: *why?*

1. *Price.* An electronic title at Ellora's Cave Publishing runs anywhere from 40-75% less than the cover price of the <u>exact same title</u> in paperback format. Why? Cold mathematics. It is less expensive to publish an e-book than it is to publish a paperback, so the savings are passed along to the consumer.

2. *Space.* Running out of room to house your paperback books? That is one worry you will never have with electronic novels. For a low one-time cost, you can purchase a handheld computer designed specifically for e-reading purposes. Many e-readers are larger than the average handheld, giving you plenty of screen room. Better yet, hundreds of titles can be stored within your new library — a single microchip. (Please note that Ellora's Cave does not endorse any specific brands. You can check our website at www.ellorascave.com for customer recommendations we make available to new consumers.)

3. *Mobility.* Because your new library now consists of only a microchip, your entire cache of books can be taken with you wherever you go.

4. *Personal preferences are accounted for.* Are the words you are currently reading too small? Too large? Too...**ANNOYING**? Paperback books cannot be modified according to personal preferences, but e-books can.

5. *Innovation.* The way you read a book is not the only advancement the Information Age has gifted the literary community with. There is also the factor of what you can read. Ellora's Cave Publishing will be introducing a new line of interactive titles that are available in e-book format only.

6. *Instant gratification.* Is it the middle of the night and all the bookstores are closed? Are you tired of waiting days—sometimes weeks—for online and offline bookstores to ship the novels you bought? Ellora's Cave Publishing sells instantaneous downloads 24 hours a day, 7 days a week, 365 days a year. Our e-book delivery system is 100% automated, meaning your order is filled as soon as you pay for it.

Those are a few of the top reasons why electronic novels are displacing paperbacks for many an avid reader. As always, Ellora's Cave Publishing welcomes your questions and comments. We invite you to email us at service@ellorascave.com or write to us directly at: P.O. Box 787, Hudson, Ohio 44236-0787.

Printed in the United States
25879LVS00001B/68

9 781843 608110